CURSE
OF SALEM

CURSE
OF SALEM

KAY HOOPER

BERKLEY
NEW YORK

BERKLEY
An imprint of Penguin Random House LLC
penguinrandomhouse.com

Library of Congress Cataloging-in-Publication Data

Names: Hooper, Kay, author.
Title: Curse of Salem / Kay Hooper.
Description: New York : Berkley, [2021] |
Series: The Bishop/Special crimes unit
Identifiers: LCCN 2021025319 (print) | LCCN 2021025320 (ebook) |
ISBN 9781984802927 (hardcover) | ISBN 9781984802941 (ebook)
Subjects: GSAFD: Suspense fiction.
Classification: LCC PS3558.O587 C87 2021 (print) |
LCC PS3558.O587 (ebook) | DDC 813/.54--dc23
LC record available at https://lccn.loc.gov/2021025319
LC ebook record available at https://lccn.loc.gov/2021025320

Printed in the United States of America
1st Printing

CURSE
OF SALEM

PROLOGUE

Megan Hales could feel her heart pounding, her pulse beating in her ears, a panicked, fluttery sensation that stole her breath.

I need to leave. I need to get out of here.

She had to move fast. Before he could stop her.

Even with the stark uneasiness driving her, she kept telling herself that was stupid, he wouldn't do that, there was no reason he would . . . but she kept remembering a look in his eyes the day before, something undefined that had caused her to go cold all of a sudden.

Fear. She was afraid of him.

The sense of safety she'd always felt in Salem, in the house where she'd grown up, was gone. The familiar bedroom felt weirdly alien, as if all the lights were on too bright, hurting her eyes. The silence thrummed in her ears, and her fingers felt awkward as she hurried.

Hands shaking, she crammed clothing into the larger of her two bags and managed, with an effort, to zip it closed, the sound loud and ragged in the early-morning silence.

She froze for a moment, listening, then pulled the bag off her tumbled bed. Her duffel bag sat waiting, also stuffed with her things, and as she hooked the strap over her shoulder she spared a brief moment to wish she didn't have to leave so much behind.

Enough. Enough of that. She had to leave.

Now.

She carried both bags through the silent house, desperate not to make any noise at all. Just enough of the dawn light came through the windows to show her the way so she didn't run into furniture or bang one of the bags against the wall or a doorjamb. She wasn't sure whether she drew a full breath until she was outside in the grayish and muggy summer morning, the front door closed silently behind her.

Megan paused only a moment, still aware of the pounding of her heart even as she told herself he couldn't possibly know she intended to leave today. No one could. And even if he had some idea, it was so early, way earlier than she ever got up, and why would he even be up himself, much less be out here in the valley near her home?

He wouldn't. Of course he wouldn't.

She had parked her car in the driveway's turnaround the night before, making sure she wasn't blocked in by any of the family cars. Still trying to be as quiet as possible, she put both bags in the back seat of her little Chevy and eased the door shut again.

It was so . . . still. Unusually hot for early morning, even in July, the humid air promised a storm later. She stood beside her car, nervous fingers toying with the strap of her handbag and then diving inside to find her keys.

She looked down at her hand, at the diamond engagement ring winking in the faint light, and pain throbbed through her, jagged and raw. She had been so excited, so certain that all her plans—all their plans—would lead them along the path to a happy life.

Today should have been her wedding day.

And now . . . she felt lost, suddenly rudderless, the whole rest of her life stretching out empty and lonely.

But that was just here in Salem, she told herself. There was nothing here for her now. Not anymore.

Still, she hesitated, breathing in the scents of honeysuckle and cut grass and, faintly, the neighboring stables. It smelled like summer in Salem. It smelled like home. She was vaguely surprised by the sudden intense regret she felt. Because it didn't have to be forever, of course it didn't. She could come back. One day. Maybe.

All she had to do—

"Megan."

Her pounding heart lodged suddenly in her throat, and she swallowed as she forced herself to turn, to conjure a faint surprised smile.

"What're you doing here?"

"I wanted to talk to you."

She glanced around at the gray morning that was just beginning to brighten and forced out a little laugh. "At the crack of dawn?"

"You're up," he pointed out, taking a step closer.

She wanted to ask how he'd known she would be, but part of her didn't want that answer. He had Talents, she knew that. Strange Talents. He was staring at her, eyes intense in his otherwise calm face, and she couldn't help shifting her weight uneasily.

"I can't talk right now," she said. "I . . . have an appointment in town. Made it days ago. I really don't want to be late." She could hear her voice shake.

Stupid. Stupid. Should have left last night.

"You're packed for a trip," he said.

Forcing surprised carelessness into her voice, she said, "Just for a week or so. I told you I might leave. For a while." She felt cold suddenly, wondering if that was why he was here. But what could he do, after all? It wasn't like he had any right to stop her.

"You can't go," he said.

"It's just for a while," she repeated. "I told you. I'd rather not watch everybody trying to think of something . . . kind . . . to say to me. Watch them feel sorry for me. It's better if I get away for a while."

She held her keys in one hand and fumbled with the other behind her for the driver's-side door. "I'll call you," she added brightly.

"You can't go," he repeated.

Megan wanted to maintain her forced unconcern, but her heart was pounding harder than before, she felt cold even in the muggy air, and some instinct she'd never before been aware of urged her to move quickly, to get away from him.

Never mind being polite, being reasonable.

Just *move.*

He looked suddenly unfamiliar in the grayish morning light, oddly . . . blurred. Except for his eyes. Those sharp, intense, strangely colored eyes. It had been exciting at first, having his focused gaze on her, looking at her in a way no one ever had before, as if nothing had existed for him except her. Seeing her, she'd thought, so clearly. But now all she felt was the overwhelming need to escape.

"I'll call you," she repeated, and forced herself to turn her back on him, a strange crawly sensation creeping over her body, all her muscles tensing. Weird. It was so weird—

"No."

Megan tried to pull the car door open, but it was as if all the strength drained out of her in a rush and she couldn't move suddenly, couldn't do anything but look down at her own hand, watch it shake, watch his much larger one covering hers, tightening until she wanted to cry out in pain.

Why couldn't she move?

"No, Megan," he said almost sadly. "I can't let you leave Salem. I can't let you leave me."

The gray, muggy morning was abruptly so cold her whole body ached, and the familiar smells were gone. All she could smell now was something sharp, acrid, something that was utterly strange and yet . . . not. It was something she thought she should recognize, even though she knew she had never smelled it before.

Something that terrified her.

She opened her mouth to scream but the only sound that escaped her tight throat was a thready, childlike whimper.

Darkness closed over her.

ONE

Hollis Templeton opened her eyes and blinked at a ceiling that looked . . . odd. She reached out a seeking hand with what had become habit, encountered only smooth sheet, and sat up abruptly.

The bed beside her was empty of her FBI Special Crimes Unit partner and lover, Reese DeMarco. That was strange enough, and unsettling enough, that it took Hollis another moment or so to realize that wasn't the only wrong thing.

The sheets she knew were pale blue looked gray. So did the duvet cover, which was supposed to be a muted but attractive print of several colors. She touched with tentative fingers and found that it felt normal—except for the chill. She felt chilled, which wasn't all that surprising since she wasn't wearing a nightgown or pajamas and it was March.

Still, the cold Hollis felt was due to something other than a chilly room and her own nakedness. It was a slightly familiar chill, and just acknowledging that made her feel even colder, especially when she also recognized the very faint, almost elusive odor that was, in an oddly primal way, unpleasant and difficult to identify.

But familiar.

Even so, she fixed her mind on *calm* mode and made no attempt to reach through the easy telepathic connection to Reese in order to wake him. In fact, she eased the "door" on her side closed. Because he could share her dreams, even from time to time walk with her through them, especially if she had a nightmare or was otherwise upset, and she did *not* want him sharing this place even if he could. Which she was reasonably sure he couldn't. At least he hadn't ever before.

And she'd probably need him to anchor her on the living side, in case she got into trouble. Or even if she didn't.

She looked up, finally, to examine the room. A pleasant bedroom in their pleasant condo, it was spacious and decorated simply and comfortably because they agreed about such things and how a home should feel even if they were seldom present to enjoy the comfort of home for very long.

But it was gray.

And it wasn't supposed to be gray.

Hollis hesitated a moment, then pushed back the duvet and sheet and slid from the big bed. She found the nightgown she had briefly worn on the floor, which was where it usually ended up, and put it on. The robe that matched it was silky and not made to warm up the body, but she found it lying over a chair near the bed and put it on as well, tying the flimsy little strings beneath her breasts.

She wondered, fleetingly, why she bothered, because it wasn't like she was really here. Or really here in body, at least. She didn't suppose her spirit required clothing, although she couldn't recall ever seeing a naked spirit. Then again, if she encountered anyone else—and she particularly *wanted* to encounter at least one other person, presumably also in spirit—she preferred to be dressed.

Hollis wasted a moment or so wondering if she really *had* dressed her spirit, or if she hadn't but had only gone through the motions because one did. If she saw herself clothed because she wanted to see herself that way. And if she saw other spirits clothed because she preferred to see them clothed. It struck her as one of those imponderable questions that often littered her life, especially in recent years, and she decided not to ponder it further. Not right now, at least.

She was very careful not to look back at the bed at first, not wanting to confirm what she knew was happening and half-afraid, as always, that she'd freeze solid like Lot's wife. But Hollis was nothing if not curious, so she finally looked back over her shoulder and saw what she expected, even if it made her feel even colder. And totally creeped out.

Herself. Lying there seemingly alone, her face peaceful in sleep, her body a bit curled near the center of the wide bed, under the covers and comfortable, one arm flung out as though it were lying across a broad chest that was not visible because Reese was not visible.

She wondered, suddenly and disturbingly, why she was even able to see her own body in the gray time. Because her spirit was here? Was that why she couldn't see Reese, because he was in their bed body and spirit, in the normal realm of existence for them?

And not this cold and gray realm of . . . wherever?

An icy finger traced up and down her spine.

"Shit," she said, and heard the peculiarly hollow sound of her own voice that was normal in the gray time. She forced her gaze away from her sleeping self in the bed and took a moment to look slowly around the room again. Everything was gray and oddly one-dimensional and featureless. The framed prints on the wall looked like smudges; even the two very colorful paintings she had attempted in recent months and Reese had had framed looked gray; and the paneled woodwork looked flat. And gray. Furniture was one-dimensional, no depth or light or shadow. And gray.

Everything was gray.

That was the overwhelming sense she got, that everything around her was gray and cold and empty, really, of color or dimension, light or shadow. Or life. Desolate. She always forgot how utterly desolate this place—or time—was. Until she was in it. She felt very, very alone.

She found a slipper half-hidden beside the bed, having to kneel on the bedside rug and reach under for its partner. She got up, slid her feet into them, and turned away toward the room's door.

Hollis wasn't a woman who hesitated much, not when it counted and these days especially, but she felt unusually adrift in uncertainty. This wasn't her world, her realm, even though she'd been warned, they both had, that the first experimental trip Hollis had taken into Diana Hayes's gray time had formed a connection between her and this . . . place. A connection that allowed, perhaps demanded, her to walk here.

Because only spirits walked here. Hollis was a medium as Diana was a medium, and she could be drawn here, especially whenever Diana opened a door into this place or time or whatever it was. Still, it had never happened suddenly, unexpectedly, when they weren't on a case.

Thinking about it, Hollis wasn't even sure where Diana and her husband and partner, seer Quentin Hayes, *were* at the moment. In the real world. She and Reese had completed a difficult case successfully, one for the good guys, had returned late on Friday, and had been given a rare long weekend off. They had fled Quantico before Bishop could change his mind or another case popped up. Even Reese had been tired; they'd needed a break. And had thoroughly enjoyed their rest and recreation for two days. (Friday night and well into Saturday morning had been pure exhausted sleep.) But they still had one day to go, which was why there had been no reason to get up early today, Monday.

Not that Hollis knew if it was early or late. Here it was just gray, without light or shadow or time, without night or day. As she moved out of the bedroom, she took care not to look at a clock because they would all be featureless and that was one of the creepier aspects of the gray time.

She stepped through the bedroom doorway into what should have been a short hallway that led to the open-concept living area of the condo, with the kitchen, breakfast nook, and a comfortable den, and another short hallway beyond that with a half bath and an extra room they had decided to use as a studio/office rather than a second bedroom.

Only that wasn't where she found herself.

She was standing on what appeared to be the slope of a cold gray mountain, slightly unbalanced for a moment as the surface beneath her feet slanted suddenly. She was looking down on what she assumed was a town in the distance.

Blinking away a momentary dizziness and disorientation, she looked harder. Not that the spider senses worked here, she had learned that, but she could see what there was to see. A fairly small mountain town in a fairly large valley, she decided, holding on to calm with an effort as she studied the scene. Gray. Varying shades of gray, but gray all the same, like some creepy eternal twilight. No lights, no people, no cars moving. Just gray squarish shapes that were probably houses and businesses, and gray streets that might have been only lines drawn on paper, and beyond them a valley vaguely marked with squares that must have been pastures and fields, and slashes and squiggles that were roads. And all around hulking gray mountains reared against an ugly grayish sky.

Everything was so utterly still. Quiet.

Lifeless.

Hollis wasn't sure what she was supposed to do now that she was here. She didn't have spirit guides, like Diana's, appearing to tell her where she was supposed to go or what she was supposed to do.

And besides, this was Diana's realm, not hers, a place where her friend and fellow agent knew the rules—such as they were.

Hollis had, so far, learned a gray-time rule only when she stumbled and fell over it.

But one thing she *had* learned from bitter experience was that the gray time was exhausting for the living, for even the spirit—or consciousness, or mind, whatever—of the living. The longer she remained, the more exhausted she would become. And unlike Diana, Hollis hadn't had the better part of thirty years to get familiar with this place.

So she started walking, down toward the town. And hadn't gone more than three paces before she heard a voice

"Hollis?"

———

DIANA HAYES HAD, in her more than two years with the Special Crimes Unit, grown somewhat more comfortable with the mediumistic abilities that had been hers from birth. She would have been far more comfortable with them by now had her autocratic father not believed, from her childhood, that the "symptoms" of her psychic abilities were a mental illness that required keeping his only surviving daughter medicated to the point of literally drifting, uncaring and almost unseeing, through her life.

Far too much of her life.

But Elliot Brisco was no longer part of Diana's life, his authority over her first severed by a doctor who saw something of the truth and had quietly weaned Diana off all the medications so she was able to see what had been done to her, and then by Diana herself, fighting for her independence and gaining it, at last, in a court and by a judge's ruling.

The final severing between Diana and her father had come when he used his money and power to back a monster in his efforts to regain control of Diana. An attempt that not only failed but had resulted in countless deaths and nearly killed his only child. She had turned her back on him for good after that. She had been unmoved by even the ruthless vengeance of another powerful man, another father, grieving and embittered by the loss of his own daughter and bent on destroying Elliot Brisco and his empire. Elliot Brisco's actions had far-reaching consequences.

And one of them was that Diana's life was her own to live as she wished.

She had resisted giving up any of her hard-won independence for a long time, which was why Quentin had had to be very patient. It was, Bishop had told Diana privately, very good for Quentin, who was inclined toward recklessness and was known for his humorous, somewhat flippant attitude, to learn patience. Even if he had to learn it the hard way.

Personally as well as professionally.

But the horrific injury in the middle of a deadly, hectic investigation had landed Diana in the hospital, had very, *very* nearly killed her, and that had taught her that protecting something Quentin would never take from her *anyway* had been a true waste of time and of her life. Their lives.

She'd wasted more than enough time.

Her life was busy now. She and Quentin had arrived back at Quantico only late on Sunday after a very disturbing case had been thankfully resolved and, after reporting in, had gone home to pretty much just fall into bed and sleep.

So when Diana opened her eyes after what felt like only a few hours and then sat up in bed, her first reaction was to mutter, "What the hell? I can't get even one night off, for crying out loud?"

Her voice sounded hollow, though she barely noticed that because it was familiar. Like the faint, unmistakable odor, which was, she had decided, as close as she ever wanted to get to the smell of brimstone.

She knew she was alone in their bed, or appeared to be; she was reasonably certain Quentin was sleeping there with her, that they were sort of wrapped up in each other under the covers, which was normal and wonderful.

But not something she was supposed to enjoy for the moment, clearly.

Dammit.

She didn't look behind her as she slid from the bed and found her nightgown and robe, knowing she would see herself lying there wrapped around invisible Quentin, which would be disconcerting even for her.

Though the connection they shared was different from that of some other bonded pairs in the SCU, not directly mind to mind because neither of them was a telepath, they had discovered that each maintained a sense of the other, an emotional closeness, of course, but also a certainty of physical nearness, and she knew he was near physically. There, in the living world, holding her.

But not with her here in the gray time, something for which she was thankful. She'd managed to get out of the gray time for a good many years without him, of course, but there had been scary awakenings in dangerous places, and she much preferred the certainty of Quentin's hand drawing her back safely, her bedrock anchor in the living world.

She found comfortable, slip-on shoes that wouldn't, she knew, protect her feet from the cold any more than her clothing would; it didn't matter what she wore in this place or time, because she wasn't here in the flesh and because the gray time was always cold.

Always.

She didn't bother to look around the cozy bedroom, because it would be gray and featureless and she didn't want that in her mind rather than the warm and colorful comfort it actually was. Instead, she just went out the door into what was supposed to be a hallway.

And nearly stumbled as she found herself in a very dense forest and had to dodge a tree directly in her path. It was a mountain forest, she thought, considering the slope. She no longer felt more than a split second of disorientation at the abrupt change of scene, but stood looking around at gray trees towering, lots of pines among the still bare-limbed hardwoods, and, between them, downslope and not all that close, what she thought might be a town.

It was cold, and still, and empty.

She waited, aware of a nervousness that never went away because this was such an alien place. Or time. It never felt . . . natural.

She didn't have to wait long.

"Hello, Diana."

It was the spirit of a little boy this time, she saw. Though certainly he wouldn't be little in any sense except appearance. He looked to be maybe ten or eleven, but she knew from experience he could easily be older than she was, with numerous lives behind him. Her child guides were always almost eerily mature.

"Hello," she responded. "And you are?"

"Daniel."

"Hello, Daniel. Why am I here?"

"Right to the point." He seemed a little amused.

"Well, it saves time," she explained. "And gives me at least a shot of getting out of here without being so exhausted I want to sleep for a day or two."

"That is a point," he agreed, grave now. "Because you're going to need your strength."

"Shit," she said. "I seriously can't get a night off? We just finished a case——"

"I'm sorry about that, but you're needed here. And I need to tell you as much as I can first. Show you as much as I can."

Diana frowned at him, aware again of crawling unease. "Show me? I really don't like being shown things here in the gray time. That tends to go badly." She vividly remembered a shocking glimpse of herself lying bleeding on a stark bright street, something she'd seen from the gray time only because she'd been connected to Quentin, and shivered.

"Why not just tell me what I need to do?" she demanded of the guide.

"Because it's more complicated than that this time, Diana."

"I knew you were going to say that," she muttered, and glanced around them at the dense, sloping forest. "Well, where are we? I mean, where would we be out in the world?"

"Salem," he replied.

"Salem?" Her frown deepened as she thought. "Assuming it's the same one, there was a case here a couple of months ago. Gray and Geneva took care of things."

"Yes, they did."

Still remembering, Diana said, "They had help. An unusual dog. And a couple of psychics Bishop would really like to get on the team. As a matter of fact, aren't there a lot of psychics in this town? I mean a lot more than you'd expect in a little mountain town? Like whole families of them?"

"Come this way, Diana." He turned and began walking down the forested slope.

"Dammit," she muttered, following and trying not to think of her numb feet, of the uneasiness still crawling over her cold skin. The spirit guides were worse than Bishop, she thought, ignoring questions they didn't want to answer. It was annoying. And occasionally dangerous.

Usually dangerous.

But Diana followed, because she was a medium and this gray time had rules she had learned over the years, one of them being that she listened to and followed guides because they needed her help. Or knew of some situation that did.

They were going downslope toward the town, and almost as soon as they emerged from the dense forest Diana saw a slender figure who appeared to have just started in the same direction.

"Hollis?"

TWO

With obvious relief, which was clear even though she was a mostly washed-out gray and eerily one-dimensional like everything else, Hollis stopped and turned to meet the newcomers. Her regular features, which became memorable if not unforgettable when animated, and her unusually striking blue eyes, which were always unforgettable, were clearly etched even without the color that filled them with life and interest.

It was, Diana thought, a quality peculiar to Hollis; the features of most in the gray time, even the guides, seemed more . . . smudged . . . than clearly etched. She made a mental note to mention that to Hollis when they got a moment to themselves. In the meantime, the other woman was, as usual, speaking.

"Thank the Universe. I thought I might be alone here, and this is *not* a fun place to be alone." She reflected. "Or even with company. What the hell, Diana?"

"No idea. Yet. This is Daniel." She gestured toward the child guide, almost absently, because she was frowning as a sudden and very troubling question occurred. "Did you get pulled in by accident this time, Hollis? Because of me? Because I opened a door?"

Before Diana could answer, Daniel did.

"You're both needed," he said.

Earnestly to Diana, Hollis said, "You know, that sort of relieves me. Because even though we were warned it would probably happen, so far we really haven't had the problem of me being pulled here just because you're here." She turned her attention to the guide, adding severely, "But it's awfully early. I think. Back home. So, why?"

The guide gave her an angelic smile and then continued down the slope, clearly expecting them to follow.

Doing so, Hollis muttered to her friend, "You know who they remind me of, these guides of yours?"

"Yes. Bishop."

"Uh-huh. At his worst. Where are we?" She sounded nervous, and her gaze swept the area around them.

"Salem, according to Daniel."

Hollis thought about that for a few steps, her gaze focusing ahead and below them at the town, which was becoming more obvious even if still only gray smudges in vague shapes. She tried to ignore her cold body and really cold feet. And how tired she already felt. "The Salem we know about from that case a couple of months ago?" Hollis read the case files and reports of other teams and investigations the way some people read biographies, just so she'd *know*.

"Apparently," Diana answered.

"Gray and Geneva took care of that," Hollis said aggrievedly. "And there was a major cleanup afterward. The file was closed."

"Yeah, that's what I heard. Maybe something new in the same town?"

"I think that would be a first. For us. The unit."

Dryly, Diana said, "I haven't been a member as long as you, but isn't that sort of normal? I mean, new things?"

"Oh, yeah. But not twice in the same place. I mean, cities, yeah, because so many people, but not little mountain towns. The rule seems to be one evil monster per little mountain town. Or always has been."

Over his shoulder, Daniel said, "Rules change."

The women exchanged a look, and Hollis said, "Okay. So what sort of monster this time? Has he said?"

"No."

Rather abruptly, as things often happened in the gray time, a cold and eerie gray mist sort of shivered around them and they found themselves standing, slightly unbalanced for a moment, on the level sidewalk of what was obviously Main Street.

"Do you ever get used to that?" Hollis asked, searching for bearings and lifting one foot briefly to rub a toe she'd stubbed painfully on the rough sidewalk.

"Not really." She looked at Daniel, who was facing them as they stood on the sidewalk.

"Look around," he suggested.

Both women looked around them at a very gray, desolate downtown Salem. The buildings were clearer, but still more gray smudges than the complete linear contours and edges buildings were supposed to have. And windows of a lighter gray, also smudged around nonexistent edges. That was all that differentiated one building from another, one thing from another, really, shades of gray. There were a surprising number of shades of gray.

Infinite shades of gray, Diana always thought when she was here.

And it was barren of real life. There were never any people or animals, never any life other than spiritual. Diana tried not to think of it as a dead place, but it was certainly not a place where anything living flourished. It dragged at her, a steady and unsettling pull she was always, on some level of herself, aware of and disturbed by.

She had more than once thought that the essence of herself, of what made Diana who she was, was constantly under assault in the gray time, as though the forces here struggled to attack her as a foreign cell was surrounded and attacked by the defenses of the human body.

And she had wondered if there was, somehow, an expiration date, a limit to the number of times she could visit here and escape alive. Scary thought. Very scary thought.

"The Universe really made a creepy place here," Hollis said. "Or time. Whatever."

"Definitely." Diana returned her gaze to their spirit guide. "Look, I'm okay for a while yet," she said, hoping it was true at least one more time, "but Hollis is going to get very tired very quickly. Because it's still new for her. So? What is it you wanted to tell us and show us?"

"Salem," he said simply.

The women looked at each other, then returned their gazes to the spirit guide.

"You'll be getting a call," Daniel said. "Soon. But I was sent to warn you first."

Hollis started to ask sent by whom, but Diana was shaking her head. "They never answer that one."

"No," Daniel agreed.

"Dammit." Hollis sighed and waited, brows raised in hopeful question that at least some information might be forthcoming.

"This is an old town," Daniel said. "Very old. And the Five have been here since the beginning of Salem. They *made* the beginning."

Diana frowned, but Hollis, remembering the case file, said, "Yeah. The original five families who settled this town, this valley, hundreds of years ago, and are mostly still in charge. Let's see . . . Cavendish, Deverell, Blackwood, and, um . . . Ainsworth. And Hales. The Five."

"The Five?" Diana asked, hearing emphasis.

"Yeah, that's the way it's written in the reports. Anyway. They still mostly run the town, like I said. Own the major businesses, employ most of the townsfolk one way or another. Oh, and one of the Five was the monster here a couple months ago. A Cavendish elder. Wanted to be a god. Or something like that. Usual psychopathic bullshit, made even worse because he was psychic. Only the Five refer to being psychic as having Talents."

Diana returned her attention to Daniel. "Okay. What about the Five? Now, I mean. Or what's coming?"

"It's already here," Daniel said. "Only not one of the Five." He considered. "Possibly not. But definitely hunting them."

Hollis eyed him. "To kill them."

"Yes. Serial. A killer murdering members of the Five. In . . . odd ways."

Hollis said, "Odd ways the local militia— No, they're local

deputies now. After that last case blew up in their faces they became official law enforcement. They can't handle it?"

"No," Daniel replied, again simply.

"Hitting too close to home?" Diana guessed.

"That. And so many of them have such good shields hiding what they can do, even from each other. Especially those they don't know about. So they can't use their psychic tools the way you usually can. To hunt monsters."

Hollis crossed her arms across her breasts and began to absently rub her hands up and down, conscious of cold silk and very cold flesh underneath. The coldness of this place was settling in her bones, aching. "Okay. And?"

Daniel smiled that oddly adult smile. "Why don't I show you?" Before either woman could respond, he waved a careless arm toward his left and the street.

Both women turned their heads to look.

"Oh, shit," Hollis murmured with hardly any voice.

Coming toward them in an odd halting or limping walk, several people who had been very obviously and very gruesomely killed were just suddenly *there*. Crossing the street. One man's head was oddly shaped, the top of it flattened just above his eyebrows in an utterly unnatural way. Another hugged his middle, where glistening intestines and other organs tried to escape from a gash straight down, from just below his chest to his crotch.

A burn victim lurched toward them, seared flesh dropping in tattered bits from its blackened body with every step. A woman staggered a bit, clutching the handle of a very large knife buried to its hilt in her chest. Another woman made an eerie moaning sound and was carrying her severed arm as though it were an infant, both the limb and her body still bleeding.

Blood was dripping from almost all of them, splashing onto the gray pavement of the street, and it was . . .

Hollis closed her eyes and turned her head away as shock rippled through her. "They aren't gray," she said in a voice that wasn't in the least bit familiar to her. "They're like real—I want to leave, Diana. I want to leave *now*."

She opened her eyes, meaning to look at Diana, to say something or ask something, but what she saw was Daniel. He was still smiling. And there was something—

Hollis felt a tug that was inner, and familiar, and instantly let herself obey, closing her eyes again against the dizzying disorientation of suddenly being yanked back into her own body.

SHE WAS SHIVERING violently, and Hollis was inexpressibly grateful for the blessed warmth of covers and the very necessary embrace of a warm man underneath them.

"Jesus Christ," she murmured without lifting her head, her voice shaking as badly as she was, eyes still closed. "I hope Quentin pulled Diana out."

DeMarco used one hand to pull the covers up higher around her, then shifted just a bit so more of her was pressed against him. "You're like ice," he said, his voice as calm as it almost always was even though he'd been yanked out of sleep by the abrupt awareness of where she had been and the urgent need to pull her back. "I didn't know anything was happening until something scared you."

It was not yet dawn, so their bedroom was almost completely dark, with only the low light in the bathroom escaping a nearly closed door to peer out doubtfully, not reaching the bed. It hardly seemed worth the effort, but Hollis disliked totally dark rooms, so there was always something on.

She wasted a moment or two wondering why it was true that she could go away in spirit, leaving a warm body behind, but that the instant her spirit, chilled in the gray time, returned, her body became icy as well. She'd have to ask Diana. Maybe she'd know.

"I wasn't scared at first," Hollis said after a few moments, her voice not shaking as badly as she became less cold and her teeth no longer chattered. "Because I thought Diana would have to be there too. And she was. And one of her spirit guides. A little boy, only not. Creepy kid. But Diana was there, so I stayed calm. Until . . ."

He felt it again, that jolt of fear and horror that had awakened him in an instant, made him reach out psychically, mentally, and emotionally for the woman he had been physically holding. The woman who had returned to him, cold through to the bone and exhausted and horrified.

"Maybe you should rest before talking," he said. "Sleep. Or take a hot shower first, to really get you warm." DeMarco wanted to reach through their connection, to find out for himself what had so terrified Hollis, but knew better than to try that often handy shortcut now. She had shut down, either deliberately or instinctively, as she had done in the past, to spare him her own ragged emotions. Which meant the horror had lingered, was still with her.

"It won't be as vivid when I'm myself again, remembering how it was," she murmured, exhaustion tugging at her. "Except . . . Jesus. A first for me. Not sure about Diana because she's gone there for years. Most of her life. So maybe not so . . . so horrible to her."

"Try to sleep," he urged again, feeling her shivering fade, her body warming, beginning to relax. To go limp, really, boneless, the way she did when she was tired like this.

She hadn't been there many times, but whenever she came back she was always cold and utterly exhausted, with haunting smudges of weariness and stress that were bruised shadows under her bright eyes, unable to share some of his excess energy as she otherwise could in order to replenish her own, even through physical contact.

And always she was almost imperceptibly thinner.

She had told him that was his imagination. That she could hardly get physically thinner because her spirit had wandered into a strange place for a little while.

Still.

"Victims," she murmured. "Past or present . . . dunno. Couldn't tell. But victims. Murdered . . . all of them. Horribly murdered. Tortured. Walking . . . stumbling . . . toward us. Knives still in them . . . One of them . . . more of them . . . making awful sounds. And the . . . the thing is . . . the thing that was so . . . so horrible . . . they weren't gray . . ."

He thought sleep had finally caught her, ending the story for now, but then she breathed something against his throat, a final word, hardly a sound, but he caught it.

"Salem."

And then she was asleep.

Salem

It was dawn when the crows began to gather.

Despite their size, they moved with eerie quiet, alighting with hushed wings on the winter-bare branches of the big tree their leader had chosen.

One. Three. A dozen. Two dozen. More.

Several flapped their wings with that strange hushed quiet, but most waited, still and silent. They gazed off toward the small town nestled in the other end of the valley, still shadowed from the morning's light by the mountains rearing, dark and massive, above the quiet buildings and streets.

Gradually, a restlessness rippled through the birds as they waited. Heads turned, bright black eyes scanning the area nearby before fixing once again on the distant town. Wings lifted and beat the air.

One crow spoke softly, not the sharp, hoarse *caw* that humans heard, but a sound that played up and down the range of notes, peculiarly intelligent. The others took up the sound one at a time and passed it along, each bird adding a note, a query, an exclamation.

The sun was still well below the peaks of the eastern mountains when their leader joined the other crows. She was larger than the rest, her black eyes brighter, her wide wings soundless as she took the space waiting for her on a broad lower branch of the tree.

She, too, gazed off toward the distant town for a few moments, her wings thrumming softly as she beat them slowly in the dawn stillness. The others grew still and silent, waiting.

Tia became still, and her quiet voice throbbed with power as she told her family what she had dreamed.

THREE

Bishop looked at the four people sitting across from him at the big table in the SCU conference room.

"It's something different for us," he said finally. "A different sort of beginning, at least."

DeMarco was impassive, as usual, his powerful body seemingly relaxed, but Bishop could feel the tension, which was not usual, not these days at least. And DeMarco's gaze rested on his partner's profile more often and more intently than was the norm for him while here at the office.

Quentin was tense as well, though he didn't bother trying to hide it. He also showed concern for his partner and wife in quick glances, and the humor that normally lightened his lean face was totally absent. He looked, in fact, a little grim. He had very nearly lost Diana once, and that haunting memory would always be with him.

Bishop got that.

Diana was still, her face closed, delicate features not revealing much even to Bishop. She didn't appear to be unusually tired; having visited the gray time for most of her life she was . . . acclimated, for want of a better word.

And Hollis, obviously still tired despite the sleep she insisted she had gotten, her deceptive slender fragility more obvious than usual, was the only one of the four who looked, utterly and completely, the way she had to be feeling: spooked, shaken, and almost angrily baffled.

She viewed baffling things as puzzles needing to be solved; it was one of the qualities that made her such a good agent and a gifted profiler. One of many qualities.

"We have to go," she said. "That was a gilt-edged invitation from the Universe if I've ever seen one."

DeMarco said, "Going in before something really gets started, assuming that's what we'd be doing, could be a huge advantage. Just being on-site and familiar with the location should help us move faster and more effectively." He had been in the military for years, and it showed.

"We haven't been invited," Bishop noted neutrally.

Hollis looked up then, her unusual blue eyes meeting his tarnished silver ones. "Salem might not know something bad is coming or already there, but we know." Her voice was tense and a little hurried. "You've sent agents into a situation on the strength of information from a spirit before. Me, for one."

"Not a situation like this one," he said.

"We have a solid contact in law enforcement there," Hollis said, her voice still tense. "Two contacts, actually, within the five families. And we don't have to worry about the usual hide-what-we-are bullshit with other cops, because Deverell is an empath and he's not the only psychic there in law enforcement by far."

Bishop nodded but said, "They also possess shields unlike any we've ever encountered before. Most of us have learned over a lifetime, half a lifetime, even only a few years, to build our shields; the psychics of Salem have learned over generations."

"Still, something we should probably try to understand," DeMarco said slowly. "Maybe those special shields provide protection. Or blindness, even to a threat." Since he himself possessed a unique double shield, he understood better than most both the pros and cons of a shield that could at times be too strong.

"We haven't been invited," Bishop repeated.

Quentin said, "And so we do nothing? Stand by and wait for the first victim to land at Finn Deverell's feet?" He had learned to keep a tight rein on his native impatience over the years, but right now it was clearly threadbare.

"I didn't say that," Bishop responded.

"You always say to watch for signs," Hollis reminded him, and said what Bishop had been expecting her to say. "That was a giant red warning flag from the Universe. We need to be in Salem."

"I've never seen anything like that in the gray time," Diana said.

Bishop didn't comment on the elephant in the room: the holes in Diana's memory due to the strong medications supposedly treating a "mental disorder" both mainstream doctors and her own father had not recognized (or had not wanted to recognize) as psychic abilities. She had drifted unaware through years, nearly half her life, and gaps in her memory still remained. How could she be certain she had never seen what she simply might not remember having seen?

Of all the agents at the table, Diana had the least experience in the field *as* an agent. On the other hand, she'd spent most of a lifetime learning to function in regular visits to her gray time, and no one doubted that experience—or the extraordinary strength that had allowed her to learn to use her abilities despite every effort to smother them.

Quentin spoke up before Bishop could respond. "Having a psychic like Deverell leading their law enforcement is a giant plus; we all know that. But even more than that, if what Diana and Hollis saw and were told is even half right, he's in danger; his *family* is in danger. All of the five families are, and probably others as well. That town spawned one monster; what's to stop it spawning another one?"

"Spawning another monster isn't a possibility we can ignore," Bishop said. "Given that particular town. Given the people there. Finn will listen, at least. Beyond that—"

The conference phone on the table rang, cutting him off.

Bishop reached for the phone, and a sudden flash of certainty made him hit the speaker button. "Bishop."

A strong, steady voice came from the speaker. "Bishop, it's Finn, in Salem. I have . . . a situation here."

Salem

He had been watching Salem for a long time.

Watching, listening, learning. All his life, really. His mother, and

34

before her his grandmother, had made sure he did. And made sure he never forgot.

It was why, he thought, they had made sure that his own bitterness and resentment were hidden. Very, very well hidden, and for a very long time. The Five were, in most ways, not hidden at all, not in Salem. They had their customs, their beliefs, but townsfolk outside the Five were aware of those. And aware of their Talents. The Five had most of the money and the land, and the authority.

The elders were very much in charge. Set themselves up fine, they had.

And held on to what they had. Built on it.

And the others, the families that had followed them or trailed into Salem in the centuries since, had for the most part simply accepted the way things were. Those without Talents saw nothing unusual about the town, accepting the "superstitions" of mountain folk with a careless shrug if they didn't believe, and accepting Talents matter-of-factly if they did. And those others with Talents of their own . . . well, they remained apart from the Five even so. In many subtle ways and a few obvious ones, they were . . . lesser.

And maybe some of them didn't resent it.

Stupid bastards.

His grandmother had told him. She'd learned from her own grandmother, and she from hers, about the way things had been here in the old days. The Five, traveling from some unnamed or just forgotten place over in Europe to arrive in a very, very young America that hadn't even borne that name for long. Not settling in any of the established places or colonies but seeking one of their own. A place of their own. Either avoiding the Native Americans along the way or managing a tenuous peace with them. And when they had settled here, the Five, there was still no conflict with natives because none had lived or even hunted here.

And nobody had bothered to ask the Cherokee as white settlers increasingly drove them and other Native Americans farther west. Nobody had asked what was wrong about the valley that held the settlement that became a town named Salem.

But he knew.

He stood on the mountain slope gazing over the valley for a moment, until his attention was caught by two crows settling on the bare limb of a big oak tree about a hundred yards from his position. His eyes narrowed as he watched them.

He considered briefly, then shrugged and turned away, moving farther back into the thick undergrowth of holly bushes and picking his way among the granite boulders and outcroppings.

It was, he thought, a good place to begin.

He checked the duct tape holding his guest securely just to make sure, ignoring the muffled, angry sounds coming from the mouth covered with tape. He studied what he could see of the face, noting eyes that were also angry—and afraid.

He liked the fear.

He stepped back, smiled at his guest, and began to concentrate. And as he concentrated, he saw those eyes grow more afraid, saw them widen, blink.

Fill, suddenly, with horror.

And pain.

———

Quantico

"What kind of situation?" Bishop asked calmly.

Finn Deverell, now chief deputy of Salem, laughed shortly. "Your kind. Hell, our kind."

Bishop glanced at the others, then said, "You're on speaker. A couple of my teams got a . . . heads-up before dawn this morning. We were just discussing it."

"Not Geneva or Grayson," Deverell said more than asked, probably assuming Bishop would have named them if so.

"No, they're both on another case. Neither of these teams has ever been to Salem, so the connection, if there is one, is something none of us can explain."

"That can't be good." Deverell sounded wary. "What Talents?"

"There's a medium on each team, and they got the warning, if that's what it was."

"A Talent none of the Five has," Deverell noted slowly. "And to my knowledge no one outside the five families has it here in Salem."

"I remember that," Bishop said. "I thought it was unusual when you told me, given the otherwise wide range of abilities in Salem."

"And I never gave it a thought until you pointed it out. No idea what it means, or even if it means anything. The partners of the mediums?"

Bishop knew what he was being asked. "A very powerful telepath and seer."

Deverell's sigh came audibly over the line. "Most of us still call that last Talent the sight, or the farseeing. That's how I was alerted. A Blackwood elder came to me yesterday, one whose Talent is farseeing. She's been uncannily accurate for a long time, and what she saw is about as bad as it gets." He paused briefly. "What kind of warning did your mediums get?"

"Very few specifics. And couched in . . . let's call it cryptic terms, which is par for the course with spiritual warnings." He explained, briefly, what Diana and Hollis had seen.

"Tallies with what Aylia Blackwood saw, at least in the broad outlines."

"No helpful details?"

"A vicious murderer killing in particularly horrific ways. And fear. I've never seen Aylia Blackwood afraid, not like that."

"Anything else?" Bishop asked.

"Well . . . I don't know if it's connected, but in the last few weeks we've been having unusual problems with communications in town, all through the valley. Cell phones, radio signals, satellite TV. A lot of interference. Other electronics seem to be affected too. No idea what's causing it."

"But something new?"

"The intensity of it, yeah. Though the valley does tend to have sporadic electrical issues, you probably remember that from last time, and summer storms here can be unusually violent."

Those around the table exchanged glances.

Finn was going on slowly. "The interference could have affected Aylia's farseeing, I suppose. But if your people also got some kind of warning from outside the valley . . ."

Bishop said, "Hollis and Diana—the mediums who received the warning—have expressed a certain urgency. If we can actually get there and be on-site before the trouble really gets started, it could offer us a huge advantage we've never had before."

"Planning to come yourself?" Finn asked. "Being here in January for the cleanup was one thing, but an active investigation? Not that I'm complaining. Just wondering."

"That depends on how workable it would be," Bishop answered. "Six or more strangers in Salem will be noticed, plenty of questions asked, and we have no cover stories prepared, so we'd have to be official, with a reason to be there other than to investigate crimes that haven't as yet happened. If we're officially there for that reason, it warns the potential murderer, which could alter his plans for good or bad, so a big risk. He could escalate—or he could go to ground and try to wait us out before doing anything at all. And our being official in any way also alerts your people that something is going on, so even more questions will be asked."

"Got a good story to cover that?" Hollis asked wryly. "I'm Hollis, Mr. Deverell."

"Finn. And I do," Finn answered promptly, surprising her. "Since the militia has disbanded, those who were not a part of the insanity back in January *and* were and are coolheaded and responsible have become deputies. The one thing we lack as a police force, though, is something more than merely adequate formal training. The county sheriff resigned before he could be fired, and his temporary replacement is mostly busy putting out political and media fires."

"Which helps keep at least some media attention at the county capital and away from Salem," Bishop noted.

"One plus," Finn agreed. "I've gone on record as saying we need solid training in order to prevent anything like that from happening again, and the other families as well as the rest of the townsfolk here have been supportive of the idea. I know the FBI has a Field Police Training Program, sending specialized agent/instructors to work with law enforcement in their cities and towns. Those instructors cover not only investigative skills but also managerial, administrative, and technical skills. I would think sending six or more agents for the job here wouldn't be considered excessive—at least not to the people of Salem." He paused. "What do you think?"

"I better not be stuck filing," Hollis said.

Finn chuckled, surprising her again. "After what happened in January, I . . . commandeered a vacant building and extra lot one street back from Main, and it's become both our new official head-quarters and a potential training facility. We've been settling in there. Still a bit chaotic, with new equipment and such still coming in, but my people have a handle on it. Though any software or hardware the FBI has designed to assist local law enforcement in maintaining good records and making use of federal databases would be more than welcome."

"You've got it," Bishop said. "I can send in a couple of strictly technical people to assist in getting that part of it set up. My active field agents are already accredited as police instructors, so—"

"We are?" Hollis's voice was startled.

"Yes, you are." Bishop went on to Deverell, "So that sounds like a reasonable explanation for our presence in Salem. It probably won't fool everyone, especially if the Blackwood elder's vision spreads as gossip does, and if the situation drags on, but it'll definitely help.

Whatever happens, we'll make sure your force has all the training and resources we can offer."

"Thanks," Finn said with real gratitude. "When can you be here? I'm not given to jumping at shadows, but I'd rather have your people here and settled in before everything hits the fan. Assuming it does."

"We should all be there by tomorrow afternoon," Bishop said. "Late afternoon, most likely. I'll make the reservations at Hales B and B. Just our names; that will give you a bit of extra time to prepare whoever you feel the need to for our official arrival."

"Thank you. I do have a few people to talk to about that. And you have a journey to start. See you tomorrow afternoon."

"Right."

Hollis barely waited for Bishop to hit the speakerphone's button to end the call before saying, "Every time I turn my back on you, my résumé grows longer."

"Or even when you don't," Bishop said.

Hollis considered, obviously, and just as obviously decided not to comment on that. She eyed Bishop. "So you are coming, huh? And Miranda?"

"That surprises you?"

She immediately shook her head. "I doubt any of us has to be told Salem fascinates you. A very unusual little town with a whole lot of psychics. Like a buffet." The last three words were said with obvious relish.

Bishop didn't rise to the bait, but he was glad to see that even Diana looked a little amused.

"We have a lot to do, so best get started," he said instead. "We'll fly to the mountain house and stay there tonight, pick up any additional equipment we might need as well as a couple of technical people to help out in Salem. And we'll gather as much info as we can before leaving for Salem tomorrow, just in case communication inside the valley does turn out to be even more of a problem than it was two months ago. The jet leaves in half an hour."

FOUR

Nellie Cavendish looked across her big desk at Finn Deverell and sighed. "Want to run that by me again?" The desk, like the big front office, had once belonged to her father, who had for a number of years before she was born run the family banking and finance business.

Her late uncle Duncan's office remained closed and locked. If it hadn't been a part of the big building, Nellie would have had it burned to ash and then buried the ashes. Deep.

"At least six federal agents are arriving in Salem later today," Finn responded, and then sat down in one of the two visitors' chairs, absently reaching to pet Leo, Nellie's big black Pit bull, who had settled down beside him after a friendly greeting. "More, probably."

"Why?"

In the nearly two months since Nellie had taken charge of the Cavendish banking and finance businesses in Salem, Finn had more than once been amused by her directness. And his respect for her shrewd intelligence and business acumen had increased steadily. She not only had wasted little time in accepting the burden of leadership of her family that was her birthright, but had also quickly made herself known—and been accepted—by the other leading families long called the Five in Salem. Including the Deverells.

"Why, Finn?" she repeated.

"Because myself and my deputies require more formal training than we've had. The FBI has a program for that, and they're sending agents down here to work with us for . . . a little while. A few weeks. Maybe."

She lifted an eyebrow at him, brown eyes holding that unusual sharpness that was both a Cavendish trait and very much her own. "And?"

"Why should there be an *and*?"

"Because there always is," she replied dryly. "Especially in Salem. The crows are gathering again, Finn. In numbers, mostly outside town, but there if you notice. I noticed this morning. Why?" Her voice was very steady.

"Why didn't you ask them?" Only a Cavendish born could command the crows, one of their several Talents—and Nellie had those talents as well as others. In spades.

"I've been doing my best to leave them alone," she reminded him, her gloved hands resting, fingers laced together, on her neat blotter. "After what Duncan did to them, they deserved the time to heal. And just be birds."

He glanced at the whisper-thin gloves covering her slender hands, also not asking why she still wore what had been designed as an outward focus point to help her control her Talents. He doubted she still needed them, but he hadn't asked. "And," he finished for her, "that's still a Talent that unsettles you. Despite everything."

She frowned. "Because I don't want to command them. Why should I? I've learned more about them in the last few weeks than I have in my entire life, even without trying and even though there's seldom been more than one or two around me. For once." Crows had gathered around her all her life, something that had baffled and frightened her until she had come to Salem and learned of her heritage.

Now it just made her uneasy.

Just.

Mildly, he said, "I didn't ask why you didn't command them. I asked why you didn't *ask them* why they were gathering again. You noticed it. You noticed it was unusual. So why didn't you ask them what's going on? Tia is usually the one closest around you, right?"

"Yeah." Her frown lingered, the rather severe expression doing absolutely nothing to mar the beauty of her finely drawn features. The Cavendishes had always had good looks, but in that way as well Nellie was rather extraordinary. "I told you. I don't want to bother them. Tia . . . communicates . . . what she wants to. When she wants to. About them, about their history. Bits and pieces. But she just offers. I don't ask."

"You don't read Tia." It wasn't a question.

Nellie answered anyway. "No. It's different, what I get from them—not thoughts, not even because of one of the Talents, I think. Not telepathy. It feels . . . unique. Concepts, images, wordless things. Wordless knowledge."

"Okay. Are you using any of your Talents?"

Her chin firmed stubbornly. "No."

So that was why the gloves still.

He sighed. "Nellie . . . that shield Bishop taught you to construct for yourself is a damned good one, but we both know what it's supposed to be used for. You don't need to call down a storm or use your telepathic Talent unwisely, but you can't keep it all bottled up."

"Says the man no one can read due to a shield built by generations of knowledge and experience." Without pausing for his reply, if he had ventured one, she went on. "And stop trying to change the subject. If FBI agents are coming here, it's for something other than to offer more training to you and your deputies. Or that isn't the only reason. So?"

Genuinely uncertain of how she would react, he reported the visit by the Blackwood elder and his subsequent communications with Bishop and his teams.

"Aylia Blackwood." Nellie's tone was thoughtful, her face unreadable. But her gloved hands moved briefly, uneasily, fingers tightening around each other. "I would say it would take a lot to scare her."

"I'd agree."

"And she's convinced someone is out to start picking off members of the Five."

"'Murder us brutally' is, I believe, what she said. And in addition to not scaring easily, she has a very strong history of accuracy in her farseeing."

"Has she ever seen anything like this before?"

"No, not that she told me. Killings weren't so uncommon in the earliest days of Salem, the times being what they were, but until Duncan came along, murders had been all but nonexistent for at least a few generations. Deaths, naturally, and a few killings now and then, but nothing like what she saw."

After a moment, Nellie said, "A stranger would be noticed, as I know all too well. And I haven't heard of any strangers in town. I get the cover story you have for Bishop and his agents, but if there's someone out there bent on murder . . . then they're already here. Living here. Is that what Aylia saw?"

"I don't think it's what she wants to believe, but believe it she does."

"One of the Five?"

"That she wasn't as sure of. But like so much else in Salem, it concerns Talent of one kind or another. Psychic abilities." He paused. "You and I both head up our respective families. No way to know for certain if elders and those like us are being targeted—and no way to know we aren't. It would make sense if we were, assuming the goal is to take down the families."

"Take down the families? That's a lot of people, Finn. That's practically Salem."

"Yes."

"Why would anyone want to destroy the town? Because it would."

"I know it would. And—I don't know why anyone would want that. But the possibility is certainly there, and something we should take what steps we can to guard against."

"How far ahead did Aylia see?"

"Not very, she thinks."

"So," Nellie said slowly, "we should probably just assume we are being, or are soon going to be, stalked by a killer."

"Probably," Finn agreed.

"You sent Robert back to school early," she said.

Finn was surprised. "How did you—"

"He came by earlier this morning. To say good-bye to Leo." Finn's nephew, taking a semester off from college, had formed a very strong empathic attachment to Nellie's dog during the events of weeks past, and had since then dropped by her office here at the bank just about daily to offer to take Leo for a walk or to the dog park just down Main Street, which made for pleasant outings for them both.

Nellie had been grateful, especially since taking charge of the extensive Cavendish affairs here *and* still being remotely in charge of a financial business in another part of the state kept her at her desk for long hours.

"His shield is nearly as solid as yours," Nellie went on, "but it wouldn't have taken a telepath or an empath to know he wasn't happy about leaving."

"I wasn't about to tell him why. He would have stayed."

Nellie started to say something, but her office phone rang just then and she picked it up. After a brief moment, she held out the receiver to Finn. "For you. Still having problems with cell phones?"

He nodded with a frown and took the receiver, wondering if he would find his cell battery completely dead. Again. It was happening way too often these days. "Yeah?"

"Finn, it's Garett," his lead deputy said, tension in his normally lazy voice. "We have a missing person."

PERHAPS TO LESSEN the impact of so many strangers descending on Salem at one time, Bishop sent the two technical specialists in both IT hardware and software and law enforcement software into town late morning on Tuesday. Sandra Convers and Mike Langtry arrived without fanfare in a light-colored Jeep, going directly to the new law enforcement center and meeting Finn Deverell there as arranged. They didn't introduce themselves as agents, and neither was openly armed.

The rest of the team came in two inevitably black and hulking SUVs, with Bishop and Miranda arriving about an hour ahead of the other four around midafternoon and going straight to Hales B and B to get everyone checked in.

"How long has Cole Ainsworth been missing?" Bishop asked Finn as he set up a rather unusual-looking laptop at one end of the large dining table in their suite. The laptop was both larger and bulkier than the current norm, with what looked like a section of extra keys whose function Finn couldn't begin to guess at since they showed neither letters nor numbers but enigmatic symbols.

Half sitting on the other end of the table despite a restless need to move, Finn said, "Far as we can tell, since sometime Saturday. There was no report because he argued with his wife and, in her words, stormed out afterward. Apparently not at all uncommon. She assumed he was staying with a buddy, which he's done before after one of their fights. It wasn't until this morning that she really got worried. Says he's never stayed away so long. So we checked with the buddy—with all his friends—and there's no sign of him. Now we're asking everybody."

"His wife is the last to have seen him?"

"My people are still running down some of his known haunts, but yeah. So far we haven't found anyone else who saw him after he left work on Friday."

"Does anyone else agree with his wife that disappearing like this is unusual for him?"

"Most of his friends agree. They say the fight wasn't unusual but also wasn't serious. Both he and Sharon are . . . passionate people. They argue. A lot. But he does tend to stay with a friend for a day or so and then come home." Finn sighed. "Like I said, I've got my people out checking places, checking with other family members, with friends of the family."

"Then that's all you can do. For now."

Finn studied the other man, thinking absently as he had before that Bishop didn't really look like any kind of cop, especially dressed as casually as he was now, in dark slacks, a white button-up shirt open at the neck, no tie, and a black leather jacket. He looked physically powerful, which he certainly was, in excellent physical condition; he likely, Finn had decided, considered his body another tool to be kept well honed and ready for optimum use. His almost too-handsome face was lent a dangerous air by the thin, faint scar twisting down his left cheek, and held the exotic additions of a widow's peak crowning his high forehead and a shock of pure white hair among the gleaming black at his left temple.

One of these days, I'm going to ask him about that bit of white hair, Finn thought.

"Family trait." Bishop looked up with a faint smile, meeting Finn's gaze steadily with slightly amused tarnished silver eyes. "In my family too, psychic abilities have been handed down for generations, though I didn't know that until fairly recently. As for the white streak, it's almost always caused by a psychic shock or extreme psychic effort of some kind. Very much so in my case. My cousin Cassie nearly died to earn hers."

"I have my shields up," Finn noted neutrally after a moment, saving the other information to be chewed over later.

"Yes, you do."

Finn eyed him. "Just how strong *is* your telepathic Talent?" he asked finally.

"When Miranda and I are together, very strong."

"Percentage?" Finn knew how the SCU rated such things.

"It's been increasing over time. These days, I can usually read seventy-five to eighty-five percent of those around me and without touching them, which used to be necessary for me. Sometimes, in some situations, the percentage is higher. Depending on whether I push . . . or just listen in."

"Can you get through anybody's shields, or am I special?" Finn managed to keep any sarcasm out of his tone. Barely.

"No idea," Bishop admitted. "I'd never tried with you before—when we met and talked outside Salem and before today—but I thought it might be advisable to know here and now if your unique shields were completely impenetrable. Even so, since you're an empath more accustomed to shielding emotions than thoughts, I might well discover the shields of a telepath more difficult to get through."

"So, is it your strength or my shields? Can any of your team read me?"

"Reese may be able to; he's the strongest telepath among the other teams. But he's also the most protected because of his own shield, the least likely to probe just for the hell of it, and his range is more limited than mine is. Hollis may pick up on emotions because . . . well, because she's Hollis."

"An empath?"

"A relatively new one, but very strong even though it's not her primary ability. And since her shields tend to be a bit unstable, she may well pick up on more than she intends or wishes to."

"Isn't she one of the mediums?"

"Yeah, Hollis has . . . several abilities."

"Sounds like a Cavendish," Finn said, wry.

"Hollis is unique. As far as we can determine, the latent ability she was born with is mediumistic, hence her primary ability. But it seems that if she needs a different ability badly enough, especially while working a case, she develops it. Spontaneously."

"I've never heard of that."

"Neither had we. And never since."

"She retains the ability after the case?"

"So far. In fact, the abilities tend to grow stronger over time."

"That does sound unique."

"And rarely easy for her. Probably one reason her shield is unstable; there could literally be too much for her mind to protect, at least for now. She even sometimes feels the emotions of spirits she encounters, which is empathic rather than mediumistic."

"What do you mean?"

"Although their abilities are highly individual, Hollis and Diana are both what we term psychic mediums; they can both see and hear the dead, and interact with them. A physical medium can do the same, but uses all of his or her senses and is able to feel physical sensations from the spirits, sometimes even the pain of their deaths. Which, if the death was violent or otherwise traumatic and especially painful . . ."

Finn winced. "That can't be fun."

"No. I've found a few strong physical mediums over the years but, given the work we do, decided against even trying to recruit them for the unit."

"I don't blame you." Finn thought about it for a moment, then said, "Hollis sounds formidable."

Bishop smiled faintly. "You won't think so when you first see her. Until you look into her eyes."

"I'll be a bit more on my guard," Finn said slowly, adding, "It's a little disconcerting, to be honest. After all these years, nobody around here can read me."

"Nellie can."

"Well, yeah, but—" Finn stared at him for a moment, then said somewhat warily, "You're dangerous."

"Sorry," Bishop said, not really sounding it.

"Please tell me that's not a . . . transparent thing to anybody but you." He was ignoring the tinge of heat that had crept into his cheeks.

"Probably not." Bishop appeared to think about it, either not noticing or more likely ignoring the other man's reaction. "Although, again, maybe to Hollis. But, if so, she won't say anything about it." He thought a moment longer. "Publicly."

"Good," Finn muttered, not quite under his breath.

Miranda came into the sitting room to join them then, saying mildly, "We keep our own shields up generally, and probing just to find out if we can isn't encouraged and isn't common. But then, neither is Salem. Common, I mean."

"But," Finn said, turning his gaze to her, "since we're reasonably sure our potential killer is already here . . ."

She nodded. "Best to probe now and then as we go along. All of us, in our own unique ways. It won't be intrusive, unless any of us finds something suspicious. You were thinking a question a little while ago, so it was easier for Noah to pick up on it."

It occurred to Finn only then that what Bishop knew, his wife and partner knew as well. Finn had picked up on their extraordinary bond the very first time he'd been in the presence of both, sensing it was both deeper and more complex than any outsider could possibly understand.

Miranda sent him a quick smile. And had he been susceptible to sheer beauty, Finn probably would have felt his toes curling in his shoes, because Bishop's wife was drop-dead gorgeous even before she smiled.

Luckily for his composure—and for the working relationship with Bishop—Finn was appreciative without being at all drawn these days.

Equally mild, Bishop said, "Quite a few of the townsfolk will probably be thinking about questions, certainly about us, but how many of them we'll be able to pick up is something we'll just have to wait to find out."

Finn nodded but said, "Outside the Five, shielding varies widely among the psychics here. Naturally."

Miranda said, "But inside the Five, you're all accustomed to shielding pretty much all the time."

"Yeah."

"Well," Miranda said, "it being more likely we'll be able to read psychics outside the Five—"

"—may or may not mean a damned thing in terms of being helpful," Bishop finished.

FIVE

He knew the feds were in Salem. He'd known long before they had arrived. They'd been invited, after all.

Not that it mattered.

In fact, he viewed their arrival as something of a challenge. After all, he'd laid his plans long ago. And now he was acting on those plans.

Sooner than they expected, he was sure. Because word was out that one of the Blackwoods had reported a farseeing, and that was what had drawn the feds here. Details of the warning were garbled, and growing wilder by the hour.

He liked that. Liked the wary glances of people on the streets, the visible tension of Finn's deputies.

He liked the fear.

He moved easily along the slope, smiling. He had left his guest alone for some time, going back twice before now just to make sure desperate effort had not managed escape.

He paused to look around carefully, making absolutely certain no one could have seen him, then slipped into the little glade and studied his guest. He was pleased but not surprised that the tough tape still held securely. He smiled at eyes blazing furiously above the strip of duct tape over the mouth. There was still anger now. Indignation.

He bet if he removed the tape, he'd be treated to pure outrage.

The earlier lessons had apparently been forgotten. He considered for a moment using his Talent again, but admitted to himself that it was more enjoyable and possibly more effective to use another of his gifts.

He bent forward slightly and swung his long arm in a smooth backhanded slap.

Above and below the tape, flesh reddened, and a convulsive swallow choked down what he guessed was blood. He was very, very strong.

Above the tape, the determinedly furious eyes had changed.

Now they were afraid again.

Smiling, he reached over among a small group of big rocks where he had placed, out of sight of his guest, a not very large but very sharp and gleaming knife.

A choked sound from behind the tape, then a steady and increasingly urgent murmuring, muttering, noises punctuated by wet sniffs.

He shifted just a bit to the side and brought the knife to the tense wrist extended out from the body and taped to a plank of rough wood. Ignoring the tape, he slipped the edge of the knife beneath the edge of a cuffed shirt and began to cut it.

He had cut the sleeve all the way up to the elbow when the sounds from behind the tape began to gurgle with understanding and even more fear.

"Well," he said reasonably, "we can hardly get started with all your clothes on, can we?"

An instant of silence, and then a wet whimper.

———————

AS HOLLIS AND DeMarco entered the suite that would serve as their base, she nodded a greeting to Miranda but continued a conversation with her partner uninterrupted.

"—because Geneva told me about it when I asked her. She always has another way out. It's handy to. I had to check to make sure I wouldn't have to stand on my head or something to use it, because Gen's as flexible as an eel."

DeMarco nodded to Miranda, who had let them in, then said to his partner, "Vanishing around a corner like something in a magician's act wasn't necessary. That's all I'm saying."

"Oh, it was only for a minute. Less. And anyway, keeps you on your toes. Hey, everybody." She looked around the sitting room of the suite, finding that Quentin and Diana had already come from their own suite, only a few moments before by the look of things, and noting that equipment and supplies had been unloaded and placed and seats in the room chosen.

She found herself being rather warily regarded by a tall blond man with humorous blue eyes, absently identifying him as Finn Deverell even before Bishop made the introductions.

Given to firm handshakes, she shook his, told him it was nice to finally meet him, then muttered, "Damn," under her breath and made for her chair.

"Want to share?" Bishop asked as DeMarco also shook hands with Finn and then took his place in a chair near hers.

"No," she said briefly, and gave the unit chief a look. "Not . . . germane." Then she shrugged and by the tone of her voice quite deliberately changed the subject when she said, "The back of my neck's sort of crawling, Bishop."

"I'm not surprised. The level of energy in the valley is high. How are you reading it?"

She thought about it. "I'm not sure about that. Doesn't feel negative. Exactly. Or positive. Exactly. It feels . . ." She narrowed her eyes, appearing to look through the unit chief rather than at him. "I dunno. Maybe it's just all the shields if everybody's feeling unusually threatened. Which I would be."

"Can you get a source?"

"Not so far," she answered immediately. "Not even a direction. Just sort of all around."

Bishop nodded and glanced at the others. "How about the rest of you?"

Diana said, "Same crawly feeling on the back of my neck. The urge to look over my shoulder." She frowned. "It's not so bad in here, but outside everything I hear seems a little . . . muffled."

"New for you?"

She nodded. "I've been affected by the energy of a storm, like most of us are, but not like this."

"And there's no storm forecast," Quentin said. "Some winter weather headed this way, but not a storm." He paused, then added,

"We all know I'm not especially sensitive to other kinds of energy, but I feel a bit jittery."

"Reese?"

DeMarco shook his head.

"Both shields," Hollis said.

Bishop nodded but said to DeMarco, "Let me know if that changes."

"Right."

Then Bishop told them all about the missing man, Cole Ainsworth.

Quentin frowned. "Missing since Saturday?"

Finn nodded. "It appears so. He didn't take his car, and there's no other sign he might have left the valley. Past behavior would indicate he's still in town or out in the valley. We're still checking with friends and family."

DeMarco said, "So we didn't get much of a heads-up after all."

Hollis half nodded. "I don't know why we expected anything else," she said, then frowned and changed the subject. "Is Nellie Cavendish going to be here today? Because I'd like to meet her."

"She's at the bank and will be until closing or after unless we need her," Finn said, continuing to look at Hollis rather warily. "Still lives here at Hales, at least for the time being. Says she's been too busy to look for a more permanent place. Since she won't set foot in Duncan's place or where her parents lived, I've been trying to talk her into taking one of the downtown condos."

"Where you live." It did not appear to be a guess.

"Yeah," he said. "Most of the single professionals around here do."

Hollis looked at him steadily, entirely unconscious of the effect on someone else when her exceptionally bright, oddly luminous blue eyes fixed on the subject she was addressing with a certain interested, curious intensity. "Do you think she will? Stay here, I mean. In Salem."

"I think she feels an affinity for the place whether she wants to or not. And a responsibility to the Cavendish family." Finn looked at Bishop, adding briefly, "You were right."

"He almost always is," Hollis said in a tone that robbed it of any compliment. "About what, this time?"

"You," Finn returned pleasantly. "I imagine a lot of people underestimate you. At first."

"A few," she conceded without visible surprise. "But they never underestimate Reese, so it evens out."

Finn imagined it did. The very big blond man, for all his calm expression and voice, pretty much radiated the kind of intensity Finn had been aware of before only in some cops and a lot of former military people. A sort of wired-and-ready-to-react inner energy that might be contained but could still be felt.

Probably from ten feet away.

Hollis was looking at her boss. "Have you been casting aspersions?" she demanded of Bishop.

From his position at the far end of the big table, he was looking at her thoughtfully. "Never. What are your impressions of the town so far, other than the energy?" His glance swept the room but settled back on Hollis.

She countered with a question of her own, mostly directed at Finn. "How many of the Five know there's a danger?"

"Only the heads and a few other elders that I know of," he replied readily. "Though Aylia may have shared her farseeing within the adults of the Blackwood family."

Hollis had no trouble following that. "She didn't see enough to point us at the potential killer, just enough to scare her into warning others, especially her own kin."

"That's pretty much it."

"So, potentially, that knowledge could have spread like wildfire by now."

"Could have," Finn agreed. "Probably more likely than not."

"And he could know people have been alerted. The unsub."

"Also more likely than not," Finn confirmed grimly.

———

NELLIE TRIED TO concentrate on work after Finn left to get his people started in searching for Cole Ainsworth, and for a time managed it. She ate lunch from a take-out box at her desk, which was the norm, her eyes on spreadsheets and other financial reports. But by midafternoon she was edgy, restless. She fought it for a time, then finally got up from her desk and went to the window.

Maybe it was a storm, forecast or no forecast. She was ridiculously sensitive to storms, and—

Outside her office window, Salem's Main Street appeared almost as it usually did on a weekday afternoon. Almost. Cars moved along at the slow speed demanded, and on the sidewalk people walked briskly in the chill, in and out of stores and the downtown restaurants and other businesses, many of them talking to each other, smiling brightly. And they hurried.

A few of them cast wary looks upward, while others kept their gazes down with a stiff, visible effort.

Nellie felt suddenly sure that if she could have overheard those conversations she would have heard voices that were a little unsteady or shrill. Frightened.

Her gaze lifted, and she studied signs, lampposts, the cute little balconies some of the downtown buildings boasted, the trees along Main and in the town square.

Crows.

Until she had seen them gathering close to town this morning, Nellie had almost been able to forget all the years of her life when the crows had always seemed to be around her. Until Finn had pushed her to use at least one of her Talents, she had been able to force them out of her mind.

But now . . .

There were dozens of them. Scores.

Black bodies glossy in the weak late-winter sunshine, they perched with almost no movement on trees and signs and balconies, not so much peering around them as directing their bright eyes toward the bank.

Toward Nellie.

She wrapped her arms around herself, almost hugging a body that suddenly felt cold. Her fingers moved one against the other, rubbing the thin leather of her gloves, reminding herself it was there. That reminder was all it took for her to half-consciously weave another layer of her shield. Protecting herself.

"Coward," she whispered.

But she was remembering weeks before and an evil darker than anything she'd known in her life. Remembering the courage it had taken to remove her gloves and lower her shields and stand with only her abilities and her determination as weapons against that evil.

She had won that battle. But . . .

Nellie did not reach out to the crows, did not open herself to anything they might have told her. Instead, feeling cold and afraid, she stood there rubbing her upper arms and staring out her window.

Wondering if the crows were here as a warning.

Or a threat.

"HOLLIS?" BISHOP WAS still watching her.

She realized she was rubbing her left temple hard, and hastily lowered that hand, lacing her fingers together in her lap. She did not look at her partner. "Think maybe that shield you helped Nellie with might work for me?" she asked her boss.

"Since it's formed of energy, quite possibly."

"You might have told me that sooner." She sounded more resigned than angry.

"So far, you haven't demonstrated an ability to . . . weave . . . energy the way Nellie can," he explained. "It's my belief that's a prerequisite to building that kind of shield, and it could be unique to her. And also, while you're still acquiring abilities and struggling to master them, it could do more harm than good."

"Figures. And no way to know, really, if and when that's going to stop. Me acquiring new abilities, I mean. Might even reach a point of having to invent a few. Told you the Universe hates me."

Bishop lifted his eyebrows and waited.

Hollis sighed. "A lot of people are feeling a lot of things, Bishop. Mostly fear. I dunno if this town could set a land-speed record for gossip or it's just because there are so many psychics around who can pluck news out of the air, but the fact there's a threat seems pretty universally known." She considered. "Or felt, anyway."

"You're really picking that up through all the shields?" Finn asked. With his shields up, he had no empathic sense other than a very low-level anxiety in the townsfolk.

"Well, catching it, more like. It's all being thrown at me. I dunno why my receiver is suddenly at max wattage, but it is. Or maybe just because my so-called shield really isn't, most of the time. Mostly there's a lot of white noise, especially here, because it's another thing that happens when there's a lot of energy all about *and* too many feelings to sort through—"

Her eyes widened suddenly, then narrowed and grew, if possible, more intense. Her face drained of color. She seemed to be looking at something in the distance. She winced. Then, softly, she said, "Oh, shit."

"Hollis?"

She drew in a deep, slow breath and let it out shakily. "I think . . . I think our unsub does have Cole Ainsworth. He has somebody."

"Where?" Bishop asked.

She closed her eyes, concentrating, fighting to grasp elusive threads of knowledge that showed up bright against the dark despair trying to weigh her down, that horrible sense of a victim all too aware of his own agonizing fate. "I can't tell. Maybe . . . north of here? The other end of the valley. North, northwest. The mountains at that end. Not close."

"Anything else?"

"Pain. Horrible pain. Fear. Terror." Her voice was very steady. "Panic. A sense of being alone . . . nobody to help. There are woods all around, I think. Really strong sense of being helpless, of being . . . doomed." She blinked and looked at Bishop, saw him. Hardly being aware of it, she shivered. "It moves in and out. Like a door opening. And closing. Maybe what I'm getting is from a psychic whose shields keep slipping, but with too much fear or pain, or too little control for that to matter. Being psychic, I mean. Not calling out for help, just feeling. God, he's so afraid."

" 'He'?"

Hollis fought to get a grip on what she felt, but for a while all she could do was sit there and endure the cold waves of terror and agony. "I think . . . yeah. He. I'm almost sure." She drew another shaky breath, still struggling. "It's . . . more than murder. What I'm feeling . . . it's getting worse, stronger." Her face went suddenly blank, wiped of all expression, only the luminous eyes starkly alive, and she added evenly, "Torture."

Finn swore, not softly.

Bishop said, "We knew our arrival here could make him move faster. Maybe it has. Maybe he sees us as a challenge rather than a threat."

"Or maybe," Quentin said, "he just doesn't give a damn."

SIX

Aylia Blackwood-Sayers was young to be considered an elder in most any place other than Salem. Not that age had anything to do with it, despite the title. Elders were made up of the heads of each family and those family members who had the strongest and best-controlled Talents.

Aylia, whose wise parents had not attempted to contain her Talents within a Barrier constructed by Duncan until she was an adult, had been a Blackwood elder since her eighteenth birthday.

She was barely past thirty now; her black hair was untouched by gray and her thin face unlined, and she moved with the easy, unthinking grace of an active and athletic person utterly comfortable inside her own skin.

The fact that she was also comfortable with the responsibilities of being an elder in her family showed in the level gray eyes and aura of dignity that clothed her always.

Even now.

She wasn't anxious for a repeat of what her farseeing had shown her on Sunday night, but with the whole town so unsettled she could feel it even without an empathic Talent, she felt it was her responsibility to see what she could.

Her farseeing was accurate—but she believed it showed her only one thread of a future, a thread that could easily be torn, snipped, or just woven into a greater whole as choices and decisions were made along the way. As events were influenced by the people involved in them, especially once her farseeing showed her that thread of potential future. The agents were here now, and since she had not seen them or known they would come when she had farseen, she was uncertain whether the future she'd seen had been one in which they'd played no part or a future in which they'd taken a hand.

Not that she could be sure of that even if she was able to farsee again. It was one of the more capricious Talents even for one of her control, apt to desert one in the event of great need and often difficult to interpret even if it showed her something.

So she did what she could to ensure the best possible conditions for farseeing, retreating to the small cottage at the rear of their backyard that her husband, Michael, had built for her years before. He called it her studio, a place for her to escape the kids and the usual day-to-day demands of being a wife and mother, or just to be alone with her thoughts and her farseeing.

Michael wasn't a member of the Five except by marriage to her, but he understood and respected his wife's Talent and her responsibilities to her family. She was lucky in that; some of those who married into the Five, especially if they married elders, had a difficult time adjusting. Aylia knew how lucky she was, and deeply appreciated Michael's acceptance of who and what she was, of all the baggage that came with being one of the Five.

He was at work today, the kids in school, so there was no one to comment when she left the house and went to her studio. It was bright even on this slightly overcast day, and comfortable; she'd furnished it with some of the excess furniture accumulated after a decade of marriage, using colorful slipcovers to hide fabrics worn by kids and pets and time, and cheerful rugs on the floor and pretty curtains on the windows.

The only indication that it wasn't just an ordinary place to get away from it all was in the exact center of the main room, and even that might have been just a meditation area, arranged with a thick rug, a low table on which were several partially burned candles, a tabletop fountain made of bamboo and copper, and a small crystal bowl filled with colorful semiprecious stones.

All part of her ritual.

Aylia made herself comfortable at the table, sitting cross-legged before it, automatically making sure the fountain didn't need more water, lighting the candles, and idly sifting through the stones with her long fingers for a few moments while she listened to the soft splashing, breathed deeply and steadily, and consciously relaxed tense muscles.

That took the most time today, required the most concentration, which didn't surprise her. Her farseeing had never before shown her something so deeply disturbing, so frightening, and there was a part of her that naturally did not wish to see anything like that again.

Coming toward her out of a strange grayness, moving in an odd halting or limping walk, were people who had been very obviously and very gruesomely killed. One man's head was oddly shaped, the top of it flattened just above his eyebrows in an utterly unnatural way. Another hugged his middle, where glistening intestines and other organs tried to escape from a gash straight down, from just below his chest to his crotch.

A burn victim lurched toward her, seared flesh dropping from its blackened body with every step. A woman staggered a bit, clutching the handle of a very large knife buried to its hilt in her chest. Another woman made an eerie moaning sound and was carrying her severed arm as though it were an infant, both the limb and her body still bleeding.

Blood was dripping from almost all of them, splashing onto the gray pavement of the street, all the more shocking because it was scarlet surrounded by that eerie grayness . . .

Aylia drew another deep breath. Then another, forcing the images from her mind. She refused to allow fear to rule her, and after a few minutes she felt calm and centered.

After that, Aylia Blackwood-Sayers followed the practice so deeply rooted in her family's history that no one even knew where it had come from, the means by which Blackwoods for uncounted generations had tapped into their Talents.

Softly, clearly, she began to sing.

———

"DID YOU SEE the crows when we drove past Main Street?" Diana asked her partner.

"Yeah. More than a little creepy. Haven't seen one out here so far."

They were following a narrow path into the mountains at the

northern end of the valley, just entering the area that Finn and Bishop had marked on the map Quentin carried. They didn't have long to search before darkness made it impossible, but all of them had chosen to get out here and begin looking for any sign of Cole Ainsworth or his captor.

But there were thousands of acres of mountain slopes, never mind the sprawling valley. It was a huge haystack.

Like the others searching, both wore their weapons openly on their hips, jackets unzipped despite the chill making them obvious. Quentin also carried a sat phone on his belt; one member of each team did, earlier tests showing that the powerful phones worked at least passably well. So far.

"I wonder why they were all downtown like that," Diana said. "And why we haven't seen any out here. I wonder if any of the others have."

Their still-new and somewhat experimental earbud coms that worked quite well in some places and with some members of the unit had been worse than useless here, emitting only a buzzing sound. Those of the team who could carry cell phones had found the same interference. So the sat phones were the only way they could reliably keep in touch while the teams of agents and Finn's deputies roamed about the mountain slopes.

It was ironic but a fact of their complicated lives that they often struggled to communicate over any distance, despite the abilities they possessed. The Universe, as Quentin had more than once noted, never made things easy.

"I also wonder about the significance of them being in town," Quentin said.

"Maybe Nellie? They tend to gather around her, don't they?"

"Have in the past. But you heard Finn, right? He said Nellie had been keeping her distance and so had the crows. Since what happened back in January. Still, they seemed to be gathered in the area of the Cavendish bank."

"Definitely creepy," Diana said. "Reminds me of that old movie."

"Same here."

Diana was scanning the area as they moved through, looking for a sign she was half-afraid she wouldn't recognize when she found it. If she found it. Changing the subject, she said, "Hollis didn't seem to be sure if the victim actually reached out to her. Or to anyone."

"Well, Finn said that Cole Ainsworth doesn't have the Ainsworth clairvoyance, assuming it is him we're looking for."

Steadily, Diana said, "So Hollis felt it because the victim she sensed was so afraid and in so much pain, not because he was psychic."

"Probably." Quentin reached for her hand.

"We don't know if the unsub is psychic."

"No. But probably not wise to assume he isn't."

"And with all the psychic abilities here the only thing we can be fairly sure of is that he isn't a medium because that's the one ability no one in Salem has ever had. Right?"

"Right." Quentin's gaze was once more roaming about them, sharp without appearing to be. "Problem is, other than Hollis picking up what she did, none of us seem to be sensing the psychics here, certainly not as individuals. Might know one if we come face-to-face, but other than that all we're getting is static. Though Bishop did say he and Miranda could pick up some thoughts from some people who were physically close, but nothing like their usual percentage."

"Dammit. What time is it?"

Quentin was one of the rare SCU members who could wear a watch most of the time, in large part because he was solely a receiver and his visions were, thankfully, rare beasts. Checking his watch, he answered, "Nearly five. I'm a little surprised it isn't already dark in this valley, even with daylight savings time going, but it will be in another hour."

Diana glanced up at the gray and brooding sky, wondering again if there was a winter storm looming. Maybe that was why she suddenly felt colder than she had only moments before.

Maybe.

THE CROW SETTLED silently onto the bare branch of a big oak just seconds after the human pair passed the tree and continued along the faint path, still talking quietly to each other. He watched them, head turning alertly this way and that, black eyes fixed on them.

On, especially, the woman.

She walked with the dead. He knew that. She walked with the dead, and that made her far more akin to the crows than she knew.

Than any of them knew.

It also made her a threat.

He opened his beak to emit a very soft sound, inaudible from only feet away. He watched the pair disappear around a bend in the path, and stretched out his wings and beat the air soundlessly, then lifted off and flew silently just far enough to perch in another tree and keep them in sight.

————

"WE'RE MOSTLY HAMSTRUNG in the dark, especially in a mountain valley we aren't familiar with, hunting a killer we wouldn't recognize if we fell over him," Quentin said to Diana. "So I'm betting the unsub is playing the odds there, doing his . . . work . . . as late in the day as he can. Especially since Finn was clear about nobody being out after dark except his deputies in pairs, and even then not on the slopes."

"Which means we'll all have to head back in soon." Diana's voice was restless, and she kept glancing up at the leaden sky. "Maybe if I tried the gray time—"

But Quentin was shaking his head. "We agreed. We *all* agreed that you shouldn't try that yet. Especially with Hollis up on one of these mountains with Reese. He still might be able to pick up on the victim or the unsub. Which means he doesn't need to be distracted, much less completely focused on Hollis, and if she's as wide-open— at least to emotions—as she says she is, I'm betting she'd be pulled in with you."

"The gray time has to be why I'm here," she reminded him, not really arguing.

"Maybe. Which means that ability may be needed here. Or it could be that your ability was needed to *get* us here. But, either way, we agreed you shouldn't try to go back. Not now when we know so little. It's dangerous, Diana."

"I know. I know it is." She was silent for a few steps, then added, "At least Hollis hasn't been able to go unless I'm there. For a while,

I was worried she could open that door. And with so many other abilities, that's one she doesn't need."

"I imagine she agrees with that."

"Oh, yeah. Says she'd much rather see spirits here in our world than there. If I had a choice, maybe I'd say the same."

"Would you?

She considered for a few more steps, then laughed ruefully. "Probably not. Creepy as it is, it's what I'm used to. Where I'm strongest and most sure of myself. I just don't know if being able to go into the gray time will be useful here."

"We'll have to wait and see. It could be an ace in our pockets."

"Maybe." Diana sighed. She hated feeling useless, especially after spending so many years *being* useless. "I never envied telepaths before, but at least they can look with more than their eyes."

"So can we," he reminded her calmly. "Our eyes are trained, like our minds. And even if we aren't telepaths, our senses tend to be more acute."

"At least you have the spider senses if you need them. I haven't been able to manage even one."

His fingers tightened around hers. "I've been at it a lot longer, remember?"

Suddenly realizing, Diana said, "You're probably trying to listen. I should shut up, and—"

"Never. And, actually, I'm not. I tried the spider senses just a moment when we were leaving the B and B, and it was like an echo bouncing back at me. Painful."

"Thought I saw you wince."

"Yeah. The spider senses are, really, probes of energy we send out, the way a telepath or empath reaches out when they want to. But the usual five senses have more of a . . . presence, for want of a better word. Something solid. More tangible to the world around us."

Diana hadn't heard it explained that way before. But it made sense. "Sort of like a radar signal? So they can hit something and bounce back?"

"Apparently. Though unlike radar they're no help here and now, with so many shields around us to bounce off. At least, I think that's what's happening. I've felt something similar, though not often. Generally there's nothing large enough or solid enough to completely block the way. But with all these shielded minds around us, it might be like looking for a chink in some pretty damned good armor to find a way through."

"There always is one." Diana's tone was thoughtful now. "A chink. A weakness. Maybe that's what we're looking for."

"Maybe it is," Quentin agreed.

FINN LOOKED ACROSS his desk at Garett Cavendish, one of his lead deputies, frowning slightly. "Absolutely nothing?"

"Still no sign of Cole Ainsworth, and we've talked to pretty much everybody who knows him. If he's not missing, he's sure as hell well hidden. And I don't know why he'd be hiding."

"Are you getting anything with your Talent?"

Garett was wearing a frown of his own that did nothing to diminish the usual Cavendish good looks. "When I drop my shields, it's like being hit with white noise. Almost deafening. And painful. I can barely sense the FBI telepaths—three of them, right?—maybe because their shields are different from ours. Can't pick up their thoughts, but I could probably look at a map of the valley and tell you where they are right now."

"But nothing from the other Cavendish telepaths?"

"No. It's like we figured, Finn. Our shields do a damned good job of hiding us even from each other. Especially from each other. I hate to say it, but if Aylia Blackwood and the FBI are right about a killer hunting here, he almost has to be one of us."

"Or somebody with no Talents at all."

"Maybe. And maybe this energy we can all feel has something to do with how someone could be killing, *torturing* someone, and none of us can sense it, shields or no shields." He shook his head slightly. "I hope the agents can function better than we can."

"So do I. When they come back in, I'm hoping they can tell us something positive. How about our search teams?"

"Nothing so far. And we won't be able to cover much more territory today. I'll get our people out tomorrow at first light, but . . . it's going to take time to search the slopes. And from what the agent got, time is something we don't have much of, not if a victim is being tortured."

"I know. And we still have to keep up our regular patrols here in town." Finn shook his head. "We can only do what we can do."

Garett nodded.

Finn glanced at the clock on one wall of his office, estimating how much longer the search teams and his own people could expect to continue the search today. Not long.

"Okay. Everybody comes back in at dark to get patrolling assignments. I want us out and visible in town tonight, at least until people have settled in for good."

"That's a lot of overtime."

"Yeah. And I don't know how long it'll be necessary."

"Until we find the bastard," Garett said.

SEVEN

Miranda, standing considerably less than a quarter of the way up the slope of the most northern of the mountains surrounding Salem, looked down across most of the valley to the town a fair distance away and absently listened to Bishop's side of the conversation as he talked on the sat phone.

". . . no victim yet, but it's only a matter of time before we start finding remains. I'd rather go ahead and get you on scene. A very good small hospital, especially for the size of the town, but they've never needed a coroner or medical examiner. Right, bring everything just in case. I'll send the chopper for you first thing in the morning. The pilot will know where to set down here, just outside the valley. There'll be a van waiting for you, as usual. Rooms in the same B and B where we're staying; it's very comfortable. Go there and check in as soon as you get here. Okay. See you tomorrow, Jill."

As he ended the call and slipped the bulky phone into the pocket of his jacket, Miranda said, "Reception is better up here than down in town."

"Definitely," Bishop agreed, moving to join her as she gazed at the distant town that was beginning to fade with darkness approaching rapidly.

"Jill and Sam?" Jill Easton was a skilled doctor and forensic specialist based in Asheville who was part of the statewide network of physicians able to be called in to act temporarily as a medical examiner. She was also clairvoyant, one of those psychics Bishop had located who was already settled and happy in a chosen profession. Sam Norris was her usual partner.

"Yeah. I notified the network last night and requested Jill if she was available. Both she and Sam are." They had long ago discovered that it was best to work with those "outsider" medical and other auxiliary technicians who understood and were familiar with the SCU as a unit; Jill had been the ME called in on several recent cases, and the fact that she was psychic was a plus.

Especially as far as Bishop was concerned.

Miranda smiled slightly, thinking about that. She was well aware that within the unit Bishop's almost uncanny ability to find and recruit—in one way or another—psychics was viewed with something rather like awe. Probably at least in part because so many psychics had felt and often had literally been alienated and alone in their lives before Bishop had found them, they'd had no idea just how many psychics had lived in the same secrecy and often quiet desperation.

She wondered idly how those within the unit would react to the knowledge that there was in truth an astonishingly vast and far-flung underground network of psychics who had found one another, coming together long before the SCU had been created, to fight a different kind of war. It was a network Bishop had discovered while searching for psychics, and his and his wife's participation in the fairly recent game-changing battle of that fight was something no one else within the SCU was aware of.

Probably.

There were, after all, few secrets within a unit of psychics, many of whom were telepaths who read minds and clairvoyants who could pluck bits of information out of the very air around them. But if the knowledge Miranda and Bishop had agreed to keep to themselves had been discovered by one or more of their team, at least the need for secrecy had been respected.

Though those within the unit might well begin to wonder when a few seeming leaps in technology would likely make their lives somewhat easier in the coming years, especially in the areas of communication and the gathering of intel. If, that is, the work being done by a handful of Bishop's trusted scientists bore the fruit he expected.

Miranda pulled her mind back to the here and now. "We won't be able to climb farther tonight. It'll be too dark to see soon, especially in unfamiliar terrain. I remember from Gray and Geneva's reports that it can be black as pitch in these woods up here. And there's no moon tonight."

They were both carrying a relatively light backpack, as were the others moving carefully on the mountain slopes, something Finn had insisted on and had, indeed, presented to them packed and ready before they set out. Anyone heading up into the surrounding mountains, he'd said, no matter how long they intended to be away from town, would carry sensible trail supplies and equipment. Because it was very easy to get turned around in the heavily forested mountains. Turned around and lost. Because they were strangers to the area and because even locals knew to be prepared just in case.

Especially in March, when the weather could change in a heartbeat and make returning to safety . . . difficult.

Bishop hadn't argued, nor had anyone else.

Now he said, "Nobody will be happy that we have to stop, but there's no real choice. Aside from darkness making searching all but impossible, most of us aren't used to this kind of terrain and should rest when we can. Probably best if we start out tomorrow at first light, or at least as early as possible."

"Want to try the spider senses again?"

Bishop shook his head and said wryly, "Every effort so far has been painful for both of us as well as the others, and I don't see that changing."

He had taught most of the others to enhance their senses, something he had learned to do himself, and he was the strongest and most accurate in the unit at using what Miranda had termed spider senses, especially when he was with her, which in this situation meant the blowback pain had been rather acute.

"I would have argued against it," she said, also wryly. "Still have a headache from the last attempt."

"The only downside of our connection that we've discovered, beloved."

"We're lucky," Miranda agreed.

"So far." Since it had to be said, Bishop said it.

They both knew that the pain they shared in trying the spider senses was just one aspect of the only real weakness of the deeper-than-telepathic bond between them. The truth was that their bond was so deep now that if one were cut, the other would in all probability bleed—and both knew the incapacitation of one, most especially if they were separated, would mean they would both go down. Temporarily at best.

Permanently at worst.

So far, that was a situation they had not had to face.

Miranda pushed that thought aside, as she always did. They would face what they had to face if and when it happened and not a moment before.

"So now we know the spider senses throw back a painful echo," she said. "But we still don't know how seriously our abilities are going to be otherwise affected here."

They were talking aloud rather than telepathically, he thought, partly because every member of the team was guarding themselves somewhat warily to the best of his or her abilities, and also because it was eerily silent up here. Far too early in the year for the summer sounds of crickets and the bullfrogs that could undoubtedly be heard from all the surrounding mountain streams, and as for birds . . .

They both heard a slight sound and looked to their right, where a crow had alighted on the still-bare lower limb of a tree. It cocked its head, shiny black eyes observing them.

"Nothing," Miranda murmured after a moment.

Bishop shook his head. "Must be more empathic than telepathic, which makes sense. Gray said it was like that, concepts, ideas, and emotions translated by his struggling mind into something like thoughts he could understand. The same with Nellie's dog. Said it hurt his brain."

"I can imagine. Well, no, I'm not sure I can. Callie's worked with Cesar since he was a puppy and says even through clear thoughts she sometimes gets no more than a concept for something he doesn't know the word for and tries to describe to her." Callie Davis was, currently, the only SCU member with a canine partner, though she and a Haven operative were working with several other dogs experimentally.

Miranda studied the bird. "He seems to be waiting for something. But what? No one commands them now. Finn said Nellie was adamant about that, just as she was to you."

"Maybe . . ."

Miranda felt a flicker in her mind that was husband rather than bird, no longer surprised that Bishop was able to open up a seemingly new or at least previously unused part of his senses, since he was a bit like Hollis in that, and she wasn't at all surprised when he said suddenly, "That's why the waiting. For us to realize, to understand."

The crow uttered a soft, curiously un-crow-like sound, flapped its wings briefly, then flew away.

She might not be able to communicate with birds, but Miranda certainly could communicate with Bishop, and at a depth below thought, where no other telepath could have reached and no external energy could affect, and she was nodding even as he looked at her. What he could sense he shared, always, with her.

"If Nellie will do it," she said.

"Their idea," he reminded her.

"If we're right about that. Just guessing, really. We could have misinterpreted the concept."

"I don't think so." Bishop took her hand and began leading them both back down the mountain slope. "We need them. And unlike most other birds, crows remember people, faces. They can help us search. I wouldn't be at all surprised if, after Duncan, they can't spot someone evil more quickly than we could."

That was a thought. And Miranda honestly wasn't sure if it was a reassuring one or a troubling one.

SHARON AINSWORTH SHOOK off her sister's comforting hand and glared at Finn, her blue eyes wide and turbulent. "I know he didn't leave me," she said. "Not for *good*. He'd never do that. It was just a *fight*, a little argument, that's all." She was a very pretty woman in her mid-twenties, but strain was marking new lines in her face and her voice was thin and high.

"I believe you," Finn said soothingly. "But we haven't been able to find him, and there has to be a reason."

"An *accident*. That must be it. Have you—"

"No sign of any accident. And he didn't take his car. So we have to keep looking for the answer. Is there—do you know of anyone who might have a grudge against him?"

She blinked. "What? No, of *course* not."

Her sister, Carrie Meridan, spoke up with a promptness that told Finn she'd already considered the subject. "Sharon, he told us not a week ago that someone had been in the dairy office after hours, re-member?"

"So what? Probably just a *kid*, just somebody wanting to *rob* the place—"

"He doesn't keep money in the office, you know that," Carrie pointed out. "It's just records, paperwork. And everybody in town knows it; it's almost a joke about how the only things of value are the cows."

"But—"

Finn broke in to say, "There was no report."

Sharon blinked again. "No. Well, of course not. There was no *damage*. He just thought somebody had been in his desk, in the filing cabinets. But it wasn't *personal*. How could it have been?"

Finn didn't know but made a mental note to check with others around the family dairy to see if anyone had any ideas about it. It might mean nothing. Or it might be important. Choosing his words carefully, he said, "So there's no one you know of who might want Cole . . ."

"What?"

"Well, say, out of the way."

"What're you suggesting? That somebody might want to *hurt* Cole?"

"I'm just trying to cover all the bases," he said. "Explore all the possibilities. So far, we haven't found anyone who saw him after he left this house."

The hectic color drained from Sharon's cheeks. "But . . . but . . . nobody would *do* that. Why should they? I mean, I know *Paul* put people's backs up, especially after what happened last summer, but *Cole* is just the sweetest guy, he really is. Nobody ever gets mad at Cole, not even *me*, really. We just have to thrash things *out* every once in a while, that's *all*."

"Okay, but—"

"Nobody would hurt Cole. *Nobody.* There wouldn't be any *reason.* I'd know if—if—"

Carrie hurried into speech as her sister faltered, saying tensely, "People are talking. About those FBI agents coming to Salem today. About what Aylia Blackwood saw. Is it true? Is there a killer in Salem?"

Sharon gasped. "Oh, *no!*"

"We don't know anything for certain," Finn said with all the reassurance he could muster in his voice. But he couldn't forget Hollis's stark words, the expression in her eyes, and was afraid his own doubts showed on his face.

"Finn—"

"We don't," he said firmly. "Look, we'll keep searching for Cole, you know that. My patrols will keep an eye out tonight, and first thing tomorrow we'll start again. I just want you to think about it, and if anyone—or anything—comes to mind, and especially if you hear from Cole, give me a call, all right?"

"But—"

"And try not to worry."

Sharon stared at him for a moment, then burst into tears. Her sister put an arm around her and soothed, glaring at Finn in a way that told him she blamed him and not her own words about a killer.

FINN SUGGESTED THEY all have dinner in one of the downtown restaurants, and since it was, after all, a Tuesday evening in a town increasingly worried and on edge, the place was far from crowded and they were able to have a rear corner entirely to themselves. And since this restaurant played soft, inoffensive music, they were able to talk in normal voices only slightly lowered without having to worry too much about people overhearing.

"Although," DeMarco offered dryly, "if there are as many tele-paths in Salem as we believe, we may not be hiding much from any of them."

"Shielded," Finn reminded him. "You say you've all felt that block."

"That doesn't mean they can't sense us, at the very least. And human curiosity can and often does reach beyond shields," DeMarco countered. "Until we know differently, I say we assume at least some of those around us are able to pick up information even through their own shields."

"Plus everybody is just plain anxious and uneasy," Hollis contributed. "Which could make them more than curious. And this weird-ass energy feels . . . stronger. Maybe." Before Bishop could ask, she added, "It's faint, but little bits of emotions keep getting through, as well as curiosity. But only people fairly near me, I think. Definitely worried."

"Because they know there's a threat?" Bishop asked.

She frowned slightly. "More because of us. I think. Partly because we're here, and two months ago it wasn't exactly a party to have the feds here, even if we were only cleaning up and trying not to disrupt the town any more than necessary. And because there's a threat, but . . . it's sort of like a game of telephone. Somebody, maybe one of the Blackwoods, told somebody else about their elder's vision, and it's been passed around and misheard and shared, anyway, until nobody's sure what's going on. Just that something is. And that it's bad."

"Maybe they're better off not knowing what we know," Nellie said. "Just worried enough to be careful."

"We can hope," Hollis said.

Nellie, encountered earlier in the town's dog park because Finn had known where she was likely to be at that time, had joined them for dinner; Leo, who disliked being left behind, lay quietly on a comfortable dog bed in the corner behind Nellie's chair.

"Apparently," she'd told them in explanation of the bed and Leo's welcome in the restaurant, "the health inspector is a Cavendish. And the owner of this restaurant married one. So the usual rules get overlooked from time to time."

"Nice to have clout," Quentin had said solemnly.

Nellie had smiled slightly but only shook her head.

Hollis looked at her with interest now, having already noted without comment the other woman's whisper-thin leather gloves. "That's some shield. I like it. I want Bishop to teach me how, but he says the timing could backfire on me. Or something like that."

Nellie smiled faintly. "It's handy at holding things in. Not nearly so good at keeping things out." Her voice was calm, but there was a faint look of strain in her eyes.

"Am I broadcasting?" Hollis asked apologetically, thinking that might be it. "I thought I'd mostly stopped doing that."

"Well," Nellie said, "not exactly. Not thoughts or feelings, but . . . I've never been able to see auras, but what I'm seeing now has to be yours." For a woman who had strenuously resisted even an admission of being psychic just weeks ago, she was taking the whole conversation, never mind her own abilities, very calmly now. Or certainly appeared to be.

Hollis looked disconcerted, which was not an expression often seen on her expressive face. "I can't see mine even in a mirror. What does it look like?"

"Sort of a gleaming white with streaks of red," Nellie answered immediately.

"Healing and power, energy," Bishop noted.

"I'm not healing anything. Or anybody," Hollis objected.

"It's also a protective ability, remember," he said. "Self-healing and self-protecting. With all the psychics around you, shielded or not, and especially with the energy, I'd expect your instincts to be protecting you at least somewhat."

"And the healing? If I'm doing that?" Her gaze was steady.

Bishop hesitated, then said, "You may always be self-healing at a certain level, below your conscious awareness."

"Because of all the abilities popping up. And sticking around. So maybe protecting me from all those potential dangers you and Miranda have worried about." It wasn't really a question.

EIGHT

Bishop nodded. "It is one theory we believe to be very likely. That could explain how you've been able to cope with acquiring so many different abilities without organic damage. You were healing yourself from the moment your abilities were first triggered."

Hollis considered a moment, then apparently changed the subject. "That isn't a shield? The protective part of my aura, I mean?" She sounded rather hopeful.

"In your case, no."

Hollis sighed and said to Nellie, "It's like being the brightest or the dumbest kid in class. Either way, not in step with all the rest."

"I get that."

"I thought you probably would. It's only my aura you can see? Nobody else's?"

"Nobody else's."

To Bishop, Hollis said matter-of-factly, "So at least some of my abilities are apparently broadcasting in that way. Perceptible, at least to a psychic as powerful as Nellie is."

"Apparently." He looked thoughtful. "My guess is that the way Nellie uses energy is just close enough to the way you do that she's able to perceive it in—or as—your aura. At least when your shield is . . ."

"AWOL?" Hollis said. "Which it is right now." She shifted slightly, almost unconsciously, bothered by the skin-crawling sensation caused by energy she could sense but couldn't quite get a handle on.

He nodded, as matter-of-fact as she was. "As Nellie said, her own shield is better at containing, not keeping things out. Energies. And the rest of us are shielding."

"So I get to be visible. Lovely." But she sounded more resigned than upset about it, sighing as she reached for her coffee cup.

DeMarco said, "Your shield is stronger some days than others. So maybe tomorrow will be better." He wasn't frowning, but it was in his voice.

"Maybe." She knew what concerned him, adding calmly, "Being visible to Nellie doesn't necessarily mean the unsub will notice, even if he's psychic."

"Doesn't mean he won't."

"We don't know enough about him to worry about something that may not be a problem. We could all be visible to him. We don't really have a clue what's possible here. Abilities, I mean. Talents. Don't borrow trouble."

"All any of us can do," Bishop pointed out, "is keep our guards up and shield as much as we can."

DeMarco half nodded, but whether in agreement or merely acceptance was hard to say.

Since they had reached the coffee-and-dessert stage of the meal and their waitress had left them to enjoy, and since the subject of abilities had been opened, Bishop said to Nellie, "Miranda and I met one of your crows up on the mountain."

"They aren't *my* crows," she objected immediately, a slight frown drawing her brows together.

Finn said, "They were watching the bank this afternoon."

"I know that." She didn't quite snap it.

"Why?"

"I didn't ask."

"Why not?"

Nellie sent him a look, then directed her gaze at Bishop. "Did you talk to the crow?"

"Not one of my abilities, though we did get the sense they expected to be asked to help us."

Finn murmured, "Maybe why they were all around the bank, watching. Waiting for you."

Nellie continued to look at Bishop. "So did you ask them to help?"

"As I said, not one of my abilities. Only a sense of what they might mean, not true communication. You can communicate with them."

"So could Gray. Why didn't you bring him along?"

"On another case. And we go where the Universe wants us to be, whenever possible."

Nellie considered that for a moment, then looked at Hollis. "It's more emotions than thoughts, really. Have you sensed the crows? You're an empath, right?"

"My control is virtually nil, so I don't count it as a full ability, just enough of one to drive me nuts," Hollis explained, then added, "I'm a medium first."

The words had barely left her mouth when Hollis was aware of a sudden, bone-deep chill. She felt gooseflesh break out on her body as if cold air had swept over her. As if a door into some icy place had opened. She was immediately conscious of time out of sync, aware that even though she was not in the gray time, she was nevertheless looking into a place and time that was not her own. Which was different. And scary.

Visiting an otherworld always carried the risk that she might not be able to return to her own.

There was a weird, muffled silence. And, oddly for her, the group at their table seemed to fade back into a sort of visual haze, leaving her able to clearly see the restaurant as she looked around. And to see . . .

Two tables over, an elderly man and woman wearing what she vaguely recognized as clothing from decades before appeared to be enjoying their dinner. Then the man turned his head and nodded at her, and Hollis felt a new chill.

He'd been shot in the head. Scarlet colored his gray hair around the awful gaping wound, a thread of it running down his cheek.

Okay, that's new. Don't usually see how they died. Damn. Oh, damn.

She forced herself to keep looking around, realizing that she was seeing only the dead, also something new for her. There were perhaps a dozen people besides the elderly couple in the restaurant, most sitting at tables as couples or in small groups, seemingly enjoying a meal. The clothing they wore was from past decades, some from very far back; one woman wore a very long skirt with a simple blouse, both that and her hairstyle telling Hollis she had lived sometime before the twentieth century.

They were all aware of her. As her gaze roamed among them, some nodded politely and returned to their meals; others stared at her as if waiting for something.

Hollis couldn't tell from looking at them how they had died— except for the elderly man.

That has to mean something. What does it mean? These things are always linked to the case we're on. Almost always. So who is he and why is how he died important? His clothing . . . he could have passed me on the street today and I wouldn't have noticed his clothes especially, so . . . recent? I think fairly recent. Men's clothing doesn't change as much as women's. A few decades ago. Less. Maybe.

She fixed her gaze on the elderly man, trying to decide what to ask him. But before she could, an odd sort of hazy shimmer above the empty chair beside the couple caught her attention. And as she stared, a huge crow assumed a solid shape, perching on the back of the chair, and bright black eyes gazed at her. It turned its head to exactly, eerily, match the elderly man's.

Hollis had the unsettling certainty that the bird was every bit as alive as she was herself.

"Wow," she murmured.

The crow uttered a soft *"Caw."*

She tore her gaze from the bird to look at the elderly man, meeting his gaze.

When he spoke, his voice was low and calm, and oddly pale eyes met hers steadily.

"You have to stop him. He isn't sick; he's evil. He's always been evil."

———————

SIMON CAVENDISH WAS late leaving the bank, which wasn't all that unusual these days. With Nellie Cavendish having taken over the Cavendish family business interests from her late uncle Duncan, and being not only whip smart but very experienced in finance *and* having her own ideas about how the business should be run, the last weeks had been busy indeed.

Simon was happy about that. He hadn't liked Duncan, had profoundly disapproved of his handling of the Cavendish finances, and had been disgusted and appalled by the older man's other . . . activities.

Simon was glad that was all over and done with.

As for Nellie, Simon had been a bit wary of one raised outside Salem even if she was one of the family and a blood heir of the direct line, but his caution had very soon been laid aside. She definitely knew what she was doing, just as clearly had no intention of enriching herself at the expense of the rest of her family, and he approved of both her shrewd financial decisions and the calm, friendly way she dealt with everyone around her.

He thought all the Cavendish cousins at the bank liked her and approved of her, a few conditionally since she was still new in Salem. There had been plenty of quiet discussions around the topic of who she'd choose as her likely successor; Simon knew himself to be in the running for the job given his own experience and skills in the family business, and while he wasn't an overly ambitious man and doubted in any case that his lovely cousin would prove to be the last of the direct line (especially if Finn had anything to say about it), he was as ready to assume the mantle of authority over his family as he was to allow someone else to should she choose otherwise.

Either way, he expected to continue his career in finance, which he enjoyed very much. He was already an elder in the family at twenty-eight, being in possession of an extremely strong Talent and a shield that had been partly innate to him and partly constructed carefully through training from other elders so that he seldom had to even think about it, far less concentrate to keep it up.

Which was a very good thing now, he knew. Aylia Blackwood's farseeing had spread, the gist of it at any rate, and even with his shield up his telepathic Talent had caught more than a few worried, anxious, and even frightened thoughts. He also knew that the federal agents Finn had called to Salem were already making their presence felt, even as calm and laid-back as they seemed, and that even those citizens of Salem without Talents were nervously aware something unsettling was going on, despite Finn's reasonable cover story for their presence.

Evidence of that was the fact that the downtown streets were practically deserted, unusual on a not-too-cold, pleasant Tuesday evening, and he saw at a glance that the three restaurants on Main were considerably thin of customers. Simon debated briefly as he walked but in the end decided he'd rather scramble a couple of eggs or maybe broil a steak in the neat kitchen of his comfortable bachelor condo and enjoy his music or a movie than eat his supper in one of the restaurants.

It was a night to be at home.

So Simon's steps quickened as he turned off Main onto a side street that would lead him home. It was dark, of course, but with the street-lights, his route was nearly as bright as day, and despite everything he had no concerns walking briskly home as he did virtually every night.

He'd seen a couple of Finn's deputies patrolling at the other end of town and didn't doubt more of them were roaming about, keeping an eye on things. Finn was good. He was smart, and he was careful.

Simon thought about that briefly, then turned his musings ahead to the next weekend as he walked, wondering with what was still little more than idle interest if maybe he'd ask Connie Taylor to go out with him on Friday or Saturday night. They'd gone out on a few casual dates, dinner and a movie and, once, to a small party held by friends, and he liked her, enjoyed her pleasant company. She worked at the bank as well, one of the loan officers. She was pretty and cheerful, she had a good sense of humor, and so far they'd discovered a fair amount in common.

Dwelling with increasing pleasure on the idea of another date with Connie, Simon turned a corner into the block that housed his condo. He didn't hear a sound, was given not even enough warning to drop his shield and probe.

Something struck his head in a brutal blow that dropped him in his tracks.

"HOLLIS?"

She blinked and looked down to see DeMarco's hand on her arm. Then she looked around the table at the team and new friends, all staring at her, all visible again and reassuringly alive.

I'm back. Thank God, I'm back.

"What did you see?" her partner asked.

Hollis forced herself to concentrate, still feeling cold. "I'm not quite sure." Slowly, she described the spirits who seemed to have lived throughout decades, longer. And the old man with the awful wound in his head and his warning. And the crow.

Bishop said, "You don't usually see how they died."

"No, thank God."

DeMarco was looking at her steadily. "So why this time?"

Hollis frowned. "Because how he died is important? Because how he died can tell us who he was? I don't know. Finn? An elderly man, shot in the head? Was that crime ever reported, as far as you know?"

"Must have been before my time. Or, at least, before my time in law enforcement."

"Figures." Hollis sighed.

"I'll have somebody go through what records we have of deaths by gunshot in Salem, but . . . Remember, it's only recently that we've had official law enforcement here. Something like that is more likely to show up in the town newspaper than anything more official. The newspaper archives are being digitized, but there's still a lot on microfilm. It'll take time."

Hollis sighed again. "So another piece of the puzzle, I guess, and good luck to us putting it together. And as far as the crow is concerned . . . I have no idea at all about the crow. Except that I got the distinct impression that it was as alive as I am. Not a spirit."

Finn was looking around uneasily now. "I never thought of this town as haunted."

"The town isn't haunted," Hollis said to Finn. "Well, I mean, there are spirits around. But nothing evil or dark or even bothersome." Despite her own words, she felt uneasy about the old man and the crow. And she still felt cold.

"Is that . . . usual?" Clearly, he had almost said *normal*.

"Pretty much. Usually I know they're around but don't see or hear them. If one of them . . . steps forward . . . and obviously has something to say, then it always means something. Not that I always understand at the time. Like now."

"So they never speak plainly?"

Hollis thought about it, absently rubbing a hand up and down her sweatered arm. "Well, sometimes they're less cryptic than other times. But they never point straight at the bad guy. Seems to be a rule."

Miranda murmured, "The Universe never makes it that easy for us."

Finn looked at her. "Apparently."

Since he still appeared wary, Hollis tried to reassure him at least somewhat. "Sometimes I see them doing the sorts of things we living do, just busy getting along. Walking along, eating in restaurants like this one, doing what most people do every day. It's only the ones with unfinished business or who otherwise need our help that tend to want to talk to us."

Finn did not look particularly reassured.

Diana said, "I rarely see them the way Hollis does, here among the living, but I've learned to feel them around me. Which they mostly are. They seem drawn to mediums even if they don't have anything to say."

Hollis wondered. She almost always saw spirits singularly; she felt them around her as Diana did quite often, but it was a distant awareness usually. When she saw them clearly, when they were trying to tell her something, it was almost always one spirit—and her own reality remained as it always had.

But not this time. This time she had the uneasy conviction that she had somehow stepped into the spirit realm. That had never happened to her before.

And she had no idea what it meant.

NINE

Nellie leaned forward slightly, clearly more than a little disconcerted as she looked back and forth from Hollis to Diana. "Bishop said you were both warned; if you didn't see them here among the living, then where—?"

Diana explained as briefly as possible about the gray time, with Hollis pushing aside troubling questions, adding a helpful word here and there.

Finn was shaking his head slightly as he looked at Bishop. "You weren't kidding when you said every psychic was unique."

"I've never met any two psychics with the same ability who used it in exactly the same way. The basic definition always holds: Mediums see and/or hear the dead, telepaths read minds, empaths feel emotions, telekinetics affect objects in the physical world, seers catch glimpses of the future, clairvoyants pick up information from people and things around them—maybe from the very air around them. But each individual person filters the abilities through their own experiences and viewpoints."

"Probably why I'm so often irritable," Hollis said, absently taking a bite of the strawberry shortcake her partner had unobtrusively pushed closer to her. "My filter's clogged." She was only half-aware of even speaking.

The others regarded her with varying degrees of interest as she continued to eat the dessert, her faint frown remaining.

"Give it time," Quentin advised finally.

Hollis finished the bite in her mouth, then said cordially, "I'd love to. Only the Universe hates me, like I said, or I did something horrible in my last life, or something like that. Because you can't push too much through a filter and expect it to not get clogged. I think I'd have a clearer idea about the old man and the crow otherwise." She frowned at him, then at Bishop. "But you were asking Nellie about the crows."

"And I was asking you," Nellie said promptly, looking somewhat relieved to move on from spirits. "Have you picked up anything from them?"

Hollis ate the last bite of her dessert, then pushed the plate away and reached for coffee. "You know, I really couldn't say whether I got anything from the crows. For sure, I mean. There were some odds and ends while we were up on the mountain, and we did see a few crows about. But I'm not sure what I was getting. I mean, I wasn't focused on birds. Or maybe it's that clogged filter."

Either way, it gave Bishop sufficient reason to say to Nellie, "We know you can communicate with them. And we could definitely use their help."

"I'm not telling them to do anything."

"Not tell. Ask." He paused, then added, "As I said, I'm fairly certain they've offered."

"Bishop—"

"Nellie, you know crows are highly intelligent. That they remember faces, people. They know who's been good to them and who hasn't. They share that information with each other. And correct me if I'm wrong, but it's not widely known that it's a Cavendish Talent to communicate with the crows, right?"

It was Finn who replied to that. "A rare Talent even among Cavendishes, the ability to communicate with the crows." He stopped himself just in time from using the word *command* rather than *communicate*, and nodded. "There are a handful of rare, extremely unusual Talents that pop up now and then across the five families, and that's one of them. It wasn't spoken of or even known to anyone outside the Cavendish family for a long time, probably because it isn't something anyone believed especially useful. Until Duncan found a way—a very bad way—to use it. I doubt many of us know now. I mean, plenty of his followers and those who feared him knew that Duncan claimed he could control them, but he made it seem like a Talent he alone had, not a family Talent. Once he was gone nobody seemed bothered by the crows. I only knew about it, that it ran in the family, not just in Duncan, because Nellie's father told mine before he left Salem."

To Bishop, Nellie said, "Your point being?"

"My point is that our unsub may not know he has any reason to be wary if he sees a crow now and then. Or, at least, not know he should be as wary as possible. Which means they could watch without being noticed. And again, crows remember people. We could use their help, Nellie. Salem's a small town, but it's surrounded by some pretty rugged mountainous terrain, and there are still too few of us to effectively cover the ground we need to, as fast as we need to. Especially if this unsub decides to keep us guessing."

"Keep us guessing how?"

"He may leave us nothing to find," Bishop said bluntly. "No body or bodies. No crime scene or dump site. Plenty of killers go out of their way to hide victims, to . . . clean up after themselves. Plus, so far at least, this unsub has apparently chosen a victim who wouldn't, for whatever reasons, be immediately missed and, so, searched for. Impossible to know for certain with only one victim, but we have to consider the possibility. And if he's doing that deliberately, if it's his game plan, it's likely intended to buy him the time he needs without the need to worry too much about people looking for him and looking for signs of what he's done."

"But he has to know you're all here," Nellie said. "By now, at least. Won't he expect you all to be searching for him?"

"Now, probably," Bishop answered. "But if he knows this area well, and we have to assume he does, he still has that advantage over us. And we've been pretty visible today. We will be tomorrow. Even if he has what he believes to be a hidden and secure place to hide whatever he's doing, he has to be feeling the pressure."

Finn was frowning. "So you believe it's more likely that he'll leave us the sort of evidence you're talking about, a dump site or crime scene?"

"Possibly more likely, which is why we have to keep searching the mountain slopes. We don't know when he took the victim Hollis sensed earlier; if it is Cole Ainsworth, we don't have any idea of the time frame he's working within. And whatever might have been his original intentions, having you and your people alert and aware and us here could certainly change his plans. But again, there are too few of us to cover this valley and the mountains, especially when we don't as yet have any possible way of narrowing our search."

"So the crows could really help," Finn said.

Bishop's wide shoulders lifted in a brief shrug. "Given the relatively small area of Salem, my experience tells me that even if he tried, this unsub would have considerable difficulty in hiding all evidence of murder, and especially of torture, not for any length of time. A crime scene or dump site would give us more information, maybe help us build a profile, at least give us some idea of what's driving him."

"And that would help." Nellie didn't really make it a question, but it was.

"Motivation is a vital part of any profile," Bishop told her. "And we don't have that. We don't know if he may try deliberately to mislead us, and we certainly don't know what's driving him, assuming it's anything sane. Many delusions have cloaked crime on a truly massive scale, murder included."

Thinking reluctantly of the crimes her late uncle had committed, Nellie had a hunch she looked as shaken as she felt. *All the bad didn't go away with Duncan. This is real, dammit, and hiding your head in the sand won't make it less real. You could have a target on your back. Or Finn could. Any of us.*

"Okay," she said. "I'll . . . talk to the crow who usually shows up on my balcony railing every night." She frowned. "Tia. I think she's one of their leaders. And even if she doesn't visit tonight, she's usually around me somewhere."

"Leo says Tia is a queen," Hollis said. Then she blinked and leaned back to look around her partner and over at the gleaming black Pit bull, who had raised his head from his bed and was calmly returning her look. "Wow. That was . . . different."

"And through a clogged filter," DeMarco murmured.

NELLIE STEPPED OUT onto her balcony with Leo beside her, more than half hoping the crow would not be there. But she was there, clearly visible in the soft sconce lights at either end of the balcony, a couple of feet along the railing, turning her head to study the woman intently.

And Nellie, who was utterly certain she'd been able to clearly understand the thoughts of a crow once before only because the spirit or energy of her dead mother had opened a door for her just for that one time, during a desperate need, was more than startled to realize that images and concepts were flickering in her mind too fast for her to do anything with them.

"Wait, slow down," she said, hardly aware of speaking aloud.

There was an instant of stillness, and then the images came more slowly, the concepts tentatively offered, but clear.

Nellie had the notion that if she practiced this she could do it silently, but for now, she spoke aloud because it was easier.

"You understand what it is we're looking for, Tia? A bad man, an evil man, has taken someone else away and is hurting them. He wants to kill. Destroy. That person and others. Maybe . . . some of my family or friends. But anybody could be hurt. Everybody."

Understanding.

"We don't know who it is. But we believe he's up in the mountains, hiding what he's doing. People are searching, but we can't search as fast as you and your family and friends can."

Understanding.

Nellie drew a breath. "I promised no one would ever force any of you to do anything again. I'm asking now, because we need your help."

Again, understanding. And a concept Nellie wasn't sure she got completely, but that seemed to mean the crows had already started patrolling the valley, looking for anything that didn't seem, to them, to be normal.

After their experiences with Duncan, Nellie wasn't at all sure most of them had ever had normal lives themselves, but she was far more sure they would be able to recognize anything unusual or wrong in the valley.

"Thank you," she said aloud to the crow, truly thankful. "Thank you, Tia."

Tia bobbed slightly as though in acknowledgment, then turned easily on the railing and silently flew away into the night.

WEDNESDAY

The first grayish lights of dawn had lightened the bedroom when Hollis opened her eyes, not surprised that she had turned in the night so that Reese had turned as well, their bodies spooning, his arms around her. She was occasionally a restless sleeper, though far less often now with him, and as usual he had adapted himself easily.

And no more nightmares now. She couldn't even remember the last one, just knew it had been months ago.

She was content and drowsy, warm against him and under the covers, and for a moment felt a flash of sleepy resentment that she was awake before his very accurate internal alarm would have awakened them both.

Then she felt an eerie but familiar chill sweep over her, a coldness she always knew bone-deep was not of her world. Blankets didn't help. Reese didn't help. Nothing could warm her as long as that connection existed.

She drew a breath, wide-awake now, trying to concentrate. She'd thought she was getting used to this, but the chill this time was accompanied by a jolt of fear. But it was okay, she told herself. Surely it was okay this time. Because she could still feel Reese behind her. Because the room was not hazy or distant.

So she wasn't actually somewhere else. She hadn't crossed some ultimate barrier into a dangerous and scary otherworld. Into a place where only the dead walked. It was the most incredible relief.

And then she saw the girl.

She stepped into view as if she had waited patiently for Hollis to come fully awake before greeting her. A girl—no, a woman— perhaps in her early twenties, with dark hair and dark eyes and pale skin. She was wearing a casual short-sleeved shirt and jeans, summer wear, and was sort of hugging herself as though cold.

Hollis felt another flash of cold herself and knew it still had nothing to do with the temperature of the room. Death. Even if she was relieved to still be here, in her own world, that chill persisted.

She was never going to get used to this. Never. The scene in the restaurant had only been a reminder of that.

Damn, damn, damn.

Softly, even now not wanting to wake Reese until she had to, Hollis asked, "What's your name?"

"Megan Hales." Her voice was a bit distant, which made Hollis concentrate harder to hold on to the connection. She was trying not to shiver.

"Megan—"

"I was the first. Before you came. They thought I just ran away last summer, left town because my fiancé jilted me, but . . . I didn't. I was going to, and packed my things, and—and then he was there. I never thought he—he would hurt me." She swallowed visibly, then went on determinedly. "He wanted to see if he could hide me away without the elders, without Duncan, knowing anything about it. And he did."

"You mean, when we had a team here in January—"

Megan shook her head when Hollis's horrified words broke off. "I was—was dead by then. Buried. Hidden. And the monster stayed quiet while all that was going on. Even though he was getting more and more angry. He had his own plans. And now . . . He took someone else just before you got here. I think you . . . you felt what was happening to that poor soul. You can't help him anymore. No one can. But the monster . . . he's taken someone else. I'm not sure who. Or even when except . . . except it wasn't long ago. If you don't stop him, he'll kill them just like he did me. Just like he killed that other man. Maybe . . . maybe worse."

Having learned the hard way how little time for useful communication she usually had with the dead, Hollis said urgently, "We need a starting place, Megan. Something. Can you— Do you know where—where he buried you?"

"The crows know. Ask them. And be careful, Hollis. The monster is afraid of you. Of all of you. He believes he isn't, but he is. Because you hunt monsters, and deep down inside even he knows that's what he is."

"Megan," Hollis began, then swore under her breath when she realized the spirit was fading. Quickly she added, "We'll stop him—I promise. Don't let him hold you here."

"I don't have a choice . . ." The spirit and her voice faded into silence until they were gone.

The room seemed darker somehow with Megan gone, but then Reese spoke quietly and Hollis immediately felt everything brighten at least a little.

"What do you suppose she meant by that last? How does a killer hold the spirits of his victims earthbound?"

Hollis half turned in his loosened embrace so she could face him, glad that he could still see spirits as she did when they were physically touching. She felt less lonely about it. "None of them has ever told me," she confessed. "But at least some of the ones I see do seem to be trying to help stop their killers, as if that's keeping them from moving on."

"Barred by some law of the Universe from simply telling you who killed them?"

"Apparently. Diana says it's still the same with her guides, even after all this time. If time even matters. She's had them lead her to physical remains, but not to killers."

"At least Megan offered us a starting point when you asked. More or less."

"The crows know." Hollis heard her own voice considering that with a calm that didn't reflect the chill she still felt. "They really are part of this valley, aren't they? The crows. I mean in an un-birdlike way. If they know where Megan is, why do you suppose they haven't told anybody so far?"

When she heard herself saying *that*, Hollis immediately said, "Oh, man, does that sound as crazy as I think it does?"

"In our world and in Salem? No." He was reassuringly prompt. "It's a reasonable question. We know Nellie is able to communicate with them, no matter how reluctant she is about it. Bishop and Miranda clearly got a message from one of them. And you did, after all, get what Leo wanted to pass along last night. Without even trying."

"It just popped into my head. Not a clear thought so much as a clear awareness of what he knew."

"Assuming she spoke to the one on her balcony last night, I imagine Nellie can confirm the offer to help and maybe even other information. Though she's reluctant enough that she might have kept the communication as brief and direct as possible."

"I don't know that I blame her. The way her evil uncle used those crows was worse than abuse. I'd feel guilty about that if I were her."

"You feel guilty about it and you *aren't* her." He kissed her, taking his time about it, then said, "We'd better get a move on if we want breakfast before we start talking to crows and searching mountains."

———

DARKNESS WAS SHADING toward dawn, coloring the sky in layers of pinks and purples, when he finished. He had chosen his spot carefully and knew the light from the two big camping lanterns had not been seen down in the valley. Or even from fifty feet away if it came to that.

He went over the site carefully after gathering up his tools, making certain he had not left any signs that would point to him. Not that he was worried about that. He'd seen them all roaming about yesterday, late, in town and on the lower slopes. But they hadn't found anything.

This he wanted them to find.

But he hadn't made it easy for them and was curious to see how long it took them. They were *special*, after all. The Special Crimes Unit. Supposed to be the best.

The first two, back in January, had been interesting to observe, if only from a distance. He granted they'd had certain skills, even Talents, but tested only against Duncan. Successful, with the help of Finn and Nellie Cavendish, against Duncan.

He wasn't Duncan.

The six here now—he discounted the two working in Finn's new law enforcement center—were a varied lot in terms of Talent. But they were powerful, every one of them, and each unique. He found that more fascinating than worrying.

It would be interesting to watch them work.

Interesting to observe their reactions.

Interesting to find out just how good they were.

TEN

None of them were taking the situation lightly, especially when Hollis related the information offered by her dawn visitor as they all ate breakfast downstairs. The innkeeper, Ms. Payton, had given them a rather private corner and large table to themselves and well away from the handful of other guests staying at the moment, either out of common sense or because Finn had charmed her the previous day.

Hollis thought it could have been either.

"Megan Hales." Bishop frowned briefly, then said, "If I'm not mistaken, she was the granddaughter of one of the Hales elders. Our researchers have gotten that far in tracing at least some of the family lines, but I don't remember anything about her leaving town suddenly."

"Last summer," Hollis said. "Suddenly last summer. Wow. Tennessee Williams, right? Anyway, it was before any of us—well before *most* of us—had even heard of Salem." She didn't waste a glare at Bishop.

Diana said, "She must have taken being jilted hard if her family believed she'd just left town and stayed out of touch all these months. How old, do you think?"

"Twenties at a guess. Early. I took everything Very Seriously at that age." She spoke as if it were eons before rather than a relatively few short years. "But getting horribly murdered isn't what anybody expects to cope with at any age." Hollis knew her voice was calm, but she felt jittery.

"And at least two more victims since she was murdered," Bishop said. "The one you sensed yesterday, possibly Cole Ainsworth, probably dead now, and a third one taken even more recently. Dead or being held or tortured."

"That's what she said." Hollis was frowning. "Yet we haven't had word of anyone else being missing. Does that bug anybody besides me? I mean, small town and all."

"Yes," Miranda told her.

"Ask the crows," Quentin muttered, his thoughts following a different tack. "Does anybody know if Nellie talked—I'm tired of saying communicated—to the one on her balcony last night?"

"She did," Bishop confirmed. "The crow's name *is* Tia, and she not only agreed to our request but let Nellie know that the crows are already—I believe the phrase used was 'patrolling the valley'—looking for anything they consider to be unusual. Easier for them to see what there is to see in the valley; not as easy on the mountain slopes, though they're likely patrolling there as well. Nothing was said about knowing the location of a grave or of human remains."

Quite suddenly, Hollis pushed away the small plate containing the half-eaten jelly doughnut that had been intended to finish off her far more substantial breakfast. "Damn. They're carrion birds, aren't they?"

Miranda said, "Not exclusively. They eat insects, grain, fruit, small mammals. The eggs of other birds."

Hollis frowned and pushed the jelly doughnut another inch or two away. "And here I was wanting to respect them."

"No reason not to," DeMarco told her, being a man who took the cycle of life pretty much for granted. "They're highly intelligent birds; we all know that now if we didn't before. What they eat isn't really relevant."

Hollis eyed him. "Unless they've eaten some of our evidence. Flesh is just the shell, I know. Intellectually I know. But the *people* look the way they were physically when I see them in spirit, and I haven't entirely gotten used to what's too often done to their bodies before the spirits depart them. In fact, I don't *want* to get used to that. Ever."

Diana said, "We talk about the damnedest things over meals. Has anybody else noticed that?" And before she could be answered, she added, "Let's hope he did bury her. Or otherwise hid her away somewhere the flesh couldn't be got at. Because I want to respect the crows too, and I don't know if I would."

"I wonder if they make exceptions for friends," Hollis mused speculatively. "Cats don't. Then again, I've never been entirely sure cats would be bothered enough to make that sort of distinction. Dogs have masters; cats have staff. Or, alternatively, if they're sensitive enough to know we're gone by then, with just a . . . a tasty shell left behind. But if crows see us as individuals—physically, I mean—surely they'd make distinctions."

"You're getting morbid," DeMarco told her.

"No, I'm just wondering how to make sure the crows like me. In case. You never know. Because if they tell their friends, one might say, 'Hey, that one's not lunch; she was nice to me once.' Which I would prefer over the alternative."

"Maybe you can just tell them that."

"I still don't know if I speak crow."

"You speak Leo," he reminded her.

"Not really, I told you. That was an impression, a concept or idea. Not really a thought, and definitely not conversation."

Bishop, well aware that they were, in their various ways, bracing themselves for what was likely to be a difficult and unpleasant if not gruesome day, contributed his bit. "According to Gray, crows have a sense of humor. Possibly sly and even malicious, but there."

"I should think malicious," Diana said. "If they eat other birds' babies."

"I doubt they laugh while they do it," Quentin offered gravely.

Hollis stared at him. "Cawing malevolently." She tested the phrase, then shook her head. "Not a nice image. At all. Though these crows around here do seem eerily silent, so maybe not. I mean, not out loud. And I'm having second thoughts about even trying to talk to a crow in that way. Not out loud, I mean. Don't know that I want to hear crow laughter in my head, malicious or otherwise."

"Gray said it was a bit unnerving. Still, you should try if and when you get the chance," Bishop told her, serious now.

"Why?" Hollis demanded. "We have Nellie."

"Nellie may be able to help at times, but she's not only not a cop, being the head of one of the five families means she's high on the list of potential targets; sticking to her normal working day at the bank is best."

"You say killers love routine," Hollis reminded him. "Especially serial killers, which this one appears to be if he's killed Megan and one more, probably Cole Ainsworth, and is holding or has already killed a third."

"True. But I believe Nellie is safe enough at the bank, and I suspect she'll have guardians other than Leo watching over her while she comes and goes."

Hollis, remembering the whole report of what had happened here in January, looked at him thoughtfully. "The crows. Guilt? Because of what happened to her father?"

Diana said, "Didn't that happen years ago?"

Bishop nodded but said, "American crows can live to be twenty or more years old, so that may be part of it, assuming crows are capable of experiencing guilt. Or it may simply be that these crows belong here in Salem and have generational memories. They do share their knowledge about people, individuals, with their own kind, and being a Cavendish—at least here in Salem—probably forms a natural bond between Nellie and the crows, especially if communication between the birds and that family has been in existence as long as we believe it has. For whatever reason, I'm fairly certain they'd protect her."

"Well," Miranda said, "there are certainly more of them than there are of us, so anything they can do to help is a good idea in my book."

"As long as I don't get eaten," Hollis said.

―――――――

FINN JOINED THEM in time for coffee and grim tidings and was able to confirm both that no Salem resident had been reported missing overnight and that Megan Hales's family had indeed believed that she had left Salem abruptly after her fiancé had eloped with another woman.

Diana winced. "With no warning at all, not even a Dear Jane letter? I'll say she was jilted."

"There was an uproar about it back in the summer," Finn said, still frowning over the new information of her true fate. "Most of the Five take care to marry outside their own families for obvious reasons, but it's still a bit uncommon for a man from one of the Five to marry a woman from another. Megan was engaged to Paul Ainsworth, which was unusual enough. Two months before what would have been their wedding day, he eloped with a cousin. Of his."

"So that was the uproar," Hollis said. "A cousin."

"Yeah, more or less, though Paul also caught hell for jilting Megan when he came back last fall. But . . . for anyone spending their lives in Salem, especially one of the Five, the gene pool is already limited by sheer lack of numbers. Aside from any religious or moral concerns, biology definitely plays a role in what any society considers the norm. Inbreeding can cause serious health issues, even between distant cousins and especially over time, so it's strongly discouraged."

"Because it wasn't always?" Miranda guessed.

"Way back, no, it wasn't. Given the times, there were thoughts of keeping family lines 'pure,' especially once the Five found this valley and settled in, because according to the lore they'd been persecuted because of their Talents."

Hollis murmured, "And once they escaped that, they fought to hold on to what had made them outcasts."

Finn nodded. "In whatever way they could, yeah. Could have gone the other way, of course, but . . . Pride or just stubbornness made them want to be who and what they were. The population numbers here were naturally even fewer then, interaction with people outside the valley almost nil. Some inbreeding was inevitable, no matter what, far too much in the early years for all those reasons. And there were quite definitely health issues that began cropping up. Too many to ignore, many of them serious. There were a lot of miscarriages, fatal birth defects. People started whispering that the families had brought a curse with them into the new land. So inbreeding was discouraged across all five families. For generations now, that's been the rule, something everyone understands, and which most everyone obeys. And like so much else in Salem, a practice based on a perfectly good reason simply became custom no one thought much about."

Quentin said, "Unless and until it was flouted."

"Why Paul really caught hell from his family, because of the cousin." Finn nodded but said, "Megan was a good kid and deserved better treatment from Paul, far better; they'd been engaged for at least a couple of years, and high school sweethearts almost from the beginning. When he jilted her after all that, I thought the same as others, that she'd left Salem and probably found herself better off.

She was a trained accountant and working in the family real estate business keeping the books; it would have been easy for her to find that sort of job in another place. And she had the strength and spirit to start over and build a new life for herself. That's what I thought."

"You couldn't have known that didn't happen," Miranda reminded him. "She told Hollis that had been her intention, that she'd packed up to leave. Her killer took advantage of that."

Hollis wondered suddenly if, assuming they found what was left of Megan Hales's mortal remains, they would also find a girlish suitcase or two crammed with whatever she had thought necessary for a life outside Salem, and felt depressed.

Under the table, DeMarco's hand grasped one of hers. *If you didn't have such a strong sense of humor to balance the compassion, you'd end up gloomy as hell.*

Hollis smiled despite herself. *I've gotten too used to being a team leader; that's the problem. That keeps me focused on business. With Bishop on-site and in charge, it leaves me too free to feel instead of think.*

Don't kid yourself. You never stop feeling.

He squeezed her hand and then let it go, and Hollis glanced around, wondering idly if anyone else had picked up on the silent conversation. It wasn't likely; physical contact made the mind talk within their connection deeper, way below the surface thoughts most telepaths normally picked up on. Still, two of the strongest telepaths in the unit were here, and there was never any telling just how strong Bishop and Miranda were at any given time.

Even when they weren't deliberately probing.

No way to know for sure, but when she focused briefly and more or less automatically to check auras, everybody's was held close to their bodies by that sharply delineated line she'd learned to associate only with shielded minds. She spent a few seconds just studying the auras of Bishop and Miranda, which were remarkable and unique in Hollis's experience because whenever they were within a couple of feet of each other, their two auras in essence became one.

One that held all the colors of the rainbow, which was also unique. She'd never told them that, and made a mental note to herself to do so. She thought they'd probably be interested.

Hollis forced herself to look away from that fascinating aura, noting finally that it, too, had that sharply delineated line because both were shielding.

So probably nobody had been listening in. Besides which, it would have been rude; those within the SCU had learned long ago to do their best to respect each other's privacy.

She glanced at Finn, who happened to be seated nearby. And his aura suddenly made her pay closer attention, because it was greenish, which was rare, but more because it held a metallic glint on the outer edge of the delineation.

"What is it?" Bishop asked, his attention fully on her.

Hollis didn't really notice when Finn turned his head to find himself the focus of all her attention, because her mind was working busily and her gaze sort of traced his outline several inches out from his body. "Finn, do you have enemies in Salem? With abilities— Talents—I mean?"

To him, the question clearly came out of left field.

"An enemy with Talents? You mean a personal enemy? Now that Duncan and the most rabid of his followers are gone, I don't believe so. Why?"

Instead of replying, she looked at Bishop. "Maybe a shield with generations of learning behind it always looks like that. More solid than we're used to. Extra protective. I haven't thought about it, or tried. Yesterday it was only exploring what we could of the nearest mountain slopes, so we really didn't see people. Not to look at. And I didn't have reason to look. But maybe I should meet a few more members of the Five."

Bishop said, "Nellie's would be different since it was developed away from here and in a different way. So maybe you should."

Miranda, taking pity on Finn's bewilderment, said, "It's one of Hollis's abilities to see auras. She sees something unusual in yours."

"My aura? What do you mean something unusual?" he demanded, returning his gaze to Hollis.

She lifted a brow at Bishop, waited for a slight nod, then looked back at Finn. "Well . . . you know it's all about the body's energy, right? The electromagnetic field around living things and some machines."

"Right."

"Some people who have stronger electromagnetic energy can be sensed by people who don't see auras but feel the actual vibrations of that energy. Which is where the bit about 'feeling vibes' came from; sensitives—generally latent psychics—can determine mood from those vibrations, so not quite the New Age bullshit you might have thought."

Wearing the expression of a man adjusting his belief system, Finn nodded.

"Those of us who see auras," Hollis went on, "that's what we're looking at. The way Nellie saw mine last night, though I still dunno— Never mind that. Every person's individual energy field, in living color, is as unique as a fingerprint. Different colors mean different things, different emotions, but that's only a baseline; every person's aura is always a combination of more than one color, and it changes as their mood changes."

"Okay," Finn said.

"So. The auras of most people who aren't psychic or don't have shields sort of . . . flare . . . in an irregular pattern of colors around them. Even pulse sometimes as their energy changes. But shielded psychics have auras that look different. Because they're guarding their own minds, their own energy fields, their auras are held closer to their bodies, and there's a distinct edge along the outside of the colors. The visible aspect of their shields. Does that make sense?"

"I suppose so," he said cautiously. "Though I always thought shields were inside our heads. Around our minds."

"I thought so too until I could see auras. And there *are* guards of a sort we all use to protect our minds specifically, but our shields are partially made up of the energy of our bodies. The energies in our auras feed the shields our minds create and control. So our most protective shield tends to be the one around our entire bodies."

"Okay."

"Okay. If there's also energy aimed at that shield from outside, a very strong psychic probe or an attack, even an electrical charge of some kind, then the outer edge of a shield has a metallic glint. If it's a powerful, determined attempt to get at the psychic, I've even seen sparks sort of striking and bouncing off." She paused. "No sparks yet, but what I'm seeing tells me someone somewhere is trying to get past your shield. And none of us is doing that."

ELEVEN

Hollis stopped on the sidewalk two buildings down from the bank and zipped her jacket against the increasing chill, sighing and watching her breath fog in the air. "That makes four elders from two of the other families, not counting all the Cavendishes in Nellie's bank. I'm beginning to think I don't need to meet other elders or family members, not for this."

Bishop said, "So still the same. The psychics have shields that look unusual compared with what you're accustomed to seeing, more dense and held closer to their bodies, but no sign anyone is trying to get through them."

"No sign at all. Only with Finn. Maybe he's just a target because he's the one in charge of the investigation. No way to really know why until we know who. I'm glad his shield is so solid. I'm also glad you talked him into staying with Nellie at the bank."

"He knows it's reasonable with the Five being targets, never mind a possible direct attack on him."

Hollis eyed him, a little amused. "And he gets to spend more time with Nellie without all her guards going up in addition to that dandy shield you taught her to build."

Polite, Bishop said, "You, of all people, should understand that some things take time and patience."

It was hardly something she could argue with. "Don't worry, I won't embarrass either of them about it."

"I know you won't."

Shifting her weight in a restless movement, she only nodded. "But I do think we should join the others in looking for Megan. For where he buried her. And someplace even remotely likely where he could have held her, and a place where he could have buried the second victim, Cole Ainsworth, assuming it's him. And wherever he might be holding the third victim. Even if we still don't have word of another person missing, Megan was sure. I'm sure, for that matter. Two more besides her, the third one taken sometime last night."

This time she sounded as restless as she looked.

Bishop said, "Even a small town takes time to search, time to determine who isn't where they're supposed to be. Some people don't have set routines to make tracking them easy. Complicating it even further is that there are quite a few away at college or traveling for business or pleasure; it'll take time to make sure of them."

"I know. And even with Finn's authority and so many in Salem comfortable with psychic abilities, it's fairly impossible to put the town on lockdown when we don't have a body or remains. Still. It bugs me."

Like anyone else who had ever worked with her or simply understood her, Bishop took serious note of anything that bugged Hollis.

Still, at this point all he could really do was take serious note.
"His deputies are canvassing the town. Businesses, residences. And
working to trace those who are reportedly out of town for various
reasons. Everyone's having trouble with cell reception, and landlines
have been dropping calls and showing other signs of interference."

"The energy?"

"Looks like."

Hollis shifted again slightly, frowning. "So it's getting worse?"

"Well, stronger."

She looked at him. "I still can't tell where it's coming from. Or
even *what* it's coming from."

Bishop nodded slightly. "Unfortunately, all the interference means
we're stuck with far slower methods of getting in touch with possible
witnesses and the residents in general."

"Maybe we should get help with that."

Bishop nodded again. "I have someone at the mountain house following up."

Hollis wasn't very surprised. "Then we should know something
soon."

"I hope so. And our search teams here are checking the spots Finn
marked on the maps for us. He knows this valley and the mountains
all around, and if he believes those are likely places where someone
could have been held without being seen or heard, then we certainly
need to eliminate them. They at least offer us starting points."

Hollis looked at him, suddenly curious. "You sent Miranda and
Reese off each with one of Finn's deputies to search, and Quentin and

Diana are together, also searching. I know you'd met the elders back in January, so you being the one to take me to meet some of them made sense."

"So?"

"So why do I get the feeling there's something else in your devious mind, Yoda?" She was the only one of his agents to use that rather mocking nickname. To his face, at least.

He didn't bother with denial. "The crows."

She frowned. "I haven't seen a single crow all morning. I assumed they were doing what the female—what Tia—told Nellie they were doing—patrolling the valley."

"Probably. But I had a hunch they might more likely approach you without Reese being present. Even shielded, his energy can be felt from quite a distance, especially when he's with you."

Hollis didn't pretend to misunderstand. "And you sent Miranda off, too, so it wouldn't look so obvious?"

"One of us was needed in the search, and I needed to introduce you to some of the elders."

"Yeah, yeah. Well, since no crows are about—"

She broke off to watch a rather large crow alight silently on one of the pretty benches placed here and there along Main Street, this one only about a dozen feet away from them, then returned her gaze to Bishop. "You planned that."

"How could I have planned it?"

"If I knew that, I could collect a lot of money from just about everybody else in the unit." She sighed, again misting the chilly air before her.

Bishop glanced around them. "Not many people out this morning, and nobody close. Now would be a good time to find out if the crows do know where Megan is. They've had time today to look specifically for the sort of signs indicating a grave, or a place where someone could have been held."

However uncertain she felt about communicating with crows, Hollis was restlessly aware of time ticking, of someone recently taken who might yet be alive and able to be found in time, of remains to be found that might help point them toward what was so far a very quiet sort of killer in their experience.

Deadly quiet.

Calm, Bishop said, "I'll be close enough to help if anything else happens when you drop your shields."

"I don't even know why they're so solid today. My shields. They've been like Swiss cheese lately."

"Maybe it's a defensive response because of the energy."

"Maybe." Hollis was willing to accept that, even though energy hadn't affected her lack of a shield before. And although she hadn't had any idea that Bishop might be able to project his own formidable shield—or in some other way deflect any energy attack against her while she left herself vulnerable to attempt to talk to a crow—she trusted him.

They all trusted him.

So Hollis turned and took several slow steps to halve the distance between them and the crow.

She lowered her unusually solid shields cautiously, almost immediately aware of both a strengthening of that crawly sensation on the back of her neck and, much stronger, way too many human feelings here in town, virtually all of them from nonpsychic people.

Worried people.

Her newish empathic ability was proving to be a real bear, even though what she felt right now wasn't as strong as what seemed to be usual for her, and she thought it was all coming from fairly nearby. Frowning, she closed her eyes and did her best to block as much of that emotional baggage as she could, even as she murmured to Bishop, "Don't be surprised if I burst into tears. Somebody fairly nearby is having a very emotional fight with her boyfriend."

He didn't have to tell her to try to block that out, just waited and watched both her and the crow, and opened up that alert place in his own mind that was more than the spider senses and something other than telepathy.

Something unique to him, and something that had not, so far, been blocked or affected by the energy in this place or all the shielded minds around them. Or both.

Hollis opened her eyes suddenly and stared at the crow, unaware that her unusual blue eyes had taken on a luminous glow. "Huh. It's Tia, the one who talks to Nellie. Yeah, I get the sense she's one of their leaders." She paused, adding, "Oh, yeah, definitely. Queenly. Proud of herself, this one."

Aware of flutterings in his own mind, Bishop wasn't surprised to see Hollis wince.

"I wasn't being sarcastic, Tia. You understand us when we talk out loud, don't you?"

After a moment, she glanced over at Bishop. "She does. Most of them do, at least enough to get the gist." Then she frowned again as she looked at the crow regarding her so steadily. "Well . . . it's clearer for them with empaths, for some reason. Understanding us when we talk out loud as well as opening up to them. Most telepaths are . . . too . . . something. Structured? Orderly. I don't quite get that concept. Never mind, Tia. I had a visit— Oh. You know about that. Okay. Do you also know where we can find Megan?"

The crow uttered a soft, curiously sad sound, and lifted both wings to flap them without taking off.

Hollis turned to Bishop, her eyes still luminous and distracted. "She can take us. Show us." She went still again, frowning a little. "Oh. It's—she's—up near where Reese and the deputy are searching. What I think I got is that the crows only found Megan really early this morning, about the same time I was talking to her spirit." She grimaced. "I really hope it's a grave and not remains, because—"

Bishop waited a moment, then said, "If they only just found her, they could have left her untouched."

The crow uttered a slightly rougher "Caw" and flapped her wings again.

Hollis looked back at the crow. "I think we've insulted her. Oh. Damn. Megan put out corn and sometimes fruit for crows she saw. She was always nice to them. And they liked her."

"Apologies," Bishop said gravely to Tia. "And condolences."

"She understands you. Which doesn't surprise me for some reason, even though you're primarily a telepath. And she accepts the apologies and the condolences."

Bishop inclined his head, still grave, to acknowledge that, and they both watched as Tia flapped her wide wings and, this time, lifted almost straight up from the bench, more or less hovered above them for a moment, and then began to fly toward the nearest slopes.

They didn't run, but wasted no time in getting off Main Street and following the bird, who clearly understood the limitations of legs rather than wings, since she stopped now and then to perch on a light post or tree limb or something else long enough for them to catch up, and seemed indeed to choose the easiest path for the following humans.

Tia led them steadily as they left the downtown area behind and began to climb the slope of the eastern mountain looming above the town.

NELLIE LOOKED UP as Elinor Cavendish appeared in the open doorway of her office, and it didn't take the frown of worry pulling at her cousin's brows, the anxious eyes, to alert her that something was wrong.

"What is it, Ellie?"

Finn, who had been sitting in one of her visitors' chairs and using her phone every half hour or so to keep in touch with his people at the law enforcement center, looked around, then slowly rose to his feet.

"I— Nellie, Simon's late. And he's never late. He wasn't supposed to come in until ten today because of getting extra hours lately. I know he stayed later than most of us last night; the security guard let him out."

"Maybe he's working at home. He does that sometimes, right?"

"Yeah, but he lets me know when he's going to do that. His schedule today was to be here." She swallowed hard. "It might not have bothered me, but . . . if somebody's after family members, well, that's a worry, right? And Simon's so dependable. He should be here. Or he should have called in."

Nellie thought of the brisk, friendly, very intelligent cousin who was at the top of her list as a likely successor to herself if necessary, and felt the bottom drop out of her stomach.

Finn spoke up before she could. "You've called his place?"

Elinor nodded. "Half a dozen times in the last forty-five minutes. Thinking maybe he was in the shower or something. But . . . I don't think that's it. I think somebody needs to check on him."

Finn swore, not quietly, and reached for the phone on Nellie's desk.

———

"SO FAR," DIANA said to Quentin, "we haven't strayed any great distance from where other people seem to walk or hike regularly up here. Would a killer really hide or—otherwise dispose of a body in an area like this?"

"It's on the map Finn marked." Quentin stepped on a short, thin piece of dead tree branch, and when it snapped rather loudly noted the way his wife and partner started. He took her hand.

"Jumpy for a reason? I mean, aside from the obvious ones."

Diana halted to stare up at him. "I think all the obvious reasons are enough. That weird energy of the valley is . . . irritating even up here. Maybe especially up here. It's very cold and looks like snow. We're searching for a body, or remains, or a grave. Maybe all three. We know there's a killer about, possibly up here with us—and he knows the valley and these mountains a lot better than we do. We're in the middle of a really dense forest, trails or no, it's unnaturally quiet up here, and the light looks funny. It does, right?"

"There seems to be a weird tint to it," he agreed.

"Gray," Diana said. "It's got a gray tint to it."

"I was thinking of fog so, yeah, gray." He lifted their clasped hands, and both looked at the sleeves of her bright green sweater and his darker but still clearly blue sweatshirt, their flesh-colored hands. "You're awake, aware, and with me," he told her, sensing as much as hearing doubt. "Not in the gray time."

She heard a little laugh escape her, feeling no amusement. "Sorry for being jittery. I don't know why, but more than once since we got here I've felt like if I could only turn my head at the right moment, I'd see the—the edge of the gray time. Like a . . . cloud of fog rolling toward me. Sneaking toward me. Maybe even hunting for me."

As he always did, Quentin took her concerns seriously. "Has that ever happened before?"

"Not that I remember." She shook her head. "We keep bumping up against things I can't remember."

"No, only the possibilities of what you may not remember. Diana, I think we're all being affected by this place, more and more as time passes. I know I feel . . . unnaturally alert, even for the kind of search we're doing. I'm pretty sure Reese has both his shields shored up, and Bishop said something earlier about Hollis's shield being stronger than usual today. For whatever reason or reasons, it's affecting us. This place. The town, the valley. These mountains. By the—what did Bishop call it?—the isolated and insular nature of Salem and its people."

"And the energy."

"And that." He continued to hold her hand as they moved on to follow the very faint trail that looked to be made by regular hikers, and which appeared to be leading them toward a clearing in the distance. They were not climbing now, but traveling horizontally.

"I guess all that makes sense."

Quentin looked at her. "You're still bothered. About something else."

"Well . . . something about that spirit guide was off. I don't know what, but I'm just wondering if I missed something. I mean, Bishop proved I could be deceived in the gray time when he sent that other psychic in to do just that to teach me to be wary. One of his lessons."

"Maybe a necessary lesson," Quentin said.

"His lessons are always necessary—I've learned that much in the past few years. And very necessary then, considering Samuel did the same thing to try to trick me. Though I still say sending that other medium in to pretend to be you just gave Samuel the idea for later." She frowned at the memory; she had forgiven Bishop when he'd confessed because they all did, but it still bothered her both because he had done that and because he'd found another psychic outside the unit who had been familiar with the gray time and able to enter it at will.

Until then, she'd believed it was a place or time completely unique to her own abilities. Bishop had told her the other medium experienced the gray time differently from her but hadn't explained just what he meant by that.

Quentin said, "Bishop also said it wasn't likely you'd encounter many spirits there just to deceive you. Samuel was . . . well, unique."

"I know."

"And that the psychic he sent in not only tended to avoid the gray time but had a few personal problems that pretty much precluded his going in for no good reason."

"Yeah, I know. And I believe him about that."

"So what was it about the spirit guide this time that bothered you?"

"I don't know—that's the problem. There was just something odd about him. The way he looked. The way he acted. Weird as it sounds, there's a feeling, maybe an extra sense that works only there, in the gray time, of what's normal. That visit wasn't normal. Daniel wasn't."

"I wonder . . . Maybe he came from Salem."

That startled her, but as she considered the idea she found her mind didn't reject it. "I've never really thought about where they come from. As in, any particular place. I mean, there were all those spirits at The Lodge, from there, but that was different. I saw most of them there, the way mediums usually see spirits, not in the gray time. Well, sort of. And I was different then, a lot more uncertain about things. To say the least. But I know more now. I'm sure of more. In the gray time . . . guides are usually unconnected—or seem unconnected—to whatever it is they need me to do. Detached, in a way."

"Just there because they were sent?"

Diana understood the question. "Yeah, pretty much. It was the way it always felt with the guides, as far as I can remember, that they'd been sent to do a job. That it was why they made contact with me. I had the same guide more than once, and whatever they told me was never . . . personal. Not about me. Not about them. Their job was to guide me wherever it was I needed to go, tell me what I needed to know. A task they'd been set. But Daniel . . . he didn't feel that way. He was just . . . different. Even before he showed us the zombie murder victims. I don't know why."

"Salem is odd all the way around. And like I said, it has to be affecting us—*is* affecting us—likely in ways we aren't even aware of. We should keep taking that into account."

"Is that supposed to reassure me?"

Quentin smiled faintly. "Not really. It doesn't reassure me. It's . . . an anomaly. And we've all learned to be wary of those. Signposts to pay attention to. It may turn out not to matter. To us, to what we came here to do. Or it may be important. Either way, we keep it in mind."

She walked beside him in silence for a bit, then said, "If Daniel is from Salem and wanted our help, why ask for it in the gray time? I mean, actually *there*. It seems like a much harder way to do it. Why not just appear to Hollis?"

It was Quentin's turn to walk in silence for a few moments, his eyes roaming their surroundings just as hers were, trained to be aware of everything around them no matter what else was going on. Then he said, "Are you afraid he's trapped in the gray time?"

"Well—" Diana stopped abruptly as they reached the edge of a smallish clearing. Staring across it at an odd tumble of granite boulders placed as if some giant had piled them there, watching as a little boy walked calmly around them and disappeared behind them, she said, "No. I'm not afraid of that. Not anymore."

TWELVE

Hollis was aware of Reese coming to stand behind her, but she didn't take her eyes off the ragged opening in the thicket of brambles and briars they had discovered only a few yards away from Megan Hales's grave. The thicket had hidden its contents from the eye very effectively, though a normal police search of the area would certainly have uncovered them. It was a shame, Hollis thought, that the extensive law enforcement search weeks before had been concentrated in the mountains on the other side of the valley.

Absently rubbing her hands together, where lacerations that had been some fairly deep gashes were healing, fading away by the moment, she said, "I just knew. That her bags would be somewhere near." She had reached the thicket several steps ahead of her partner and had already been tearing branches and brambles away when he'd joined her to help.

Reese put his hands on her shoulders. "I know."

There were two of them, the bags, a girlish pink, faded by the passing of months out in the weather. A duffel with a shoulder strap as well as wheels at one end, and a much larger suitcase, also wheeled. Obviously part of a set. Each had an ID tag.

Hollis didn't bother to look at those.

"I don't really want to know what's inside them. What she wanted to take with her. Thinking she'd never come back."

"No reason why you should. I doubt it would tell us anything about who her killer is or why he chose her."

"The bags do that. Tell us why he probably chose her. If she was really his first and he was just learning to be a predator. They grab a tempting target they can't resist at first. Often close to home or work, because they haven't yet learned that's a bad idea. Convenience. Maybe just opportunity in this case. Because she was leaving and he knew or just saw her and realized. Because she wouldn't be missed. Maybe he was close enough to watch her pack. Or maybe in a town this small, she might not have lived or worked close to him, but he still somehow knew she was leaving. Maybe when gossip about her being jilted got around." Hollis turned suddenly to stare up at her partner. "I do wonder. Cole Ainsworth stormed out after he and his wife had a fight. So leaving in a way. Megan was packed and ready to leave town. And what about whoever he has now, the third one?"

"Might have been leaving too. It would be a good way for the unsub to hide what he was doing, at least for a while, grabbing people very likely to not be missed right away. In this case, at least, it probably would have been a while longer if Megan hadn't come to you. Though I'd call it stretching coincidence that three members of the Five—assuming they really are the targets—were so conveniently leaving Salem right when he needed victims."

"Yeah, especially this time of year. Not really the usual time for vacations. As for colleges and universities, the winter term is going on, right? Through the end of this month?"

He nodded. "So less likely someone would be leaving to begin a new term. Though Finn did send his nephew back to school early."

Hollis was frowning. "And saw him safely out of town, *and* talked to Robert once he was back at school just to be sure he arrived safely, I know. One we can hopefully cross off our list. But . . . if two victims have been taken in just a few days, at least one of them is probably already dead . . ."

"Then he's working fast. Or is still holding at least the one grabbed most recently."

"Maybe he hasn't been held . . . long enough. Maybe he's still okay."

" 'He'?" Reese questioned.

She nodded slowly, still frowning. "A man, I think."

"Any sense of the victim we believe is Cole Ainsworth?"

"No, nothing. I believe Megan; he's dead." She shifted uneasily. "This morning I was getting emotions down in town when I dropped my shields, at least from nonpsychics, getting what Tia wanted to tell me. Up here, nothing, even when I tried. My shields are back up, and still weirdly strong. For me, I mean."

"The luggage?"

"I just knew it was there. Maybe something that got through my shields."

It was Reese's turn to nod slowly. "From what the clairvoyants in the unit have said, that sense is less likely to be blocked by the interference of energy. In fact, energy tends to make them more open even with shields."

Hollis's frown deepened. "Storms. Every clairvoyant I've ever talked to is bugged by storms on some level."

"As you are."

"Yeah, but that isn't a new thing."

"Isn't it?"

She stared at him. "Worse now, maybe. I remember being nervous about storms when I was a kid."

"And a latent."

Hollis allowed herself to be distracted from horrors. "Are you saying *all* these abilities were latent in me all my life, and are being triggered one by one, taking their own sweet time to make themselves known?"

"Why not?"

"Not even Bishop ever suggested that."

"I'll bet he's suspected it, though."

Hollis considered that for a moment, then shrugged it off to return to more important things. The horrors. "Anyway. If Megan was this monster's very first victim, he could have waited months afterward, just like she said. To make sure he wasn't suspected, wasn't caught. That she wasn't found. That's common enough when a serial first kills. And then there was the thing in January. Megan said he was quiet, he laid low during all that. The whole town and half these mountains crawling with feds and other cops for weeks. Even more of a risk she might be found. But she wasn't found. And now we're here, and he's killing again. Do you suppose he waited for us?"

"How could he know? The Blackwood elder's farseeing, yeah, that probably got around, the gist of it, at least. But to know it would draw us . . . it's a leap."

Something flickered in the back of Hollis's mind, but it was gone before she could grasp it.

Knowing from experience that it would come back to her only if she didn't force it, she shook the uneasiness of that elusive thought away.

"Maybe he knew Finn would call us. Because from the reports of what happened, it's obvious, had to be obvious then, that Finn knew Bishop before. That Nellie did. They didn't try to hide that, not really. People would have seen, even without any extra senses. And Bishop is . . . memorable. He tries to keep out of the spotlight, but he's good media, and these last few years he's led so many pretty damned public task forces around the country."

"And it's one small step from Bishop to the SCU."

"Not even a step. We're not a guilty secret anymore—there's information out there on us. Stuff even a civilian could find if they knew how to look. Hell, if they know how to Google they could find us eventually. The basics, at least. What's fit for the public in the eyes of the FBI, the stories and articles that made it to print. And hackers are everywhere, maybe even here. They could have gotten into law enforcement databases. We can't assume they didn't do that. Even with all the Bureau's precautions, Bishop's precautions, we can't assume."

DeMarco had kept his hands on her shoulders after she turned to face him, a quick glance showing him that her hands were nearly healed. She had cut them up badly in dragging heavily thorned under-brush away from the luggage. He knew she hadn't even felt the pain. He also knew the scratches on his own hands were gone now.

She didn't even need to concentrate to heal herself now; he wondered if she realized she didn't need to concentrate to heal him as well, at least when they were touching. And maybe when his extra energy helped her.

"Okay," he said. "Say he knew we were coming. That he was able to find out about us and knew what to expect. What should that tell us?"

Hollis thought about it, her head tilting slightly as she looked past her partner to where Bishop and Miranda stood talking to the two grim deputies, one male, one female, both staring down at the partially uncovered remains of Megan Hales.

He hadn't buried her very deep.

"That he's committed." She pulled her gaze from the pitiful grave, unwilling to look again at what had likely attracted the attention of the crows, what they would have seen themselves if they had managed to discover this odd little glade more than half-hidden from anyone both downslope and upslope by large boulders and more of the thick brambles and other undergrowth and at least three clusters of fairly low, thick blue spruce evergreens.

It was very visible now.

The mocking glitter of the diamond engagement ring, winking brightly even on this grayish day, on one of the long, withered and blackened fingers jutting up stiffly from the loose soil that had covered the rest of her body.

The pink nail polish tipping the ends of those withered fingers had, eerily enough, not faded a bit.

Hollis looked again, and again yanked her gaze away and looked up at her partner's grave face.

"That he won't stop until somebody stops him."

HE KEPT TO his observation point because he was sure they wouldn't look for him, or for victims, here. The only downside was that he wasn't close enough to see much, and heard nothing.

Well, not the only downside.

The goddamned crows.

He wasn't sure, even now, whether they were acting at the bidding of someone, some *person*, or if the crows themselves had chosen for some unknown reason to get involved.

If it was the former, he needed to identify that particular enemy, and fast. If it was the latter . . . well, the crows hadn't figured into his plans. They were just birds, after all, and even if Duncan had claimed to command them, he was gone.

But they were around; he had noticed that days ago. And it seemed to him there were more about, flying around the valley almost like they were patrolling it.

Not only that, but he'd been near enough to watch Nellie Cavendish walk to the bank this morning, her dog beside her—and more than one crow had seemingly held positions along her usual route, perching on lampposts and benches, watching her.

And watching the people around her.

That had been . . . unexpected. Not shocking; he had to at least consider the possibility that communicating with the crows could be a Cavendish Talent not at all exclusive to Duncan no matter what he'd said, very rare but still perhaps one Nellie held. Especially if the tales told about what had really happened back in January were even close to truth.

And he was reasonably sure those tales were true, because he'd heard more than one of them from an actual witness, one of the few to have survived the purge of Duncan's more fanatical followers.

So the Talents Nellie possessed had to be taken into account; he knew that.

She had, after all, defeated Duncan.

If the crows *were* following someone's orders, it almost had to be hers. Not so surprising; she'd worked with the feds before. With Finn before. So maybe she'd set the crows to searching the valley and the slopes.

For Megan? How could she—how could any of them—know about Megan? Aylia Blackwood's farseeing, rumor had it, warned only that something bad was stalking the Five. And rumor was garbled as hell when it came to more than that, as was normal for rumor, especially rumor driven by fear.

So how had they known to search for Megan? She wasn't the one he'd left for them to find.

That bothered him. It made him uneasy. But even so, he wasn't willing to change his plans. Certain things had to happen in a certain order.

Finding Megan didn't matter.

It didn't matter at all.

———

QUENTIN AND DIANA moved around the odd pile of granite boulders that were stark and gray surrounded by the heavy branches of evergreens rising all around and forming a sort of screen that gave the small clearing a hidden, secret look. Both held their weapons ready, moving cautiously, halting abruptly when they saw what waited for them in that small, secret clearing.

In the still, cold air, the acrid smell was seared flesh and blood. So much blood.

Diana felt her stomach clench and churn, and fought to keep the sickness down as she slowly holstered her weapon. She had seen more than one dead body in her years with the SCU, but it was not something she had ever gotten used to. And this . . .

The first visual impression was overwhelmingly one of raw flesh, and jagged white bones, and blood.

To say that this victim had been tortured did not begin to define what had been done to him. He was quite literally in pieces, bloody flesh and bones, some of the bones clearly and brutally broken and others showing the hauntingly clean edges of some cutting tool. It looked as if the skin had been removed, torn from the body at some point and cast aside in strips that showed blackened, seared edges.

The head sat by itself in the center, a horrific centerpiece of bloody muscle and sinew barely covering the skull. It had been scalped, the eyes gouged out, the open mouth showing jagged, broken teeth.

The internal organs had been removed and, bizarrely, were draped, glistening wetly, over a single small, flat-topped boulder to one side of the clearing, the intestines dangling over to touch the ground. Also bizarrely, several of the long bones, stripped of flesh and muscle, had been jabbed upright into the ground around the rest as though marking the outer edges of the killing field, the dump site.

It was impossible to tell from looking how much had been done while he was living. In fact, it was almost impossible to determine that the remains were those of a man.

Almost.

Diana half turned away to look at Quentin as she breathed jerkily through her mouth. "Jesus," she muttered.

Quentin took another long look at the remains, then turned away as well, his face still. "Come on," he said, his voice a bit hoarse. "We need to call Bishop."

It took nearly fifteen minutes for Bishop and one of Finn's deputies to arrive from, he told them, the grave of Megan Hales.

"He—the guide, Daniel—was there for just a minute," Diana explained steadily to their team leader. "Less. Seconds. Beside the boulders. Sort of . . . smiling at us. At me. Quentin couldn't see him, but he looked so alive. And then he walked around behind the boulders, vanished behind them. He wasn't there when—when—"

"When you found the body."

"What's left of him," Quentin said, only years of experience in standing over the horrific evidence of what human beings could do to one another keeping his voice level, even detached. "Honestly, I doubt we would have gone back there behind the boulders otherwise. That little trail we were following more or less faded out at the beginning of the clearing. We probably would have just crossed the clearing and gone on into the woods again."

Diana, with much less experience, was struggling to manage detachment. She said, "I didn't see any clothing. Isn't that supposed to be evidence of a sexual crime?" She was still in the learning stages of becoming a profiler.

"Often," Bishop responded. "Though it could just as easily be a sign that the unsub removed the clothing to give us less to work with, since TV and books have made the science of forensics well-known. Or because he wanted the maximum shock value, which could also be the reason for the way he arranged everything. Anyone moving around the boulders was going to get a shock. But, in any case, with this much damage, we'll need a good pathologist to tell us exactly what was done to the body and when, if it's even possible."

"You said this morning that Jill Easton was on her way?"

"In town and on her way to Megan's grave now, since it's closer for her. Since Finn doesn't yet have crime scene techs, she and Sam will need to check the scene and supervise the removal of Megan's remains. And then come here and do the same. We need to know for certain who this victim was, and I don't think a solid ID is likely or even possible from—appearance. With the face battered, discolored and swollen, the teeth knocked out, hands and feet so badly burned, all the rest of the damage to the body, we'll probably have to rely on DNA. But there is that scrap of hair left. Finn's on his way up to take a look."

Bishop had gone around the boulders to see what Diana's spirit guide had led them to, but hadn't lingered, returning to join her and Quentin on the valley side of the odd granite formation. The only indication that what he'd seen had affected him was the faint scar twisting down his left cheek; as always when he was disturbed, it became whitened, more obvious, a visible barometer of his emotions.

Diana said, "Finn isn't coming up here alone, is he? Since he's a member of the Five, I mean."

"One of his deputies is coming with him," Bishop answered. "He agreed it's worth the risk to see this victim ASAP and try to identify him."

"You called him before you got here," she noted.

Bishop nodded. "As soon as Quentin told me the remains were

recent and not buried. From what Hollis sensed yesterday, and given how long it must have taken to destroy the body this way, it's more likely this could be Cole Ainsworth than Simon Cavendish."

Quentin said, "We should be able to get some info here just from the area. That's a crime scene, not a dump site. And not a grave the way you said Megan was buried. What was done to him was done there."

"Agreed."

"This is the first time we've been in this area. And with the boulders and the angle, all the evergreen trees and bushes, no one down in the valley would have seen a thing even if he worked on the vic yesterday—and all night surrounded by some kind of lights. Hikers don't come near this area even in daylight, not in winter; the little trail we were following was a wildlife path to the nearest water. I didn't need any paranormal sense to hear a stream in the right direction."

"But you nevertheless tried to use the spider senses," Bishop said.

"I decided to give it a try up here," Quentin admitted. "Hoped maybe it wouldn't be the same as down in town. Unfortunately, I didn't pick up a thing." He didn't add that the effort had caused the same sharp pain they had all experienced and in addition left his head throbbing.

He didn't have to.

Bishop nodded. "Well, our normal senses say that a great deal of what was done here was postmortem. And it took a while. Even so, it's fairly obvious the victim probably died sometime last night. Though could be as late as dawn."

"And this place—the victim—was screened well enough by the

boulders and all the trees and undergrowth that even the crows were less likely to see it if they patrolled this area before," Diana said. "Especially while—while it was probably happening. Unless he—"

Quite abruptly, her trained and experienced imagination offered a new detail, so clear and vivid she would have sworn she could hear screams of agony.

THIRTEEN

Quentin said steadily, "I'm betting he made sure the victim couldn't make a sound."

Diana nodded and hurriedly changed the subject, mostly to try to divert her mind from thoughts of a gagged victim who had certainly tried to scream in agony. "The crows. They usually roost at night, right? And they prefer more open areas, not as heavily wooded as this. Usually."

"Yeah," Bishop answered. "And the crows in this valley have returned to most of their normal habits, according to Finn, at least until now. The one named Tia who's been communicating with Nellie and now Hollis definitely seems to be one of their leaders, so a night visit from her was maybe timed then simply in order to meet Nellie alone and establish the communication. Normally, they do roost at night. But we don't know for certain they haven't disrupted that habit recently as well as begun patrolling. Tia didn't say how long they've been doing that. Or even how, whether individually or in a—"

"I don't have to be a telepath to know what you're thinking," Quentin said when his boss broke off. "A flock of crows is called a murder, isn't it?"

"Yeah, though I would guess the average person doesn't know that."

"With ravens, it's a conspiracy," Diana murmured. "I remember reading that somewhere." She had spent much of her free time the last few years reading virtually everything she could get her hands on, simply trying to catch up on all those lost years. "But we don't have one here, right? A conspiracy of the other kind? Tia led you guys to Megan's grave low on the eastern mountain, and we find this— these remains at nearly the same time fairly low down on the northern mountain. It doesn't mean two killers. Does it?"

"No, I don't think so," Bishop replied. "We have too little for a preliminary profile detailed enough to help us, but can make some educated guesses based on what little we do know. Even with months between the first and second killings, we very likely have a single killer. One victim last summer, probably his first, because he took care to hide her remains and because killing her was enough for him—for a while. And he likely would have waited for quite some time to see if he was going to get away with murder. Realizing he had would have emboldened him. But to move like this, to take Simon Cavendish so soon after taking Cole Ainsworth . . . something may easily have changed his plans."

"Or," Quentin suggested, "the escalation is because he was forced to wait longer than he wanted to in the beginning, after he killed

Megan. Need has to be driving him, because it always drives this kind of killer."

Diana was frowning. "Or maybe . . . though need drives him, something else is also driving him to move fast, especially now. External more than internal reasons. If this victim is Cole Ainsworth, and Simon Cavendish is in the unsub's hands now, hidden somewhere or being . . . tortured, then . . ."

Nodding, Bishop said, "If he knows about the Blackwood elder's farseeing, knows there was any kind of a warning specifically to the families, that we know who to look for, that could easily be additional pressure. He could feel pressed to move faster in order to satisfy his need to kill before we can shut down his victim pool."

"Or time could drive him in another way," Quentin suggested.

"Yeah, it could. The valley isn't huge, but we aren't an army; the faster he moves, the more likely he could keep *us* moving constantly without giving us much time for gathering and evaluating evidence, for strategy, for time to do much more than identify the victims he leaves for us. But if we *can* very clearly identify his victim pool, that still gives us an edge. I hope. At least enough of an edge to alert potential victims and protect as many as we can."

"And give potential victims an edge," Quentin said. "Hopefully, at least. It's a town filled with psychics. Maybe they can use those abilities to protect themselves."

FINN CAME BACK around the boulders to join the others, his face set. His previous experience of torture victims had been only dump-site photos taken by Geneva back in January. That had been bad enough, and didn't make viewing the remains of this victim any easier.

Steadily, he said, "I can't identify him for certain other than knowing he's male. But at a guess it's Cole Ainsworth. I don't believe it's Simon Cavendish. Simon is dark; correct me if I'm wrong, but I'm—guessing—this victim was blond, and that fits Cole Ainsworth."

Bishop nodded. "There's enough hair left untouched by the blood to tell that much." He frowned. "Just enough."

"Think it was deliberate?" Quentin asked.

"Could be. He hardly left a square inch of the body untouched in some way, before and after death, yet just enough blond hair to make that visibly clear."

"Why would it be deliberate?" Finn asked.

"Maybe taunting us. Playing games. He might have believed there'd be more time before we could be certain Cole Ainsworth is actually missing, and grabbed Simon so quickly to further muddy the water, make us uncertain who the victim is, at least for a while. Or he could be making certain we know or at least guess there is or will be a third victim, since Simon is dark."

"To keep us looking for someone we might be able to help instead of looking for him," Diana said. "Another thing to keep us concentrating on to slow down our gathering and analyzing of evidence."

"If he knows how we work," Bishop agreed. "How most law enforcement typically works. Or if he can just reason it out. The priority is always going to be on locating victims we can still help. That's true of any law enforcement officers, including us."

"I really hope he doesn't know as much as you believe he might," Finn said.

"We always hope that," Quentin said.

Diana was glancing around them almost absently, and her voice was restless when she asked, "Finn, are you sure Simon is missing?"

"All I'm sure of is that he isn't at work, isn't at home—and it doesn't look like he got home last night. He left the bank later than usual and walked; it's only a few short blocks to his condo and he very seldom drives. His car's parked at the condo, keys on a table by the door. He didn't stop at any of the restaurants or cafés. He's been taking work home these last weeks, with Nellie making some changes at the bank, but his briefcase isn't in his condo or his office. His regular cleaning service came yesterday, and while I happen to know he's a neat guy, no way he's *that* neat: There isn't a thing out of place at his condo, just like the service left it, including clean sheets on a bed that hasn't been slept in."

Diana wondered if Finn was even conscious of his determined use of the present tense.

"We've already checked with his coworkers at the bank," he went on. "Most left before he did, and none of them have any useful information. We've found no witnesses along his usual route home. I've got a team following up on his friends outside the bank, and Cavendishes who don't work there but might know something. Many have already been questioned generally about anyone potentially missing because of Cole. I just don't know if we're going to find out any more than we already have."

Bishop said, "It should have taken Simon how long to walk home?"

"No more than half an hour even if he strolled. According to security, he left the bank just after six thirty. Home by seven, say a quarter after at the very latest."

"A forty-five-minute window." Bishop shook his head slightly. "And he left the bank later than usual; if the unsub had targeted him, he had to be lying in wait somewhere along Simon's usual route home."

Quentin nodded in the direction of the victim they had found here. "And we're fairly certain because of what was done to him and what's left that this man was being tortured for hours, that he was almost certainly still alive when Simon was taken."

Finn said, "So from that and from what Megan's spirit told Hollis this morning, this victim had already been taken before Simon disappeared, and was . . . suffering . . . even then."

Quentin said, "Which likely means that last night the unsub had to leave this victim, probably here, then get himself down to town, snatch Simon—planned or because the opportunity was there—then take Simon somewhere he felt it was safe to leave him. While he came back here and . . . finished up with this victim."

"Taking one victim while he had another," Bishop said, "even if he felt rushed for whatever reason, means planning and preparation, a lot of it. I doubt Simon was taken because he just happened to be where he was."

Quentin nodded. "So the unsub had to lie in wait, maybe longer than he planned because Simon was later than usual, then immobilize Simon quickly and quietly, and get him out of downtown because you had people patrolling the area."

"And then take him to whatever place he had ready," Diana said.

Nodding again, Quentin said, "Even if most of the downtown businesses were closed by then, there are restaurants all around. Plus the patrols. It would have been at least reasonably likely that someone might have seen something. He couldn't waste any time getting Simon out of the area."

"Simon would have passed very close to two of the restaurants on the way to his condo if he took his usual route." Finn paused, then added, "As nearly as I can figure, we were all at one of them at just about the right time."

Quentin said, "Man, I hate knowing that."

"We weren't near the front windows," Finn reminded him. "Even if any of us had been looking, we wouldn't have seen anything."

"And that's assuming he was grabbed off Main Street," Bishop added. "The condos I've seen are all at least a block or more off Main."

Finn nodded again. "Yeah, his is. Two blocks back. One of my patrols was downtown about the same time and reported nothing unusual along Main. We're trying to get a list of who was still downtown and in the general area and might have seen him. Might have seen anything. As for a hiding place . . . we're checking every building, looking into storage areas, basements. Again."

"He has to know you would be." Diana was frowning. "So . . . the unsub could have just had his car there, right? Knocked Simon out, probably tied him up, dumped him into his trunk. Driven away."

"That's probably more likely than having a hiding place downtown," Bishop agreed. "Nobody's going to openly carry a grown man any farther than necessary, even after dark, and especially in the downtown area. But he couldn't have driven all the way up here to get back to this victim; there are some forestry and other service roads on these mountain slopes but none close."

It was Finn's turn to frown. "Yet he transports *this* victim, somehow, into an area with no road access for hundreds of yards minimum. Maybe sometime yesterday, fairly early. Even though your team had people moving all over town and up here on the slopes as well?"

"We hardly covered the area," Bishop pointed out. "Not even down in town, and certainly not up here. And we got a late start yesterday."

"Still, do you see a killer taking that kind of risk?"

"We've all known killers to take bigger risks. He could see that sort of thing as a challenge. But I'd expect this unsub to be more cautious, at least until he gets a better sense of what we're doing to find him."

Quentin said, "From what Hollis picked up yesterday afternoon, the unsub had already started working on this victim by early afternoon, and it's clear most of what was done to him was done here. So I'm betting this victim was here, at least by then. Whether the unsub was still working on him while we were moving around . . . maybe. Or maybe he knew we were searching and settled in somewhere to watch. Plenty of places all around the valley where he could have kept an eye on activity, then come back here after dark."

"He may have deliberately left us another sign, something he wanted us to see," Bishop said. "One battered hand and wrist, one battered foot and ankle. Ligature marks around wrist and ankle. Deep. This victim was held immobile for quite some time. Probably securely enough that the unsub felt safe leaving him here, especially if he knew none of us were near this area or likely to be."

"Then it got dark," Finn continued. "And he knows any of the search teams on the slopes would be pulled in. Decides to grab

Simon as planned. Gets himself into position and waits. Goes after him. Disables him. And Simon is not a small man and is in fairly good shape, so it pretty much had to be a blitz attack. Stashes him maybe in a trunk because it's easiest, quickest. Comes back up here." He shook his head. "I'd prefer to hope he saw an opportunity and took it rather than followed a plan to grab Simon when he already had this victim in hand."

"So would I," Quentin said. "But I agree with Bishop; it's more likely Simon was planned."

"We need to establish a timeline," Bishop said. "Dr. Easton can help with that. We need to know how this victim died, and when. And how long he could have lasted under the kind of torture evidenced here."

Diana hoped the sudden return of her queasiness didn't show. She had seen mangled bodies before, in the field and at the body farm. Too many. Still, it was so hard to be professionally detached from horrors. From seeing them and knowing all the terrible things that had been done to what had been a living, breathing, feeling human being. And especially so when she was very afraid more horrors were waiting.

SIMON CAVENDISH TRIED to wake himself up, wondering fuzzily why his alarm hadn't gone off. Because he thought he'd been sleeping a long time. His eyelids scratched against his corneas, and his head felt stuffed full of cotton and ached. Pounded, really, right on the edge of a migraine.

Maybe that was why it was so dark.

That must be it. He had a migraine, and so he'd gone to bed and used the blackout drapes in his bedroom to make sure no light got in to disturb him. So his head would stop hurting. That was why it was so dark.

For a while he lay there, his eyes closed again, vaguely satisfied now that he understood why his head pounded and why he was lying in the dark. But then he tried to shift slightly, because he thought one of his arms had gone to sleep.

He couldn't move.

Simon stopped trying for a bit, thinking about that. Trying not to listen to the little voice in his head that was telling him a lot more was wrong than just one of his thankfully rare migraines. He tried to remember going to bed with a migraine, but the last thing he remembered . . .

He'd left the bank. Yes. Walked home. No—started walking home. Turned off Main to walk the two more blocks to his condo. And then . . . what? And then the migraine had hit him all of a sudden, hadn't it? It must have, because he couldn't remember . . .

He couldn't remember anything. Just a blinding pain in his head, and then nothing.

That wasn't a migraine.

Simon opened his eyes, admitting to himself that this was not the darkness of his bedroom. This was . . . this was too dark. It had weight, this darkness. Substance. It pressed against him, threatened to smother him because he couldn't seem to catch his breath. And not a sliver of light showed anywhere.

He tried to move again, cautiously this time. He could move his legs a bit, but his ankles were pressed together. Tied together. And his arms were . . . his hands were behind his back, he thought, and numb; he tried to move his fingers and couldn't. Because his hands were tied together too.

He was lying on his side; he knew that. But not in a bed. He was lying on something hard.

Simon lay there for some amount of time that felt like forever. Or a few seconds. Trying not to listen to the voice in his head that was louder now and telling him he was in trouble, bad trouble. The voice that was edging past panic and into something that felt like terror.

Swallowing, he tried to call out, "Hello?" and heard his own voice sounding both hoarse and oddly muffled.

When he tried to move his legs more, his knees bumped against something hard. He managed to move his aching head back, and felt a flash of new pain when he pressed against something hard behind him. He wanted to turn over onto his back, and tried, but when he moved his heavy legs his knees again bumped against something hard.

Above him.

He could hear himself breathing in short, jerky pants, and he imagined it was getting even harder to breathe. Surely that was his imagination. It had to be. His heart was slamming against his ribs, and his head was still pounding sickly, and he knew he was shaking. Maybe that was why it seemed harder to breathe.

Maybe that was why.

The darkness wasn't getting any lighter even though his eyes were wide-open. And suddenly the voice in his head was too insistent to ignore, even though listening to it terrified Simon.

You're in some kind of a box. A small box. You never got home, Simon.

Somebody hit you. Aylia Blackwood said a monster was hunting in Salem, hunting the Five.

The monster's got you.

And he's buried you alive.

That was when Simon Cavendish began to scream.

FOURTEEN

Bishop said, "As far as I've been able to tell, there are no real telltale physical characteristics identifying any member of the Five as being from the specific families. Coloring, build, height, that sort of thing."

Finn shook his head. "No, there's all the variety within each family you'd expect to find within most any family. Among the adults of the Five, blonds, brunettes, redheads, and fair skin are the rule."

Quentin said, "Yeah, figures."

Steadily, Finn said, "If he kills again, and if he leaves his next victim the way he left this one, knowing what anybody looks like isn't going to help us identify them." He looked at Bishop steadily. "How sure are you that the remains found at the other site are those of Megan?"

"Her name is on the luggage tags; the luggage itself will be taken back to the law enforcement center so the contents can be searched and catalogued by your people. That diamond ring should be traceable." He paused, adding, "You're thinking about notifying her family."

"I'm thinking I need to. Before rumor spreads around the valley at warp speed. We need to be more certain of the ID of this victim, but Megan . . . Rumor and conjecture isn't the way her family needs to find out, not when they believe she's living somewhere safely outside the valley and didn't want to get in touch with them. It's going to be a hell of a shock."

Bishop knew what he was being asked. "I'm as sure as I can be without a DNA test that it's her. Her family should know. And there's another reason they should be told."

Finn was already nodding. "Now that we know she's dead, family and friends have to be questioned. Her movements last summer traced as well as we can trace them. That's going to be a really cold trail, Bishop."

"But still an important one. She was his first victim. And he buried her in a spot we might easily have missed without the help of the crows. Hidden well enough that she remained undiscovered for months. Maybe she was never meant to be found. Chances are good she knew him. Or that he believed he knew her. He may have lived near her or even worked with her. And even in a town as small as Salem, with all the overlaps, not everyone knows everyone else. It could help us narrow the field, give us a place to focus."

"Yeah, okay. As soon as I've notified her parents, we'll start interviewing friends and family, get as many as we can today, start again tomorrow." Finn sounded restless now. "I don't want to pull too many off the search for Simon, though. We might still be able to help him."

"How far can you stretch your resources?" Bishop asked bluntly.

"Not as far as I'd like, especially having to send deputies out in twos to search or just to canvass. Even once we're absolutely sure of his—his victim pool, I don't want any of my people out alone, members of the Five or not. Right now every deputy is out either searching for Simon or still canvassing to try to trace Cole Ainsworth's movements and determine when and where he was grabbed; I've got administrative people manning the phones at the office, helped by the two agents you have there. The office is still chaotic, but they're managing. I have barely enough manpower to run a third shift patrolling in town and the rest of the valley overnight. Everybody's getting overtime and nobody's complaining, but I just don't have enough trained people to keep this up for long."

Quentin said, "Let's hope it won't have to be for much longer. We have to catch this monster sooner rather than later."

"Amen," Finn said soberly. "Look, I'm going to get back to town so I can notify Megan's parents."

"Make sure you keep a deputy with you when you're moving around," Bishop warned him. "Even with clear evidence that the unsub is targeting the Five, we don't know how he's choosing his victims. And you're very visible."

"Megan wasn't an elder, much less the head of her family," Finn pointed out.

"And Simon Cavendish?" Bishop asked.

"An elder. And a likely successor for Nellie unless and until she has kids. I'm pretty sure he's on her short list."

Diana was curious, and willing enough to offer a distraction from horrors by following that tangent, but she didn't have to be an empath to feel Finn's restlessness, and knew he needed to be doing something. Even if that something was notifying next of kin.

Bishop was saying, "Better safe than sorry. You have to consider yourself a possible target, and act accordingly."

Finn grimaced, but nodded. "Yeah, okay. Are you guys going to keep searching up here while your ME works?"

"One of us plus a deputy needs to stay with each victim until Jill's able to get them down to town and to the hospital so she can do full autopsies. Miranda and I will do that. Reese and Hollis are already moving again, continuing to search the area you marked for them."

"Diana and I will keep going," Quentin said. "Search as much as we can while we have the light for it." He frowned suddenly. "The crows." He looked at Bishop.

Nodding, Bishop said to Finn, "When you've notified Megan's parents, and assuming there's still no sign of Simon, maybe you should ask Nellie to contact Tia. We need the crows helping us search specifically for Simon."

"Copy that," Finn said. He headed off, gathering with a slight gesture one of the two deputies standing several yards away. The remaining deputy stood her ground, but her expression clearly told anyone who wanted to know that she wasn't going to go near the remains on the other side of the boulder without a direct order to do so.

"What about Hollis?" Diana asked Bishop. "You said she was the one who talked to the crow that led you to Megan's remains."

"I'll get in touch and ask her to keep an eye out, to try to talk to any crow she sees."

"Try?"

"So far, we're only certain Hollis has been able to talk to Tia. It could be easier to communicate with Tia because she's their leader, or one of them. She's likely one of the older crows, with more experience of people. We don't know enough to be sure of that yet."

"One more thing we need to know," Quentin said.

———————

BY DUSK ON that overcast and very chilly Wednesday, they had transported the remains of Megan Hales and the unidentified male victim to Salem's small but modern hospital, where Dr. Jill Easton had the assistance of both her usual partner, Sam Norris, and one very clearly spooked but nevertheless steady older doctor who had performed more autopsies than any of his colleagues in town.

Dr. Dean Brady was not one of the Five, but he had married Belle Deverell more than twenty years before and they had two teenagers at home, so he very much felt a vested interest in any threat against the families.

"I've treated people in Salem for twenty-five years," he told Bishop when the agent had arrived at the hospital with Jill, Sam, and the remains of the unidentified victim they had carefully collected. "If this poor soul was one of my patients, I may be able to identify him."

"It's possible it's Cole Ainsworth," Bishop told him.

Brady's rugged face paled slightly. "He's one of my patients," he said.

Bishop exchanged a quick glance with Jill, then told the other doctor bluntly, "There isn't much left intact."

"I won't say it's something I'm used to." Brady's voice was calm. "But I did a stint in a major trauma center a few years ago. I can handle what I have to."

Bishop merely nodded. "Then I'll leave you to it. Jill, we're set up at Hales rather than the law enforcement center, as I told you, whenever you have anything new to report. If we don't hear from you before, someone will come by tomorrow."

"Right."

"In the meantime, I'll have my sat phone, and Finn has one as well."

Jill Easton, who was petite and blond and didn't look nearly as tough and experienced as she was, said again, "Right. We'll do what we can with the unidentified victim first since the ID on Megan Hales is all but certain."

"Thanks." Bishop left them to it. He had already determined from Jill that she'd had no better luck here in Salem using her clairvoyance than any of his agents—less, in fact—saying only that she hadn't picked up anything except a faint headache and planned to keep her shields up for the duration.

There was a Jeep from Finn's motor pool waiting for Bishop outside the hospital, along with a deputy, whom he dropped off at the law enforcement center on his way to Hales.

He sat for a moment outside the center after the deputy had gone in, his gaze fixed on a freestanding sign near the entrance. Perched on the sign were two crows.

Bishop opened his mind as he studied them, but this time all he got was the odd white noise, a kind of static interference. It was getting stronger. And it was becoming almost as painful as any attempt to use the spider senses.

One of the crows stretched its head out and bobbed slightly, bright black eyes fixed on the nearby human. It was . . . watching. Waiting.

Bishop glanced around and saw several more crows close by, perched on signs, on the bare limb of a tree, on a bench. He hadn't been conscious of them up on the mountain once Tia had led them to Megan Hales's grave, but now he felt as well as saw them.

Definitely not a telepathic sense. More like . . . something fluttering at the edge of his awareness.

After a long moment, Bishop raised his shields once again and left the center. He had been the last down off the mountainous slopes and was aware that Miranda and the rest of the team waited for him at the B and B.

It was still relatively early but already dark, and he noted that the downtown area was again very quiet, too quiet for a reasonably pleasant Wednesday evening in March, especially with snow tentatively in the forecast. People tended to want to be out and about with bad weather looming, either stocking up on supplies or just being out while they could be.

Not tonight.

He was willing to bet that at least some details of what had been done to the unidentified victim had made it off the mountain long before his remains had. And there had certainly been enough time since Megan Hales's family had been notified for that news to spread like wildfire.

So now the townsfolk of Salem knew that at least two of their neighbors had been brutally murdered and that a third was missing.

There had been no sign of Simon Cavendish, Finn's deputies had discovered no one who had heard from him since he'd left the bank the previous day, and Finn had officially logged him as missing.

Whether the majority of Salem had any clear knowledge that

members of the Five were the most likely targets of the killer was very much up for debate, at least for now. It was doubtful *anyone* would assume themselves to be safe.

Bishop knew that members of the Five made up around forty percent of Salem's population of less than ten thousand people and probably more if the families were traced through marriages beyond a couple of generations. The longtime practice, as Finn had explained it to Bishop, was for females born in any of the five families to keep their family names, usually hyphenating them officially if and when they married, and those combined names were passed along to offspring. Beyond that generation, however, it was pretty much an individual choice as to whether to keep surnames that were bound to grow cumbersome.

Bishop knew enough about human nature to know that there were undoubtedly men who disliked the idea of their own family names disappearing down the line when they married into the Five, so that was undoubtedly an influence on at least some choices made through the years.

Still, according to Finn, most people were aware if they were descended from one of the five families whether they bore the names or not, and many could trace that ancestry back, sometimes over many generations. In addition, all five families tended to have a higher percentage of sons than would have been the average.

It interested Bishop, especially given the psychic abilities passed down for many generations.

"Like a buffet," Hollis had said, emphasizing their unit chief's focus on psychics. Bishop had to smile, remembering that, but his smile faded. He would have much preferred to study Salem only in terms

of its psychics, but that hadn't been an option when Finn had first gotten in touch with him the previous year and wasn't now.

He stopped at an intersection, watched one crow light on a street-light near him and another perch on a bench only a few feet from the Jeep.

So he had an escort. Maybe. And if he did, it was likely the crows were also keeping an eye on the rest of the team. To watch what they did? To stand ready to help?

Or because they had their own agenda?

After how Duncan had used them, they would have been justified, after all, in having a less-than-positive opinion of the humans around them. That Nellie had gained them their freedom was good, but they had been prisoners of Duncan's dark ambition much longer than they had been free of it.

Bishop shook his head slightly and drove on, still thinking about Salem. In only a few short months, this town had been the site of too many brutal murders, and if the majority of its citizens had been un-aware of or able to ignore the deaths of victims just passing through or otherwise visiting Salem back in January and earlier, they were bound to feel very differently about family, friends, and neighbors being killed so viciously.

Between Aylia Blackwood's farseeing, Simon Cavendish officially being missing, and the remains of two victims brought out of the mountains today, it was no wonder most of the people of Salem had apparently chosen to go home from work and stay home, keeping children home as well.

The town was shaken. And Bishop was very much afraid it was only going to get worse.

————

IN THEIR MAKESHIFT command center at Hales B and B later, after an evening meal no one had done justice to, the team considered what they had.

"Which is pretty much nothing," Quentin pointed out. "The remains of one victim murdered six months ago or more. The remains of one murdered sometime last night or early this morning. A third potential victim missing. Unless Dr. Easton can tell us something we don't already know, the only thing we're more certain of than we were when we got here is that the targets do appear to be members of the five families."

Diana stirred restlessly in her chair. "Nearly half the citizens of Salem are members of the Five—more if we try to add up all the descendants, right?"

Bishop nodded. "Do you doubt the Five are targets?" he asked her directly.

"No. Not really." Her gaze met their team leader's. "What's happened so far seems to confirm it, right? And it was clear enough in the gray time that someone's hunting the Five."

"But?"

"I don't know that there is a *but*. Except . . . it really can't be just that, can it? The goal? To destroy the Five?"

"It's certainly ambitious, if so."

"I'd call it insane," Quentin offered.

Diana nodded. "The Blackwood elder saw someone hunting the Five, killing them horribly. Hollis and I were told in the gray time someone was hunting the families, killing them, and Daniel showed us torture victims. Okay, we have two victims, so far, horribly killed. Tortured, or at least we're sure the second victim was tortured." She held her voice level. "And we have Simon Cavendish missing. All are members of the five families, if the tentative ID on Cole Ainsworth holds. But . . . if nearly half the people of Salem belong to the five families, even if what we believe we know is true, can we still just assume they're being targeted *because* of that?"

"No," Miranda said, "we can't. Wiping out the families as a goal, an endgame, for this unsub doesn't make sense, if only due to the sheer scale. Wiping out just the elders doesn't make sense because Megan Hales wasn't an elder, and if Cole Ainsworth is the second victim, he isn't an elder either."

Bishop said, "Megan could turn out to give us a lot more information than any other victim might. He killed her first. But the gap in time between her and the second victim has to be significant in some way in terms of his motivation—though not necessarily negating whatever the endgame is. Maybe she was killed because of convenience, or because something about her or his response to her triggered his initial need to kill and in her case he acted impulsively. Maybe he's spent the time since he killed her developing his plans."

DeMarco said, "Plans we can't yet know."

Bishop nodded. "No sane killer could hope to eliminate even a substantial number of the five families without being caught."

"Which begs the question," DeMarco said.

"I doubt he's clinically insane. He was careful after he killed Megan. He buried her in a remote location not likely to be found, waited to find out if anyone suspected she'd never left Salem. Waited during everything that happened with Duncan Cavendish. And if what

Megan told Hollis is true, he waited and watched while this whole area was crawling with law enforcement weeks ago. He's patient."

Quentin said, "If he snatched Simon Cavendish when and where we believe he did, that was planned and efficient. Coolheaded."

"Agreed," Bishop said.

Hollis stopped chewing on a thumbnail to say, "Two men and a woman. Is that significant?"

Miranda said, "Megan was the first, and I think we've all agreed his motives for taking and killing her could have been different from whatever drove him to grab the men. More impulsive, without real planning. Megan really could have been opportunity and circumstance. He knew her or watched her or both, realized she was leaving, and took advantage of that opportunity."

"Or," Diana said slowly, "she gave him some kind of reason. Something personal."

FIFTEEN

"Definitely possible," Bishop said.

"Okay." Hollis was nodding slowly. "So Megan is impulse. Something about her triggered him. Possibly something she did or said. Something personal. Which would mean he knew her."

"Possibly very well," Miranda said.

"Yeah. We really do have to talk to her family, people who knew her. Look for somebody else in her life around about the time she was being jilted by Paul Ainsworth." She blinked. "Um . . . how was Paul related to Cole?"

"Cousins," Bishop answered. "Not especially close, according to Finn."

Hollis nodded again. "So we look for somebody in Megan's life last summer. He knows her, something maybe happens between them, he kills her. And he's very lucky or very good, because he gets away with it. It was his trigger, and now he has a need to kill again.

Months later, and not long after a pretty bright spotlight was shining on this town for weeks, our unsub takes another victim. Most likely it's Cole. He stormed out after a fight with his wife, and she was too mad to care that he—she assumed—was staying somewhere with a buddy for a day or two. So he wasn't missed right away. Just like with Megan. So maybe a second victim chosen for opportunity, because nobody would immediately realize he was gone."

"Maybe," Miranda agreed.

Hollis frowned. "Wait. Megan's car?"

Bishop said, "According to Finn, there's no sign of Megan's car. There was no search for it months ago, obviously, since everyone believed she had driven it out of Salem herself, but deputies are on the lookout now and he's officially put out a BOLO statewide. Nothing yet."

Quentin said, "The unsub's had more than enough time to get rid of that car. I doubt we'll ever find it."

Hollis nodded. "One car missing for months, yeah. Cole didn't take his car, which his wife assumed meant he was somewhere nearby with a friend. But we can't assume that because we don't know where he disappeared *from*."

"Probably not too far from home," Quentin speculated. "Educated guess says the unsub grabbed Cole from the downtown area at or near his condo—somehow; immobilized him—somehow; and hid him—somewhere."

Diana asked, "Did Megan live in one of the downtown condos too?"

"No, at her family home out in the valley," Bishop replied. "No one in her family and no one else who knew her saw her leave. With everything that was happening then, her clothing and car gone, it was just assumed she had left to get away from all the unpleasant attention."

Hollis muttered something under her breath, then said, "And last night he grabbed Simon Cavendish, who was walking home, as usual, through part of the downtown area. On a weekday. No car to ditch, but still the unsub had to be careful, fast—and lucky. Because he still had Cole stashed somewhere, and if what I felt yesterday was right, he'd already started torturing him. Started—and then stopped to go grab Simon? Does that make sense?"

"Still depends on the why," DeMarco said.

"We were here," Hollis pointed out. "And by late yesterday everybody knew it. Some of us on the slopes, some in town, at least until it started to get dark. Pretty damned visible. But obviously not a deterrent."

"Wait," Diana said. "Once we knew yesterday there was already a victim, we weren't just searching the slopes and being visible in town; Finn's deputies were canvassing here in town, looking for anyone that might have been missing. Literally going door-to-door. Businesses as well as homes. Could the unsub take the chance of not being where he was supposed to be?"

"Good point," Quentin told her. "He might have stopped working on Cole *because* the deputies were moving through town knocking on doors, others calling citizens, trying to find out who was missing. All of us were out. He might have realized what was going on."

"Especially," Hollis said, "if he's psychic. Just because we've been having trouble with our extra senses doesn't mean a psychic born and raised here has the same problem. Dammit."

———

HE WAS AS comfortable on the mountain slopes as he was on a paved street, and he had the sharp night vision of an owl, so he was able to find the precise spot quickly and easily even in the dark. The tools he had hidden remained undisturbed, as did his earlier work.

Maybe that was luck.

Or maybe it was something else.

He had the night to complete his work. He knew very well that the search teams had returned to town, and he knew the patrol routes of Finn's deputies, so he wasn't worried about discovery.

And Simon would keep.

He could feel the unease of Salem, and it made him smile. Most were shut inside their homes for the night. And most were anxious but felt somewhat protected, he knew. Those with Talents counted on them to help them survive, unwilling to believe the Talents themselves might make them targets. And everyone knew about the FBI agents Finn had called in, the ones with their guns and their own Talents.

So even members of the Five, uneasy though they were, were also calmed somewhat by that knowledge. But he couldn't allow them to feel safe. That's what they had to understand, all of the Five and all of the very smart cops.

They had to understand no one was safe.

———

"IT'S AT LEAST possible that he is psychic," Bishop said. "And if he's psychic and possesses one of the very solid shields you were able to see today when you were studying auras, whatever abilities he has are likely to be hidden from us."

"And he doesn't have to be a member of one of the five families in order to be psychic, right?"

"We know there are psychics outside the Five."

Diana asked, "Do we know who they are? I mean, we know the elders of the Five *are* elders because they're among the strongest in their families with Talents. Has anybody kept track of psychics in other families? Their strengths and weaknesses, their particular abilities?"

"Not officially," Miranda said.

Diana frowned at her. "How about unofficially?"

It was Bishop who said, "There's no real way to be sure going back generations. According to Finn, there was a general awareness—maybe a psychic awareness—as recently as twenty years ago that there were maybe a score of people at that time outside the Five with abilities. Talents. Not handed down in their own families but occurring fairly randomly as psychic abilities do. Some approached members of the Five asking for help in learning to understand and control those abilities."

DeMarco asked, "Was that help given?"

"For a while, yeah. Then Duncan Cavendish began building his power base, recruiting loyal followers, and whispers began that he was interested in Talents."

"Scary interested?" Hollis answered her own question before Bishop could. "Yeah, I remember. Scary interested. He wanted energy, wanted other abilities for his very own. Basically wanted to use whatever he could steal in his ambition to become a god. Steal . . .

fatally. If word about that got around, I imagine that would have made any psychic think twice about being open about their own abilities."

"It did."

"So, for the last decade or so at least, psychics outside the five families decided to keep quiet about it."

Bishop nodded. "It was one of the reasons why we believe Cavendish targeted descendants of the Five who lived outside Salem; at least he could be relatively certain abilities were possible in them. In Salem, those who hid their abilities hid them well. Including from other psychics. Even as powerful as he was in the beginning, Cavendish didn't dare target the five families here in Salem. He recruited some psychics from the other families and found various ways of using the abilities of both them and the few Cavendishes who were rabidly loyal to him as tools, but he didn't kill them."

"But he killed other psychics. I mean, before he started targeting descendants outside the valley."

"Looking back, there was a pattern very early on, but at the time it went virtually unnoticed. Over roughly two decades, there were some people who either supposedly left Salem or simply disappeared. No bodies were ever found, not that Finn could discover. And he couldn't be absolutely certain those who vanished had been psychics. But he suspected. And given what we now know for certain Duncan was doing over the last year, it's at least highly probable he's responsible for some if not all those missing people and that they were psychics."

Diana said, "So fear of Duncan would have kept psychics outside the Five quiet. And now that he's no longer a threat?"

"There hasn't been a lot of time for any long-term wariness to change," Quentin pointed out. "Not nearly enough, if you ask me. I'm betting any surviving psychics figured out how to stay alive by being very quiet about their abilities, probably suppressing and denying, and even with Duncan gone that'll be a hard habit to break."

Hollis shook her head slightly, frowning. "So we really can't be sure our unsub is one of the Five. No matter what Daniel hinted to Diana and me in the gray time, it's probably more likely he isn't, especially if he's psychic and had to hide that for years in fear for his life. He could have worked up quite a grudge against Duncan and those helping him. Right?"

Bishop nodded. "Yeah. But he doesn't appear, so far, to be targeting people who helped Duncan. Though that could be something else dictating his actions. The rabid loyalists are virtually all gone, their cases working their way through the court system. Because of the severity of the charges, none were granted bail."

"And none of the victims we know about so far were among those who helped Duncan even in . . . less illegal, criminal ways."

"No, Finn's certain of that."

Hollis was still frowning. "So whatever the unsub's endgame is, it could very easily have nothing to do with Duncan."

"That seems more likely than not."

"And we don't know that it's about power for the unsub. Attaining more power, I mean, by specifically killing psychics. He's just . . . killing."

"Just," Diana murmured.

"You know what I mean." Hollis shook her head slightly. "Targeting the Five, but not because of Duncan's crusade. And his victims so far . . . We're sure Megan wasn't psychic?"

Miranda said, "According to Finn, she wasn't."

"And Cole wasn't. But Simon is."

Bishop nodded.

"Abilities that didn't help him," Quentin pointed out.

"Ours don't seem to be helping us very much," Hollis said. "Not so far, at any rate."

"So he really could have an edge," Diana said steadily. "An edge over his victims, and over us. Be a step ahead of us."

Hollis moved restlessly in her chair. "Hell, maybe more than a step. He knows the town better than we do, the valley, the slopes. The people. He has his plan and there's been plenty of time for him to work on that, perfect it, if we believe he's been planning since Megan if not before. He could have more than one place he can . . . work. Different places ready where he can stash victims. Dammit. Why do I have the feeling that our getting here, what we believed was early in the game, is not going to do a single thing to help us stop him." It was not a question.

Clearly just as frustrated, Diana said, "What's the point of a heads-up if it doesn't help us at all?"

"Who told you the Universe was fair?" Quentin asked dryly.

"You did."

"I said it was balanced; I never said it was fair."

"*Balanced* means we catch a break now and then, right?"

"One would think."

"The crows could be a break," Hollis pointed out. "They've certainly been visible today. Tia said they'd look for Simon specifically tomorrow and keep patrolling the valley."

"Which could be a big help," DeMarco agreed.

"Yeah, but . . . the crows don't figure into the profile, right? I mean, however they're able to help, we still need to figure out this unsub, and sooner rather than later."

There were nods all around.

Bishop said, "We know he's physically strong, he's mobile, and he knows the area."

"He's a sadist," Quentin contributed. "The victim that may be Cole Ainsworth was certainly tortured before death, his body dismembered and defiled after death. Broken bones stuck into the ground like some weird . . . I don't even know what to call it. Megan's remains were more or less intact, but basically skeletal, so we don't know what he did to her, or whether he returned to her body after she was dead. Maybe to experiment."

Hollis stirred. "Finn said there'd been no reports of animals going missing or being found dead or inexplicably hurt, right? And no reports of arson in the valley, not even small fires?"

"No," Bishop replied. "None of the early signs we might expect from a budding typical serial."

Diana said slowly, "Can we even consider him a typical serial? I mean, killing a series of people, yeah, but chances are better than good that he knows some if not all of his victims, right?"

"Given the size of the valley, the population, the time period we're talking about, it's likely," Bishop agreed.

"Which affects the profile."

He nodded. "They used to be called stranger killings; it was what made them so difficult to solve, because the killer had absolutely no connection with his victims, unlike in typical murders where connections and motives are usually pretty obvious. In this case, we're all but certain he's a part of the community here, the town, but victimology will likely be filled with too many overlaps to be helpful. Same church, same gym or grocery store, same doctor or clinic."

"So again, all we can be fairly sure of so far is that victims are chosen from among the five families," DeMarco said. "Which tells us he has a grudge and a plan."

"And doesn't tell us much more," Bishop agreed.

"I wish Megan had told me more," Hollis muttered, voicing a common complaint because she'd learned through bitter experience that spirits were seldom very helpful. "If she was his trigger, why? Just because she was leaving? People had left Salem before, for jobs, school, just to move away. What was it about Megan, about her leaving, that made her his first target? That's what sticks out to me. Megan. And the way Diana and I were alerted in the gray time."

DeMarco looked at Bishop. "Finn talked to her family?"

"He did, though they were so overwhelmed by the news of her death they couldn't tell him much."

"All due respect to Finn, we need to talk to them."

Bishop nodded. "On the list for tomorrow. Miranda and I will talk to them."

"And we'll have Jill's post by then," Hollis said. "Maybe know more about what he did to the latest victim, to Megan, if there's anything at all consistent. Maybe more puzzle pieces. But I don't see that adding to the profile, not unless Jill finds something none of us is expecting. And we saw what was there." She sighed. "Still not seeing much benefit to our heads-up. So why bother? Just the Universe messing with us?"

There were several rueful smiles at another common complaint, and it was Miranda who said, "Maybe *how* we got the heads-up is the important thing."

"Because it was in the gray time?" Diana frowned.

"It does stick out, as Hollis said. You two have both been able to gain useful information in the gray time, but before it was always after we were already on a case. Right?"

"Yeah. So . . . why was it different this time?"

Still frowning, Diana looked at Hollis, noting that the other woman was also frowning. "Hollis?"

"What?" Hollis looked at her, saw her, then blinked. She became aware she was chewing on a thumbnail, forced herself to stop, and crossed her arms as she leaned back in her chair. "It's your time or place a lot more than it is mine," she pointed out.

"Yeah. So maybe you can think about it, about what we saw with . . . clearer eyes than I can."

Hollis frowned back at her. "Something didn't seem right to you. You thought it was strange. Unusual."

"Well . . . thinking about it more since then, maybe."

Bishop said, "Sure that isn't a little self-doubt talking?"

Diana immediately shook her head. "Not at all sure. There are still plenty of blank places in my memory of *most* of my visits to the gray time in those early years. That's why I think Hollis might have a better take. I'm certain when I'm *there*, confident of what I know or don't know. I'm usually certain afterward that what I saw, what was told to me, was something I could trust, especially in the last few years."

Quentin was watching her steadily. "But not this time? You were sure even right after that visit that something had been different. Because the supposed victims you were both shown were in color. Right?"

Diana nodded. "We both saw them in color. Which really, really stands out in the gray time."

"Signposts," Bishop said.

She nodded again. "So far, everything I've ever seen in color in the gray time was important."

Quentin said, "Is that why you keep thinking about going back?"

"Maybe." She looked at him for a long moment, then returned her gaze to Hollis. "You've been there a few times now. Is any of it bugging you? I mean other than those . . . victims . . . all in color?"

Hollis was still frowning. "Being in the gray time was just . . . creepy. More than usual. Maybe because we weren't on a case and it was . . . startling . . . to be yanked there. Maybe. Those victims being in color made it extra creepy."

"What else?" Miranda asked her.

"I don't know." She shook her head, then said, "Something about the guide, I think. About Daniel."

Quentin looked at Diana and said, "You were bothered about him earlier. About him maybe being stuck in the gray time. Until he appeared to guide us to a victim on the mountain."

"I think . . . I know I was bothered by something about him. Maybe that was it. Even him appearing to me on this side of the gray time was different. That's rare for me; we all know that. And him leading us to a victim—that was also rare." She frowned at Hollis. "What about Daniel was bugging you?"

"I dunno. Something about the way he talked to us, the way he smiled. Maybe." Both her uncertainty and her frustration with it were clear.

"How did he talk to you?" Bishop asked her. "What was different?"

Hollis said, "Like I said, it's really more Diana's time or place than it is mine; I haven't been there that many times. So maybe it wasn't as odd as it felt to me. I mean, Daniel was fairly unhelpful, which is the rule with spirits and spirit guides, we all know that, but . . ."

DeMarco was watching his partner steadily. "Which of your senses are strongest there?"

She looked at him, surprised. "I hadn't thought about it that way."

"So?"

"Well . . . it's a disorienting kind of place, at least to me. It's cold and looks weird and smells weird, even sounds weird when I speak or Diana does or the guide. I feel cold and tired there almost at once. None of my senses seem to work right there."

"None of them?"

"The usual five are sort of muffled or just different there. The spider senses definitely don't work. At all. At least not for me, not so far. Empathy . . . Huh. This is the first time I've been there since I became an empath. I think. I don't remember feeling any emotions other than my own."

"Clairvoyance?" Bishop asked.

"I'm not clairvoyant." But it was said more or less automatically, and she was still frowning.

DeMarco said, "Gut feeling. What did you *know* when you were there? About Daniel."

"He didn't belong there." She looked surprised again.

"Why not?"

"I . . . don't know."

SIXTEEN

It was a bit later than normal that evening when Nellie and Finn shared a table at one of the downtown restaurants, late enough so that there were only half a dozen other customers, including the two deputies who ate their own supper at a table near the front windows while they waited to escort Nellie and Finn home.

"Is it really necessary?" Nellie asked for the second time.

"Bishop says so, and I agree with him," Finn replied. He kept his voice low. "We might not know much about this killer, but who he's targeting seems clear enough. We're potential targets, Nellie, both of us."

"You're always armed and I have Leo," she pointed out, glancing to one side to see her big dog relaxed on his bed out of the way of foot traffic. She did, in fact, own a gun, but it had lived in the drawer of her nightstand for the last few weeks. When there hadn't seemed to be a threat to her in Salem any longer.

"Still. We know this killer is vicious and . . . on a mission. We don't know how he chooses individuals, how he decides who he wants to kill and when, or even if he's working from some kind of kill list he's had ready for a while. We don't know how he's managed to take three people without any witnesses. We don't know how he was able to hide or dispose of Megan's car. We don't really know what he's capable of, except the extremes of violence and cruelty. So we take precautions. That's sensible, right?"

"I guess." Nellie pushed her plate a few inches away, frowning. The food was excellent as usual, but her appetite had vanished completely when she'd learned about Simon. The friendly cousin she liked very much was seldom far from her thoughts. "Still no word about Simon?"

"You know I would have told you. No word. No sign. And not much more we can do to search for him until morning."

"No searching after dark."

Knowing what she was asking, Finn said, "Having regular night-time patrols on the slopes before, especially weeks ago when Duncan was so dangerous, was different, Nellie. We knew who and what the threat was. But now? This? Most of my people are members of the Five. Potential targets. And even aside from that, I've barely got enough manpower to do a thorough search during the day and keep up regular two-deputy patrols here in town and in the rest of the valley at night, to keep people on the phones, manning the station just to take ordinary calls."

"I wasn't criticizing," she murmured.

Finn nodded.

"I hate this."

"I know. So do I."

Nellie shook her head slightly. "With Duncan gone, his followers, I thought things would be better. It's like you said: At least what he was, what he planned, was pretty damned obvious. And why. We knew he was behind what was happening. But this killer . . . how could he have been hidden for so long, for months? Longer if there were signs nobody noticed, and there had to be, right? You don't just wake up one day and decide to butcher another human being. I didn't have to see the . . . the remains brought down out of the mountains to know how viciously they were killed. The more recent one, at least. Everybody's talking about it."

"Yeah, I know." It was something he had expected, small towns being infamous for the speed at which knowledge spread.

"How could a killer like that hide what he is? How could he be walking around looking normal like the rest of us?"

Finn regarded her steadily. "You know as well as I do that human monsters hide in plain sight. They always have. It's the Talents you're thinking about, isn't it?"

"Well, they should help. Shouldn't they? The whole reason Bishop created the Special Crimes Unit was to have agents able to investigate using senses most people don't have. Senses, Talents, like we have. Like a lot of people in this valley have. So why aren't they helping us?"

"Aylia Blackwood's Talent at least told us something was happening."

"A warning that doesn't seem to have done much good. She hasn't had another vision, right?"

"Not so far. It takes a lot out of her to try, but she keeps doing it. Michael's worried about her."

Nellie frowned. "Her husband? I haven't met him, right? He wouldn't have been at the meeting of the elders last month."

"No. But he's supportive of Aylia and respects Talents. He owns that electronics store on the other end of Main Street."

Nellie half nodded. "So Aylia had that one vision, the one that scared the hell out of her. And us. And none of the rest of us has sensed anything helpful."

He eyed her. "Have you tried?"

"I talked to Tia," she reminded him, not quite defensively. "To ask them to search, and then again to search specifically for Simon."

"Talking to the crows isn't the only thing you can do."

"It's the only thing useful right now."

"How do you know that?"

Nellie looked at her gloved hand, fingers toying with the stem of her wineglass. "Calling down a storm would hardly help," she said. "Even if I could."

He didn't argue about whether she could; they both knew the answer to that despite her words. Conversationally, he said, "Sooner or later you're going to have to accept all your Talents. And use them."

She made her voice light with an effort that showed. "Give me a break. I'm still getting used to them myself."

"You mean openly having them."

"Whatever. I just . . . what happened with Duncan was driven by extreme need; you know that. What he would have done to Bethany was—" The little girl who would have been Duncan's final victim was safe and well now, the trauma of her abduction softened with a Talent Nellie had not even known she possessed. She shook her head. "I couldn't let him kill her."

"I know."

"And you know I'd help Simon if I could. But nothing I can do is going to find him. I *have* tried. To open up. To listen. All I get is some kind of static. And a pounding headache."

It didn't surprise Finn; the same thing had happened to him. And, from all he could gather, to most of the members of Bishop's team. He frowned slightly. "Funny thing, that. There's been energy in the valley a long time, enough so that many of us could sense it, but as far as I know it's never interfered with our ability to use our Talents. Not like this."

"Maybe it was something Duncan did?"

"I don't think so. I've thought of that, but . . . If he could have found a way other than that constructed barrier of his to dampen our Talents, he would certainly have done it long ago."

Nellie stared at him. "It wasn't me, was it?"

He smiled slightly. "Well, that was a hell of a storm. But if anything it seemed to lessen the energy in the valley, at least by the time it was over, and at least for a while."

"Then what's causing it?"

"Bishop told me it was unlikely to be coming from a single source."

"Unlikely. Not impossible. Great. Something else we don't know." She drew a breath and let it out slowly. "Okay. Our Talents aren't helping us figure things out. So all we really have is a possibility that either family ties or the Talents seem to be making us targets. Why?"

"I don't know. Envy. Jealousy. I doubt it's fear."

She frowned briefly. "Because of what he did to—to Cole Ainsworth? If it is him?"

"I'm no profiler. According to Bishop, the extreme violence and cruelty of this killer is something that tends to come from some kind of anger, with some other nasty kinks in his nature. He buried Megan, but . . . what was left of Cole wasn't hidden except behind a few boulders."

"You're sure it's Cole." It wasn't really a question.

Finn nodded. "I'm as sure as I can be until DNA results are in."

"Cole wasn't missed right away. Like Megan. But not at all like Simon. That can't be good. Not that any part of this is good, but you know what I mean."

"I know. And you're right. The killer certainly doesn't seem to be much worried by either my deputies or Bishop's team crawling all over the slopes and the valley."

She heard something in his voice and said, "There isn't anything else you could be doing. Not you and not Bishop's team. Aylia's warning wasn't specific enough to tell anyone where to look or who to look for."

"Yeah. That doesn't make it easier."

———

"THINK IT THROUGH," Bishop suggested to Hollis. "Why didn't Daniel belong there?"

"I don't know why I feel he didn't belong there."

"Go through the experience, step by step."

She frowned at him. "All of it?"

"If both you and Diana feel something was wrong, different, about that visit or about Daniel, something you saw or heard or felt could be important, Hollis."

"Well . . . we were both yanked out of sleep. I just started walking through the condo, knowing from experience it would . . . become a different place. Diana?"

"Same. And didn't make it to the door before I was suddenly on the slope."

Bishop said, "The slope. Not down here in town?"

Both women shook their heads, and Hollis said, "Weird, feeling the ground suddenly tilt under your feet. But it did. The town was . . . distant. But in front of me. So I just started walking. And Diana was there within a minute or two, with Daniel."

Quentin looked at his partner. "Did Daniel say anything to you before you met up with Hollis?"

"He said . . . I'd need my strength. That I was—we were—needed here. In Salem. I said something about how Gray and Geneva had handled things weeks ago. Then he said come along or something like that, and started leading the way downslope, toward the town I could sort of see. We came out of a denser part of the forest, and that's when I saw Hollis."

"Go on."

"She was relieved."

"I was," Hollis agreed. "That place is bad enough with company. Alone, it's spooky as hell. And I always sort of worry if Diana isn't there pretty quick. That I might not be able to find the way out on my own. And she said something about that, asked, I think, if I'd been pulled in by accident because she opened a door."

They all knew it was a possibility that worried Diana.

She said, "And that was when Daniel said we were both needed. But he wouldn't say why then, just started toward the town again."

Hollis said, "And while we were walking, there was a sort of mist that swirled around us—and just like that we were on the sidewalk down on Main Street. It was so sudden I stubbed my toe. Because pavement."

"That mist," Quentin said to his partner. "I don't remember you mentioning anything like that before. It was different? Something new?"

"Far as I can remember, yeah."

"It was weird," Hollis said. "Always before, when I've been there, it's just blink and you're somewhere else."

"Same here," Diana said slowly. "I think."

"So maybe another signpost," Bishop suggested.

Diana frowned at him. "What could that mean? A weird sort of mist?"

"Portal," Hollis said, then blinked.

DeMarco was watching her. "Why do you say that?"

She thought for a few moments, then swore under her breath and answered him with even more frustration in her voice. "I have no idea. Dammit." She looked at Bishop. "Do you?"

He was frowning very slightly. "You know the only sort of portals we've dealt with have been energy portals. Closing and sealing them was the goal, not stepping into them."

"I know that's the only kind Reese and I have dealt with," she said. "I don't recall seeing anything about them in other team reports, but that doesn't mean there haven't been any."

"There haven't."

Hollis nodded, accepting. She looked at Diana. "So it really was a first for you in the gray time?"

"Right."

Quentin spoke slowly. "Something for us to remember, but I don't see how a portal of any kind in the gray time helps us here and now."

Bishop shook his head. "Neither do I. It's quite likely a quality of the gray time, even if it seemed to be something new to Diana. The fact that it's a place for spiritual energy means the laws we deal with likely don't apply, so what seems strange here is normal there. It could easily be just another way to move—or be moved—from one point to another. Hollis, what happened next? Daniel talked to you and Diana?"

Slowly, Hollis said, "He told us someone was after the Five. A killer, serial. He waffled about whether the killer *was* one of the Five, which bugs me. Said something about all the psychics, in the five families and outside them. About all the shields keeping them from using their psychic tools the way we can, to hunt monsters. One of us asked him . . . something. And he said why didn't he show us. He gestured for us to look, toward the other side of the street. Main Street. We saw all those poor people. Cut and burned and bleeding, walking toward us. It was horrible. I wanted to leave. And just as Reese started to pull me out, I looked at Daniel. There was something about him. Something wrong."

DeMarco was still gazing at her steadily. "You were looking at him. So something *looked* wrong to you. What was it?"

"His eyes."

"What was wrong about his eyes?"

After a frowning moment, Hollis shook her head, frustration again tightening her features. "I don't know. I mean, I still *feel* that there was something wrong, something about his eyes, but when I try to remember, it just isn't there."

"I thought I was the only one with memory problems about people and things in the gray time," Diana said.

"Apparently not."

Miranda said, "So maybe both your memories are affected at least somewhat by the gray time. I mean, maybe that's a natural attribute of the gray time."

That struck Diana as something potentially good, at least as far as her own memory issues went. If there were things she wasn't *meant* to remember in the gray time, for whatever reason, then maybe her uncertain or missing memories of visits in the past had a lot less to do with her own mind than she'd realized. She dragged her attention back to the less personal discussion.

"Interesting, I guess," Hollis said. "But not really a lot of help. Just one more frustrating thing about this case."

Bishop said, "Maybe the interference here affected both of you in the gray time."

Diana stared at him. "Is that possible?"

"We don't know enough about the gray time to rule it out."

Hollis was even more uneasy. "That sounds weird. And . . . spooky. If the energy here could reach one of us even there, it's not like any energy I've ever experienced or even heard about."

Quentin said, "Well, it's also reasonable that if it *could* reach you in the gray time, it would have a blocking or muffling effect on your abilities. Because that's what it's doing to us now."

"Not completely blocking us. I was able to communicate with Tia here. And a bit with Leo." She didn't mention the easy communication with DeMarco, especially when they touched; that was another thing entirely, something that was a part of their connection, and something she knew the other two couples also shared. It was not, strictly speaking, an ability, and was not affected by external energy.

"That was more empathic than telepathic," Bishop said.

"Okay. But as far as I can tell with a new ability, it's not as strong here as it was before. I'm picking up emotions from people near me, but that's all."

"So probably affected at least somewhat by the energy here, as all our abilities and spider senses seem to be. We have to find a way of dealing with that energy," Bishop said. His gaze was on Hollis steadily.

She frowned at him. "Well, I don't know how. It isn't something I can see, like I've been able to during other cases. I'm not even aware of it in any real sense, not the way I have been before. Except when I try to use my abilities. It's . . . diffused. It's not a doorway or—or a dome, not a force."

Miranda said suddenly, "Does it have a consciousness? A mind behind it?"

"No." Hollis turned her frown to the other woman and added slowly, "No, it doesn't. Not a single mind, a personality. I don't feel any sense of identity. Just . . . energy."

SIMON CAVENDISH HAD no idea how much time had passed. He was in total darkness, cramped, his limbs senseless. It was icy cold. His throat was raw from earlier screams, his mouth dry as dust. His head pounded. He was vaguely sure the fluttery throbbing he felt in his ears was his own heartbeat. Astonishingly, he thought he might have slept, but he wasn't sure. The panic had not so much gone away as become something dark and crawly beneath the level of his conscious awareness.

That was because his conscious awareness was taken up by something else.

It was getting harder to breathe.

He focused on that, and at first told himself it was only because his throat was sore and dry, his nose clogged by tears he didn't remember shedding. And for a while that occupied him as he thought methodically about forcing his throat to relax, forcing himself to breathe shallowly, slowly.

Simon focused. *Just breathe. Shallow. In. Out. In. Out. Don't think. Just breathe. In. Out. In. Out.*

He kept his eyes closed because the darkness was so absolute it had weight, heavy weight, and he was afraid it would crush him. He refused to think about how numb his arms were, his legs. About how his head pounded worse than any migraine he'd ever had in his life.

He refused to think about people and the things he'd taken for granted. Like just being able to move, to breathe easily. To have a hot shower and feel clean. To sleep in a warm, soft bed between smooth sheets. To drink water or whatever else he wanted, when he wanted. To eat good food when he was hungry. To talk to friends and family, listen to them. Enjoy them. To enjoy their companionship.

He refused to think about dying.

Time passed, he thought, but nothing changed. Except he was certain, way down deep where those dark and crawly things were, that it was getting even harder to breathe.

He tried not to wonder if anyone had missed him. If anyone was looking for him. Tried not to wonder if this box that was his prison was buried where no one would ever think to look.

He carefully didn't think of his prison as a coffin.

He had no idea where he was. Maybe no one would think to look for him wherever this was—

He drew a sudden, deep breath of the terrifyingly thin air, his eyes opening to stare incredulously into the heavy darkness as another realization jolted his mind.

Stupid! Stupid!

Simon closed his eyes again and, ignoring the thin, stale air, ignoring numbness and pain and terror, began to concentrate as he never had before.

SEVENTEEN

Nellie Cavendish opened her eyes with a jolt, a wordless cry escaping her, and realized she was sitting up in her bed, that her arms were held out as though reaching for something. She heard a whine, and automatically relaxed enough to stroke the broad head of her anxious dog where he lay near her feet.

"It's okay, Leo," she murmured, half closing her eyes again to focus, to reach mentally, psychically, exercising what was still a largely unused muscle. "It's . . . I think it's . . ."

Leo whined again, but when she pushed back the covers, swung her legs over the side of the bed, and reached for the lamp and the landline on her nightstand, he was instantly on the floor, watching her with bright eyes.

Nellie quickly punched in a room number, unsurprised when he answered before it could ring twice.

"Bishop."

"I think I know where Simon is," she told him as steadily as she could manage. "We need everybody. And shovels. I'll meet you downstairs in ten minutes."

She didn't wait for a response, immediately cradling the receiver and rushing to get dressed. She realized it was still dark outside because she'd needed the lamp but was vaguely surprised when a glance at the clock across the room from her bed—as far away as possible so she couldn't short the damned thing out—told her it was just after two in the morning.

She'd been in bed barely three hours.

Nellie?

Finn. I think I know where Simon is.

On my way.

She didn't even think about the easy, assured touch of his mind or her equally easy response, just kept moving.

She automatically dressed in a couple of warm layers and chose thick socks and her virtually new hiking boots, grabbing her quilted jacket on the way out of her room, with Leo close at her heels.

She did not remember to put on her gloves.

It didn't occur to her until she was hurrying down the quiet lamplit hall toward the stairs that she hadn't even bothered to brush her hair or so much as glance into a mirror, but the thought was fleeting. Nothing mattered but getting to Simon as fast as possible.

She was downstairs in the lobby area in minutes, and before she could do more than pace a few steps one way and then another, the others were coming down the stairs toward her. She wasn't surprised to see that Bishop's entire team was there, all dressed warmly, seemingly wide-awake—though Hollis yawned and rubbed her eyes with one hand.

In the other hand she held a big flashlight, as did everyone else.

Hollis was, predictably, the first to speak to Nellie.

"That's some transmitter," she said.

Nellie was startled. "Did I—?"

"Loud and clear. From you and Bishop." She eyed her unit chief. "Didn't know you could do that."

"Saves time." He didn't add anything else to that, instead saying, "We have a couple of collapsible shovels in the SUV."

"We need more," DeMarco said.

They had all arrived so quickly that it was only then that the B and B's night man appeared behind the registration desk from his office in back, his eyes wide and startled. "What—"

"We need shovels," Bishop told him. "And a crowbar or two."

"It's Simon, Jim," Nellie said quickly. "I think I know where he is."

Jim didn't hesitate. "The outside utility room's around the side. I've got the key. Come on."

There were several shovels, a pick, two big claw hammers, and a crowbar. The tools were quickly distributed among them, along with two large battery lanterns, and they followed Nellie as she led them toward the parking area of the B and B.

"I can—" Jim began.

"Call EMS," Bishop instructed him calmly. "Get an ambulance, but tell them no lights or siren, and have them wait right here."

As most did when Bishop gave an order, Jim obeyed without argument, turning to hurry back to the building.

Quentin said, "Think the unsub might be watching?"

"He has to sleep sometime, but best not assume anything where he's concerned," Bishop replied. "If we can keep him in the dark about anything we do, it could give us an edge."

Diana's voice was tight. "If Simon's been buried underground all this time—"

"It's getting harder for him to breathe," Nellie said, her voice equally strained. "But he's alive."

"Can you—" Hollis began.

Nellie cut her off with a shake of her head. "I can sense him, I know he's struggling, but I can't talk to him."

"Figures," Hollis said, resigned.

Diana started to say something, then exchanged a grim glance with Quentin and merely shook her head.

Nobody questioned Nellie as she led them away from the building in the direction of the mountain slopes to the east, or when she stopped abruptly and turned toward the parking area's entrance, where a Salem police Jeep was turning in.

Finn parked the Jeep and turned off the engine, then got out along with two of his deputies. All three looked wide-awake, and all three were armed and carried flashlights. The two deputies pulled two large backpacks from the Jeep and shrugged into them as they followed Finn to join the others.

"This way," Nellie said, and immediately hurried through the parking area and then picked a vague path that meandered up the gradually steepening slope.

"Is he close?" Bishop asked.

"Pretty close, I think. But not easy to get to. We can take this path for a while, but then it's straight up the mountain." Nellie would have said more but decided to save her breath for climbing. The flashlights the others held made it easier than she'd expected to find her way, especially when Leo moved from his automatic heel position to go ahead of her, his nose to the ground almost constantly as he ranged back and forth but kept heading in the direction Nellie knew was the right one.

With snow in the forecast, however vaguely, it was cold, and the heavy cloud cover made it even darker than it usually was at night on any of the mountains surrounding the valley, especially once they were well into the heavy forest. There was no wind at all, and the utter silence was broken only by the faint noises they made in climbing.

Nobody was wasting breath on questions or comments.

Nellie had been far too busy since coming to Salem to have had time to do much hiking, and was wishing she'd done far more when her legs very quickly began to burn from the unaccustomed climbing. But she gritted her teeth and pushed on, all her concentration fixed on keeping hold of the frighteningly faint thread she could almost see glowing in her mind.

Simon.

She turned off the path at almost the same moment as Leo did, dimly aware that he was being guided by her more than by any scent he'd found. She didn't have to wonder to know that the killer had not taken this route to wherever he had buried Simon. Probably he'd found an easier way, especially if he'd been carrying his victim. They were really climbing now, and she heard Hollis's breathless voice behind her as she spoke, apparently to her partner.

"Add the occasional . . . mountain hike . . . to our . . . workout schedule . . . okay?"

"Good idea," he answered, with less effort.

Hollis made a smothered sound that might have been humor or something else, then continued to climb in silence broken only by an occasional curse muttered under her breath.

The climb was far steeper now, and with no path to follow they were picking their way quickly among winter-bare saplings, through underbrush, and around granite boulders, some of them very large. Hardwood trees reared above them, bare limbs occasionally catching the light of one of the flashlights to glitter with frost, and the evergreen pine trees were heavy and still.

They had probably been climbing for half an hour or more when Nellie and her dog abruptly turned to the right, following rather than trying to get past a lateral ridge of boulders and heavy brambles. She followed it, moving faster because they were no longer climbing, until the ridge abruptly ended and there was a small clearing with what appeared to be a tangle of holly bushes at its center.

"Under that," Nellie said breathlessly, pointing.

Willing hands very quickly pulled at the bushes, to find they were not rooted but had been cut away at some different location and used here as camouflage.

Beneath was a rectangular patch of recently turned earth.

Between the flashlights and the battery lanterns there was plenty of light, but little room for more than four of the strongest among them to begin digging. The others stood back, holding lights and trying to catch their breath from the hurried, difficult journey up the mountain.

Barely twelve inches down, the first shovel hit something hard, and immediately they knelt on the hard ground, still digging quickly but more carefully. As soon as one end of the box had been uncovered, Bishop and Finn tossed aside shovels to begin prying up the very solid lid.

Hollis was close enough to hear Nellie whispering, "Still breathing, still breathing," but she was still both relieved and surprised when the lid was yanked up with a jerk to reveal Simon's white face, eyes blinking and tearing in the brightness of the lights turned on him and his prison.

Or maybe it wasn't the lights.

He opened his parched lips, but Finn said quickly, "Don't try to talk, Simon. We'll get you out."

He lay on his side in the box, which was just barely large enough to hold him in his bent position. There were plastic zip ties binding his wrists behind his back and binding his ankles, and more than one of his rescuers winced in sympathy when the ties were cut and he groaned as circulation began to return to his cramped limbs.

Finn's deputies removed from their backpacks a collapsible stretcher and an emergency rescue blanket, both positioned close so that Simon could be lifted carefully out, his shivering body wrapped warmly in the blanket and belted securely onto the stretcher.

Finn gave him as much water as he wanted and then, no doubt more warming, something from a flask he produced, and it was only then that Simon cleared his throat and looked steadily up at his rescuers.

"Thank you."

———————

THE TWO DEPUTIES, DeMarco, and Quentin carried the stretcher down the mountain to the waiting ambulance, with the deputies set to return and keep watch over the site until it could be exhaustively searched and studied in daylight. Simon tried to protest that he could walk, but Nellie told him calmly to shut up and enjoy the ride, and he grinned rather weakly in response.

As soon as they were on their way, Nellie turned to the others, noting in the surprisingly bright light that Bishop was gazing thoughtfully down at the open box and that Finn was frowning.

"What?" she demanded.

Miranda said, "He was taken Tuesday evening. It's almost dawn on Thursday."

Diana added, "He can't have been buried in this box so long and still had air to breathe. Look at the box. It's pretty much airtight, barely large enough to hold him in that cramped position, and it was buried with a foot of dirt over it."

Hollis was nodding. "Maybe five hours of ambient air. Less."

Nellie frowned, watching as Bishop knelt once more and searched the inside of the box with his flashlight. He stopped when he reached a spot in one corner of the end where Simon's feet had been, and they all shifted position slightly until they could see a very small, round hole.

Bishop reached down and held his fingers near the hole for a moment or two. "Air," he said. "Under pressure."

Finn helped him clear away more dirt around the outside of that corner of the box, both of them digging carefully until a large silver oxygen tank was revealed. It had a short, narrow rubber tube running from the tank to the small hole in the box that had imprisoned Simon. For the first time, all of them became aware of the very, very faint hissing sound of oxygen escaping.

At the end of the tank with the valve and tube, there was also a plain metal box surrounding the valve.

Finn hesitated. "Prints?"

"I doubt it," Bishop replied. "Still . . ." He removed a pair of exam gloves from a jacket pocket and put them on before carefully prying the small box open. There was a tangle of electronics inside—and a cell phone whose lighted surface showed plus four hours and forty-seven minutes and counting upward.

"Is that how long he was buried?" Nellie asked.

Miranda said slowly, "Plus. If that's a timer set to begin releasing oxygen just before the ambient air in the box would have run out, the clock would have started at zero. So we can add approximately five hours to that time. Which means he was probably here close to ten hours."

Hollis said, "Since around dark last night. So where was he for the twenty-four hours or so after he was taken? No sign of a gag, and we can assume he would have yelled for help if he could have. Unless he was unconscious or otherwise unable to make a sound. Either the blitz attack left him out for quite a while or he was drugged."

"Which," Miranda said, "could tell us more about the unsub. Drugs could mean possible medical training. We really need to talk to Simon. Find out what he remembers."

Bishop very carefully stopped the timer on the cell phone, and immediately they heard the soft hissing stop. He produced an evidence bag from a pocket and put the gadget into it. He looked at Finn. "As soon as your deputies come back to watch this area until we can conduct a thorough search after daylight, let's get down off this mountain and talk to Simon."

Nobody argued.

———————

"I DON'T REMEMBER anything," Simon told them ruefully. He was in bed and in a very spacious room at the hospital, torn between being glad of the warmth and comfort, for which he had a new appreciation, and the awareness that he really was all right and should have been up and about now that he was. "Walking home, feeling my head explode—and then waking up in that damned box."

Bishop and Finn had stopped to talk to the doctor, and exchanged glances now before Bishop said, "You were also injected with a sedative strong enough to keep you out for nearly twenty-four hours before you were placed in the box."

Simon blinked. "I was?"

"Given when you were taken, and everything that was happening before and after you were taken, our guess is that you were probably kept in the trunk of a car or some other relatively safe place until he could transport you up the mountain. Either he took some of that time to prepare the box or else already had it ready. For you or someone else."

Simon drew a breath and let it out slowly, looking from one grave face to the next. "So . . . why am I alive? From what I've heard, Cole Ainsworth wasn't given any chance at all."

None of them commented on how fast word of the tentative identification had spread.

Miranda said, "There's always a reason, even if it doesn't make sense to us until we understand motivation."

"Scaring the shit out of me?" Simon offered with forced lightness.

"I doubt it was personal," Finn said. "Unless it was, of course. Is there anyone with a grudge against you, Simon?"

"What? No. I mean—no. I don't make enemies, Finn. Hell, I don't even deal with customers at the bank."

Miranda smiled at him. "What about your personal life?"

"Don't have much of one. Friends, sure. An occasional party or date."

"Any bad breakups recently?"

"No. Wait, you're not saying a woman could have done this to me?"

"It's unlikely," Bishop told him. "Not impossible. What was done to the other victim required a great deal of strength. And women very seldom dismember victims; when they do, it's virtually always to make it easier to dispose of the body. That didn't happen in this case; the remains were left out in the open. Almost on display. Extremely unlikely that a woman did that."

Simon lost a little of the color he had so recently regained, and no telepathy or empathy was required to know he was thinking of the near escape he'd had. And picturing that dismembered victim. "Okay. Well . . . no, no bad breakups. I haven't had time for anything but casual dates since I left college. Honestly, I can't think of a soul who'd want to—to do that to me." He drew a breath and let it out slowly. "Or who would want to bury me alive."

EIGHTEEN

Hollis said calmly, "So probably it wasn't personal at all. Maybe the unsub wanted to find out if you could reach out telepathically. If anyone could hear you. Did you try right after you woke up in the box?"

Simon immediately shook his head. "Honestly, it didn't occur to me for a long time. I don't know how long." His voice was very steady. "I was . . . panicked. Didn't know for sure I was—was underground, but it's what I thought. What was so terrifying. When the panic sort of died down, I started wondering if anyone would ever find me, ever even know where to look—and I suddenly realized I should have been trying to reach somebody, anybody."

He looked at Nellie. "I didn't try to reach you specifically, but within just a few minutes, I thought I had. I wasn't sure, though. I don't use my Talent a lot, but when I do there's a pretty strong connection. This time the contact felt . . . tenuous. Almost muffled."

She nodded. "To me as well. I was certain it was you, but not at all sure I could hang on to that thread long enough to find you."

"Thank you."

Nellie smiled at him, then looked at the others. "This . . . unsub . . . had to know Simon is a Cavendish, an elder, and so a telepath, probably a strong one. Wouldn't he have expected him to reach out?"

It was Finn who said thoughtfully, "Maybe not. We've all been having trouble using our Talents in the last few weeks. Maybe he *needed* to know if Simon could reach anyone."

Miranda said, "Maybe because the energy we've all been aware of is his doing and he's not sure how effective it is."

"Or," Bishop said, "it's affecting him, affecting his own abilities, and he wanted to know if any of us have the same problem."

"So I was a lab rat." Simon managed a smile. "A very lucky lab rat."

Finn glanced at Bishop, then said, "We mean to make sure your luck holds. I'll have a deputy outside the door here, and when you're discharged, you'll have an escort."

Uneasy now, Simon said, "You mean he might not be finished with me?"

"I mean we're not going to take any chances. We're doing our best to keep a close eye on all the elders, especially when they're in transit. Listen, the doc wants to keep you here at least until afternoon. Get some rest, okay?"

Simon didn't bother to deny that being held for long hours in a nearly airless box that could very well have become his coffin had been exhausting. Instead, he merely smiled, thanked them all again, and settled back to rest.

They left his room and gathered in a waiting room just down the hall, the area nearly deserted at such an early hour. The sun had not yet come up.

Finn didn't have to ask if the others, like himself, were up for the day. He merely said to Bishop, "Does this help us at all?"

"Maybe. That he was drugged is a new wrinkle—we believe—but the drug used, like so much these days, can be easily found and obtained on the Internet. Backtracking every citizen in Salem looking for that purchase would take far more time than we have."

Nellie perched on the arm of a chair, absently petting Leo when he sat by her feet. Nobody had questioned her dog's presence in the hospital, which vaguely surprised her. "Two people dead so far—that we know about. One of them this week. I'm sure I don't have to tell anybody how glad I am that Simon is safe, but burying him alive for whatever reason doesn't seem to fit with the rest. Am I the only one waiting for the other shoe to drop?"

"No," Hollis said instantly. She was frowning. "I really don't understand this . . . test, or game, or whatever it is. Keeping Simon alive, making sure he'd *be* alive all those hours. Except for the bump on his head and ligature marks from those zip ties, he doesn't have a mark on him. From brutal torture and dismemberment to that? It doesn't make sense. And another thing. We're sure the first two victims weren't psychic, and there are plenty of members of the five families who aren't. Simon very definitely is. Why grab a strong telepath, mess around with some kind of injection and oxygen tanks, and then hang him out like bait on a hook?"

"To offer us a puzzle?" DeMarco suggested wryly.

"Or just to see if he could lead us around by the nose?" She sighed. "I know unsubs play games with law enforcement sometimes, and we've sure as hell known them to play games with us, specifically, but . . . that tends to be after we've been following them around for a while, right? Maybe even when we're close to catching them, or believe we are. So they start playing games, to throw us a curve or two, make us rethink. Only that doesn't apply here. At all. We've only just started building a profile. So, why now?"

Bishop said, "To slow us down, maybe, keep us from building that profile."

"Every time he leaves us a victim or potential victim he gives us more information," Hollis objected.

"True."

"To muddy the water, maybe," DeMarco said. "Two victims who were family members but not psychic; a third victim who is definitely psychic. Two men and a woman. Two who weren't missed right away, one who was. Two brutally killed, one left alive for whatever reason—but who would certainly have died if Nellie hadn't been able to read him and lead us to him. No real pattern we can grab onto."

"Still family members," Hollis said. "That's all they have in common. Members of the Five. If anything, that's even clearer now."

"I don't have enough deputies to watch every elder, much less watch them twenty-four hours a day," Finn said unnecessarily. "Even just trying to protect those who have to be out alone is going to be difficult. Obviously, we'll do what we can, but . . . I've spread the word that none of the Five should be alone, even at home if possible, for the duration, but I don't know how much protection, if any, that'll provide when we don't have a name or a face to put to the threat. And every deputy I have on escort duty is one less I have to patrol and keep an eye out for trouble."

Quentin said thoughtfully, "Which could also be something the unsub wants to make sure of. To tie up your resources and keep the rest of us spread thin, give himself more time and more room to . . . work."

"And we still don't know what his endgame is," Diana added. "A grudge against the families is possible—we all know that—maybe because of the Talents or just their importance, their power, in Salem, but that would be more about *what* they are, not *who* they are. It doesn't make sense that a motive like that would lead the unsub to just randomly take out members of the five families, whoever he can grab. Does it?"

"Unless we should be looking somewhere else entirely for a motive," DeMarco said. "Maybe he's been playing games all along. Maybe we're looking exactly where he wants us to look."

Hollis frowned at him. "At the Five."

He nodded. "As you said, that's even clearer now than it was when we got here. So that's where we're looking. At the Five. At them as potential victims. Around half the people in this valley are members of the five families. Three victims so far, all three members of the Five. Everything we know or believe puts the families at the center of our focus. And yet we've all agreed that doesn't make sense. Wiping out the Five as an endgame would be crazy ambitious, never mind insane."

Hollis said slowly, "We're looking at the Five *because* of the victims chosen. Looking for a reason that ties in with their identity as members of the five families. Which is mostly why we've been spinning our wheels."

"So maybe," DeMarco suggested, "we should look at it another way. Maybe his motive, his endgame, is a lot more specific."

"Specific to his victims?"

"Maybe . . . specific to only one victim."

"One victim intentional, everything else he does window dressing?"

"We've seen it before."

Hollis nodded. "Sleight of hand. I want to kill C, but I kill A and B first to divert suspicion."

"Or the water is muddied because everything we know so far has led us to be focused on the Five. But all three victims could be connected by some reason other than their being members of the families. Three victims doesn't give us enough to be certain of conclusions, not statistically. Especially in an area where there are so many overlaps in victimology. These people could be targeted, for all we can know, because they went to the same doctor or graduated from the same high school."

"Great," Hollis muttered.

"You know it's as likely as anything else. Probably more likely."

"I know. I don't have to like it."

Bishop said, "But we have to consider possibilities."

"Yeah. But I still say the timing of this unsub is . . . off. Even if he wants to play games, or test us, or whatever," Hollis said slowly. "Mostly serials are obsessed with satisfying their own twisted needs, killing one victim and then moving on to the next. They don't have the desire or the time to lead us around by the nose."

"So why is he bothering with games?" Quentin mused. "Why

follow a brutal murder by burying Simon alive and allowing us the chance to save him? I think Reese is right. The only other answer I can think of is that he wants to distract us."

"So what is it he doesn't want us to see?" DeMarco finished.

"Megan," Hollis said immediately, frowning. "His first victim. For months his only victim. But . . . if she was his real target, why would Cole Ainsworth's murder have been so vicious? You don't torture somebody just to kill them. You don't torture somebody unless you're sick enough to enjoy it."

"True enough," Bishop agreed.

Diana said, "Killing Megan could have triggered a lot of twisted urges. Couldn't it?"

"Yeah," Quentin said slowly. "Especially if he killed her in a rage and that rage wasn't satisfied by killing her. Add that to the months after her death when he was lying low and couldn't do anything about his feelings and urges and . . . Yeah. Her death could have triggered him in more ways than one."

"So," Hollis said, "we have to find out everything we can about Megan. About her life. And about her death."

THEY RETURNED TO Hales B and B long enough for showers and breakfast, then split up. Finn and Nellie, after some argument, went to Nellie's bank, where she had work waiting and where Finn could coordinate with his deputies and the team. And where neither would be alone.

Quentin and Diana headed back up to the site where Simon's box prison waited so any evidence there could be tagged and collected, and Hollis and DeMarco went to check in with their acting medical examiner.

Bishop and Miranda went to talk to Megan Hales's family. It was still early when they reached the Hales home out in the valley, but since Finn had called ahead they found her parents and teenage sister sitting around the breakfast table with coffee, all three still clearly in shock.

It was a comfortable, sprawling house, innumerable family photos the clearest indication of strong family ties. In virtually every grouping, Megan's bright smile as a baby and child and young woman beamed out.

"I thought she was safe," Megan's mother, Sylvia, said to the agents, her voice curiously hollow. She stared down at the hands wrapped around her coffee cup, then lifted her anxious gaze to search their faces. "She'd talked about leaving ever since Paul . . . So I thought she had. She was—was embarrassed and self-conscious because everybody knew, and she just wanted to get away. To escape from the goldfish bowl, she said. I wished she'd write or call, of course I did, wished she'd let us know how she was doing, but I didn't really expect . . . She was young, and a new life would be— would have been—exciting. There would have been so much to do. Starting a new life. She was—would have been—busy. We knew that. So when she didn't call or write—"

Miranda, hearing the desperate need for reassurance, said quietly, "There was no way any of you could have known she didn't leave the valley. Every indication was there that she did. You can't blame yourselves."

Frank Hales said, "Is that why she—why he picked her? Because she was going to leave? Because she was alone?" There was something in his voice that said it was a question that had tortured him.

"We aren't sure," Bishop told him. "Can you tell us about Megan? What she was like? Who her friends were?"

"You don't think one of her friends—"

"No, probably not, but everything you tell us can help us to understand her. And understanding her could help us to find her killer."

"She was a good girl," her father said harshly. "No trouble at all as a child. Just like other little girls, she was horse crazy, rode all the time. She grew out of that by the time she was a teenager, when she—when she and Paul started to go steady." He hurried on. "When she finished her schooling she went to work as an accountant, helping to keep the books for us at the office. She was busy. She didn't have time to—to fool around. She was working for her future, for a good future. Planning it all out . . ."

"It wasn't Paul. Was it?" Sylvia's voice was thin.

Bishop shook his head. "He left Salem two months before and didn't return until late last fall. His movements have been accounted for."

"So he just jilted her." Chloe Hales spoke up for the first time, her voice unnaturally steady.

Miranda looked at her. "Sisters talk," she said quietly. "Did Megan say anything to you, Chloe? Was there anyone in her life she was . . . uneasy about?"

The teenager's brows knit over bright blue eyes that remained fixed on her coffee mug. "What do you mean?"

"Just that. We have some reason to believe that Megan was killed by someone who knew her. Perhaps knew her well, or believed he did."

"Believed he did?"

Miranda glanced at her husband, then said, "He may have been an . . . admirer. Watching her but not able to get up the courage to actually interact with her. Or he could have been a friend, one she may have confided in without any romantic interest."

"Or?"

Miranda studied the girl for a moment. "Or . . . it might have been someone she turned to after Paul left. All those weeks of everyone around her knowing she'd been jilted, maybe feeling sorry for her. The day she'd planned for her wedding getting closer and closer. That had to be rough. Painful. It would have been natural to turn to someone else, another man, for comfort. Did she, Chloe?"

"She never would have cheated on Paul."

"But after Paul ran off with someone else? That wouldn't have been cheating."

"She didn't say anything to me about that," Chloe muttered, still frowning and staring at her mug.

Frank Hales looked at his daughter, surprise and something else crossing his strong features. "Chloe? If you know something, you have to tell us."

"She didn't talk to me," Chloe repeated.

Bishop said quietly. "But you noticed something, didn't you, Chloe? Or maybe someone else noticed something, saw something, and told you about it?"

There was a long silence, and then Chloe half shook her head, but said, "Gabby Douglas was always jealous of Megan. Always. She couldn't wait to say nasty things about Megan after Paul ran off with his cousin."

"What did she tell you?"

Chloe hesitated again, then looked up, finally, and met Bishop's steady gaze. "She said she'd seen Megan sneaking around. She said . . . that Megan must not have loved Paul after all, because she didn't waste much time crawling into bed with someone else. And she said it was worse than being with a distant member of his own family like Paul had."

"How was it worse?"

Chloe bit her lip.

Miranda said gently, "We need to know, Chloe. How was it worse than being with a distant member of his own family? Who was Megan seeing before she disappeared?"

"Danny Dryden," Chloe whispered. "He's . . . he's one of our cousins. A first cousin."

HOLLIS AND DEMARCO went to the hospital, where Dr. Jill Easton, her assistant, and her colleague Dr. Brady had pulled an all-nighter to tackle the two postmortems.

Though all three looked tired, nobody complained. The two men sat on either side of a metal desk in one corner of the large, sterile morgue, drinking coffee, while Jill joined Hollis and DeMarco next to the remains that lay underneath sheets on two stainless steel tables.

Hollis had never been fond of morgues, but she was accustomed enough that neither the harsh lighting nor the eye-stingingly harsh odors of chemicals and the faint, underlying smell of death distracted her from her job. Much.

"Please tell us something we didn't know," she asked Jill in a tone that really was almost pleading.

Jill smiled faintly, but there was a tiny frown between her delicate brows. "Well, with Cole Ainsworth—the ID is now official, thanks to a healed fracture from football and a small scar on the sole of his left foot—I can't tell you anything any of you couldn't see for yourselves. He was likely rendered unconscious by a severe blow to the head, and COD was massive blood loss and shock.

"Between those two events, he was tortured by somebody with enthusiasm and a very sharp knife, maybe a scalpel but likely something as common as a kitchen or pocket knife. Your unsub didn't stop when his victim stopped breathing, which is why Ainsworth looks the way he does. The unsub had fun removing most of the skin in strips, some of which he seared apparently just because. He both cut and crushed muscles and some organs, the latter probably with some kind of common tool like a hammer or mallet. What organs he didn't destroy by crushing he removed and left with the other remains. He didn't exactly dismember Ainsworth so much as crush some of the long bones of the arms and legs—with pliers, I think— badly enough that nothing but a few tendons and shreds of muscle held them in place. It was afterward that he cut or broke most of the long bones to separate them from the other remains."

She shrugged slightly. "I don't know if time of death matters to you in this particular case, since I understand you believe he was held for quite a while before he was killed. And TOD isn't easy to determine because of what was done to the body and the cold temperatures. But I estimate he's been dead about forty-eight hours."

DeMarco said, "Do you know if he was drugged?"

"Preliminary tox screen doesn't show alcohol or drugs or other toxins, but I've sent samples to the lab. Results in a few days, probably."

"If you had to guess?" Hollis asked.

"If I had to guess, I'd say he was awake and aware while all of it was going on."

"Awake. Jesus. Any signs he was restrained in any way?"

"Yeah. Ligature marks on one otherwise unmarked wrist and ankle from a fairly thick rope. He was tied that way for quite a while. Hours at least. Longer. But traces of an adhesive were found on the arms, wrists, and ankles. There were also some wood slivers embedded in his back, arms, and legs. My guess, after he was tied up for a while, he was then duct-taped to some kind of wooden frame, something as simple as a cross, that held his body fairly stationary while the unsub worked on him."

Hollis winced and exchanged glances with her partner. "A cross that might have been symbolic?"

"Maybe. Though I'd guess it was more likely the simplest, strongest frame he could construct and use without much effort and using tools ready to hand. No special knowledge or skills required, and judging by the splinters the wood was likely from some old woodpile or tumbledown building."

"Okay. And Megan?"

"Died sometime last summer, approximate."

Hollis nodded. "Fits our time frame."

Jill looked at her thoughtfully. "You saw her, right? Her spirit?"

"Yeah, yesterday morning. Why?"

"She happen to tell you she was pregnant?"

With another glance at DeMarco, Hollis said, "No. How far along?"

"Six, eight weeks. She may not have known herself, but chances are she at least suspected."

Hollis was thinking about Paul Ainsworth and that very sudden jilting of his fiancée, thinking about how an unexpected pregnancy would have compounded the misery of that hellish situation for Megan, but all she said was "Okay. Can you tell how she died?"

"Hyoid bone is fractured, pretty nearly crushed, so I'm thinking she was strangled by someone with very powerful hands. With so little flesh remaining it's hard to be sure of bruising around the throat, but I am." She didn't have to explain to them how she was.

Hollis merely nodded.

"I don't believe he tortured her," Jill went on. "In fact, he appears to have buried her with care. And possibly caring. We found enough to be certain there were flowers placed in the grave. Not held in her hands, but spread all around her, under her, like a bed. And one more thing. I don't believe that diamond ring went in the ground with her. Best guess, it was placed on her finger within the last couple of weeks."

"But it was hers."

"The report I got is that it was traced to the jewelry store where Paul Ainsworth purchased it just before they got engaged. Anything over a carat is traceable, and the setting was custom. It was her engagement ring."

"That's interesting," Hollis said slowly.

"I thought you'd like that."

"Any idea why he would have put the ring back on her finger sometime after she was originally buried?"

"Maybe as simple as he didn't want to be caught with it in his possession."

"Or as complicated as——?"

"Well, we can safely infer at least one thing. I can tell you she'd been uncovered and then reburied numerous times since she was originally buried."

Hollis drew a breath and exchanged glances with her partner. "Did you find any foreign DNA?"

"Yes. Some pretty degraded, some not so much. A good defense attorney might make mincemeat of it, but I know what I know."

"Semen?"

"Semen. He visited her. A lot."

NINETEEN

Hollis had been at this too long to feel sickened. Much. She was even able to hold on to professional detachment, outwardly at least. Steadily, she asked, "I gather you didn't get enough for a positive ID?"

"Well, I'm running what I have through all the databases, but so far nothing close to a hit. Which, even if it might otherwise identify him, only tells us he probably isn't in those databases—which is true of most people. If you find a viable suspect, the DNA may at least point at him. Probably not conclusively, though."

Hollis considered for a moment. "What about the remains of the fetus?"

"You mean DNA?" Jill frowned a little. "I may be able to get a better sample there. You're thinking paternal DNA?"

Hollis half nodded. "Her fiancé is ruled out fairly conclusively as a suspect in her murder because he wasn't anywhere near here when she went missing and for weeks before and months afterward. No indication he didn't believe she had left Salem only weeks after he jilted her. Apparently both families and friends gave him hell over it. But it still might be interesting to find out if he was the father."

"I'll get right on it." Jill looked at them both rather curiously. She had been called in on serial murder cases often enough to be at least aware of how such investigations generally progressed. "Doesn't sound like a typical serial. A world of difference between how each of these victims was killed and treated afterward."

"And," Hollis said, "the third victim was knocked out, tied up, drugged, and buried alive. But left with an oxygen canister pumping air into his would-be coffin. With a timer on the tank. If a very strong telepath hadn't picked up his call for help, he would have died. We barely got to him in time."

Jill whistled softly. "Games, a test, or a distraction?" She had certainly been at this long enough to consider the possibilities.

"We're wondering the same thing."

DeMarco asked, "Anything else you can tell us?"

Jill's faint frown deepened. "Something I know but can't yet prove, at least until all the lab tests come back."

"Which is?"

"Megan Hales might not have been able to carry the pregnancy to term. And even if she had, the child likely would have been born with severe birth defects."

Slowly, Hollis said, "There's usually a reason for that, right?"

"Yeah. In this case, everything I saw was the likely result of inbreeding. Probably not between first-degree relations—siblings, parent and child. Maybe cousins, but if so, first cousins, and there almost had to be a history of inbreeding within the family line to cause the sort of damage I saw."

———————

THEY EMERGED FROM the hospital into the gray and very cold morning, the heavy clouds still promising snow to come, and Hollis absently zipped up her jacket. "From the timing and what Jill suspects, it certainly doesn't sound like the father was Paul Ainsworth."

"No. And if she's right about the birth defects, it's very likely the father was a Hales."

"Wonder if that was what caused the breakup. I mean if she started seeing another man and Paul found out there was someone else."

"You think she wouldn't have told him?"

Hollis sighed, her breath misting the air. "That after all those years of being with him, she'd had sex at least once with a blood relation—just before she was supposed to marry Paul? She was very young. So I'm guessing probably not. Maybe the sort of thing that would come out in one of those passionate arguments a very young couple tends to have. But not something she'd have done deliberately, I think, confessing something like that. Plus, from what Finn said, everybody in the town blamed him for the breakup, not her. If she had been the one to cheat first, I doubt he would have taken the blame for the breakup. Sounds more like she was dumped and turned to someone else, someone she already knew. Maybe for comfort. Or revenge. Either way, he caught her on the rebound. At least once."

"Do you think it could have been rape?"

"I dunno. Possible, at least. She might have been too afraid or ashamed to tell Paul—or anybody else—if she'd been raped, but I doubt she could have hidden it, not with all the trauma and other aftereffects of rape."

DeMarco accepted that with a nod. "If she even knew she was pregnant, she might not have known which one was the father."

It was Hollis's turn to nod, but she was still frowning. "Since he was the one to run off with someone else, it just seems more likely that Megan would have turned to another man after she was dumped practically at the altar. Because wouldn't it be a bit of a coincidence if Paul realized he loved his cousin too much to marry someone else right after Megan cheated on him?"

"I would think. And I know neither of us has much faith in coincidence. But it does happen."

"Yeah."

He glanced at her, but Hollis remained silent until they were in their black SUV and the engine was running.

Then, slowly, she said, "If this is our unsub, if he was the father, he couldn't have known. About the baby, I mean. That it was . . . wrong. Birth defects. And even if he did, if he thought there was something in his bloodline or hers, that they were too closely related and it could cause problems maybe because there was already a stronger history of inbreeding in the Hales family—we need to check with Finn about that." She blinked. "Where was I?"

"Even if he knew or suspected birth defects were possible."

"Thank you. Even then, even if he expected such a tragedy, what about that would have made him decide to go on a killing spree, beginning with Megan? He strangled her, Reese. That's about as up close and personal as you can get. And nearly always done in rage."

"One way or another, she had to be his trigger," he said. "Whether it was because he found out about the baby or because she was leaving Salem, leaving him, something happened between them, something that caused him to totally lose it and strangle her."

"Okay. But the question stands. Why decide to go after others and kill at least one of them horribly months later? He must have known for certain back in January that he'd gotten away with killing Megan. Cops and agents combed the slopes after Duncan went down, searched for evidence against him and his followers. They didn't find Megan. Didn't find any sign of her grave. So . . . she was gone; everybody thought she'd run off after being jilted. Paul had come back here married to his cousin and had taken a lot of flak about all that. Nobody suspected murder. The unsub was safe."

DeMarco considered for a few moments. "Then it wasn't enough for him to be safe. Killing Megan wasn't enough."

Hollis grimaced. "He visited her grave. Had sex with the body, for weeks if not months. That sounds very like an obsession with her."

"I would say so."

"A sick and twisted obsession."

"Hardly the poster child for a good boyfriend," DeMarco agreed dryly.

"If he was a boyfriend and not just a little solace or revenge." Hollis gave him a look. "Yeah. And we're still left with the same questions. If killing Megan was personal, and since he'd clearly gotten away with it, why grab and kill Cole Ainsworth?"

"Paul's cousin. Something there?"

"Cousins all over the place," Hollis muttered, then said, "Finn said Paul and Cole weren't close. As in friends, I mean. Cole was married himself, and in a relationship that appeared pretty demanding. Not to say volatile."

"So not much interested in Paul and Megan's relationship."

"I'd think not. Of course, the unsub is right here and has been all along. We don't know what he's seen, overheard, suspected, much less what his feelings have been. About Megan, about his relationship with her. Cole could have been personal too, in an entirely different way."

She looked at her partner steadily. "I think we need to call Bishop while he and Miranda are talking to Megan's family. They may already have found out Megan had been involved with someone else, but if not, there's maybe a different set of questions they need to be asking."

———

AYLIA BLACKWOOD HAD done what she could to calm her family members, but ever since two victims of the killer had been discovered up in the mountains and brought down late the previous day, it was all anyone could talk about. Worry about.

Including Aylia.

Because the more she thought about them, about Megan especially, the more troubled she became. Like everyone else, she had believed that Megan had packed her things and left Salem to start a new life elsewhere.

Unlike everyone else, Aylia had known the real reason why Megan wanted to leave. Not because of all the pitying looks and overt sympathy after she was jilted. Not because she would have had to see Paul and his new wife virtually every day.

Because she'd been afraid.

Aylia had not dismissed those fears. She had believed Megan had been unwise in her own actions, careless and even reckless, that Megan had acted out of hurt and only further complicated her life, but she had certainly not deserved scorn for her very understandable actions. She had, after all, done no more than many a young woman—and quite a few not-so-young women—had done before her, turning to another man in hurt and bitterness after being dumped.

A man she had trusted, a man who had been her friend. Or so Megan had believed. But after their one afternoon together, after Megan had "come back to my senses" and told that other man she'd made a mistake . . .

He hadn't taken it well. And though Megan hadn't gone into detail, it had been clear that whatever had passed between them had scared her. Scared her enough to prompt her decision to leave Salem.

But . . . it had still not seemed such a serious situation to Aylia. Young people hurt each other. They were careless. They were selfish. They got over it. Usually. Now, looking back, Aylia wasn't at all sure she herself had taken the situation as seriously as she should have.

Because Megan was dead. And the shock of that was compounded by the fact that she had apparently been killed last summer before she could leave Salem.

Had Aylia's own counsel somehow made a bad situation immeasurably worse? And if so, was there, now, anything she could do to make up for that? Was there anything she could tell Finn, tell the federal agents? She had never known who the man was, just that he had been . . . possessive. Possessive enough to have refused to allow Megan to leave?

Aylia went out her back door, still frowning in thought, and headed across the yard toward her little cottage. She knew she needed to settle her mind, to think clearly so that she could decide what to do.

Perhaps she could tap into her farseeing again and that would help her to decide. Her Talent had helped her in all the difficult moments of her life, after all. Surely it could help her now.

She was vaguely aware of how cold and still the air was, a glance upward showing her gray clouds growing darker and heavier. It was supposed to snow. There hadn't been much snow this winter, though lots of bitter cold, and she had the notion that the valley needed a good storm right now.

Everyone was so tense——

It was no more than a faint sound behind her, but suddenly Aylia felt a wave of overwhelming cold that had nothing to do with the gray day, and before she could do more than begin to turn, something struck her head, pain exploded in a red burst, and everything went dark.

———————

"WAIT. WE NEED to stop here."

DeMarco immediately pulled into the lot beside a small and beautiful old church not far from downtown Salem, but even as he was parking in the otherwise deserted lot, he asked simply, "Why?"

Hollis was staring at the church, unconsciously rubbing her left temple. "Hmm? Oh . . . just a feeling. We need to talk to the pastor."

"Why?" DeMarco repeated.

She looked at her partner, then gestured toward the sign outside the church where there was an invitation for all to attend Sunday school and Sunday services. Atop the sign was perched a large crow, staring at them.

"The crow called you?" DeMarco guessed.

"Nothing as definite as that. I think." She rubbed her temple harder and watched as two more crows joined the other on top of the sign. All three were gazing directly at them. "Just . . . we need to talk to the pastor."

"About?" DeMarco was patient.

Hollis frowned at him for a moment, then said slowly, "About Danny Dryden." She turned her head and stared at the crows, the fluttering sensation in her mind distinctly unsettling. "Damn. That's . . . weird. Not images and concepts this time. His name is clear as a bell. Almost in neon."

"The name Bishop and Miranda got from Megan's sister. Who Megan was involved with before she decided to leave Salem."

"Yeah."

"They're going with Finn to talk to him."

"I know, but . . . I think . . . the crows have been sharing information with each other. Connecting things they've seen. One of them saw Danny Dryden up where Megan was buried. More than once."

"So more evidence he could be the father of Megan's baby and so possibly our unsub?"

"Yeah, I think so." Her voice was a bit absent. "They really didn't think anything about it, about him being up there, because he was up in the mountains a lot. It didn't seem strange to them until Megan's remains were found. Until . . . Tia . . . started asking her family and friends if they'd noticed anything odd during the last few months."

DeMarco eyed her. "Another coincidence is bothering you." He didn't have to explain how he knew that.

"Well . . . yeah. Danny. Daniel."

"Don't spirit guides have to be dead by definition?"

"You'd think. But living people do appear in the gray time. Diana and me. That psychic Bishop sent in to prove to Diana that she could be deceived there. God knows who else."

"Okay. But Daniel the spirit guide was a kid. Right?"

"Appeared to be. But one kind of deception in the gray time pretty much clears the way for other kinds. Samuel certainly was able to appear as someone—something—else. To be something else or project the image of someone different."

"But?"

"But . . . mediums aren't even supposed to exist in Salem, at least as far as we know. Not an ability any of the five families has. So if Danny *is* Daniel, then how did he even know about the gray time, much less be familiar enough with it, or strong enough, I guess, to go there and draw Diana there?"

"However he discovered it, he must have visited it more than once."

"Maybe lots of times, yeah. Which is really going to creep Diana out. It creeps me out."

"I'm not surprised."

"But what's *really* bugging me is why. Assuming he did know about the gray time, had visited it before however many times, why use it the way he did? Why go there, appear as a kid, a spirit guide, and offer a warning to Diana and me about what was happening in Salem?"

After a moment, DeMarco said, "It was the warning that brought us here."

"But Finn called Bishop later that same day. Asking for help, because of the Blackwood elder's farseeing. That was going to happen, him asking Bishop for help, because the farseeing had happened. Maybe Finn wouldn't have had quite the urgency, maybe we wouldn't have, but Bishop wouldn't have said no. Some of us, if not all of us, still would have come."

"Agreed. And Daniel might have heard about the farseeing, might have known or deduced that Finn would ask Bishop for help, because he had once before."

"Makes sense." She brooded for a moment. "So, did he just want to make sure we came? Why? All that so-called warning in the gray time really did was . . . spook Diana and me. Convince us the threat was real, and awful." Slowly, she added, "Convince us that the threat was from a serial killer, out to destroy the Five. No other rhyme or reason."

"Convinced you that the victims were only that. Members of the Five."

"Yeah." She looked at her partner. "Maybe that was the distraction all along. From the very beginning, even before we came here. What he didn't want us to look at, to pay too much attention to. Megan. Personal ties and motivations. The longer we were focused on the idea of a serial killer, the longer it would take us to look at those victims for personal ties."

"Maybe." DeMarco nodded slowly, then looked at the neat little church, so quiet on a Thursday morning. "And we're at this church because?"

"The family goes here. Danny Dryden's family. And—because the crows want us here. To talk to the pastor about Danny Dryden and his family."

"Okay," DeMarco said. "Let's go see the pastor."

TWENTY

As soon as Hollis set eyes on the Reverend Joshua Matthews she was nagged by a vague familiarity. He was past middle age, a tall, thin man with a shock of silver hair and gentle brown eyes, and didn't look . . . substantial enough . . . to host the customary deep, booming voice of a Southern Baptist preacher.

"Danny Dryden's family?" He looked from Hollis to DeMarco. "He isn't a suspect in these terrible killings, is he?"

Hollis smiled at him. "His name came up in our investigation, Reverend, and we have to cover all our bases. He and his family attend your church?"

"His mother and grandmother do. As long as I've been here. But I don't know that I can tell you anything."

"Danny doesn't attend?"

"Well, not regularly, not since he was a child. He's one of my holiday members. He comes Christmas and Easter, and that's about it. Not terribly uncommon, especially among the younger members. Not that he's as young as all that. He must be past thirty by now."

"He's not married?"

"No."

Hollis tilted her head slightly as she gazed at the preacher. "Girlfriend?"

"I really couldn't say, Agent. Although——"

"Although?"

Matthews was frowning a little, clearly troubled. "Is it important, Agent?"

"It could be very important."

"I was just going to say that from all I've seen, Danny has always seemed pretty much . . . absorbed in his own concerns. Not very interested in mixing with others. His family has always been the sort to——as the saying is around here——keep themselves to themselves. They were never active in the Hales family real estate business, except that they own a considerable number of rental properties and land they lease to farmers, which provides an income for them."

"Danny doesn't have a job?"

"He handles the properties for his mother, I understand."

Hollis studied him, her head still tilted to one side. "So not a job with regular business hours, I take it. Does he have hobbies that you know of?"

"He likes to hike. Always out roaming in the mountains."

"I see." She focused without really being aware of what she was doing, reaching deeper than what she could see and hear. "Reverend . . . what is it about Danny that makes you uneasy?"

He looked somewhat startled. "Uneasy?"

"Yes. Something about him disturbs you. What is it?"

"It's—it's nothing I know firsthand, Agent. My father, Lucius Matthews, was pastor of this church before me, twenty years ago, and he had certain reservations about Danny. But Danny was only a child then, and it was so long ago."

"What sort of reservations did he have?"

"I gather it was more a matter of temperament than anything else. He thought Danny was too quick to strike out at other children when he didn't get his way. He was especially prone to do that whenever any other child took something that belonged to him. Apparently there were some troubling scenes during Bible school one summer."

DeMarco was also studying the reverend, his gaze intent. "What happened after that, Reverend?"

"What happened? I don't know what you mean."

"What did your father do? About Danny?"

Matthews frowned. "He didn't do anything. He was *going* to talk to Angela Dryden, suggest that a therapist might help the boy deal with his temper."

"Why didn't he talk to her?"

"Because he died, Agent."

Hollis exchanged glances with her partner, then said, "I'm sorry if this is painful for you, Reverend, but how did your father die?"

Somewhat stiffly, Matthews said, "It was an accident. In this very office, Agent. He was cleaning one of his guns, and . . . There was no question of suicide, I promise you. His cleaning supplies were all out on the desk, his shotgun cleaned and set aside. We never knew for certain why it happened, but somehow one of his target pistols went off. He was shot in the head."

"Do you have a picture of your father here, Reverend?"

Looking a little bewildered now, Reverend Matthews pointed to one of the walls, where a large grouping of photos hung. "There, in front of this church. It's the last photo we have of him."

Hollis went to look at the photo, and it only required a moment for her to be certain. Lucius Matthews was the spirit she had seen in the restaurant with the gunshot wound in his head.

The one who had warned her that the monster they hunted was not sick but evil. And had always been evil.

———

THEY MET UP back at Hales in the early afternoon, all the team plus Finn, Nellie, and Leo.

"No sign of Danny Dryden at his condo here in town," Bishop told them after filling in Quentin and Diana about what they'd learned from Megan's sister and from the postmortem. "The family home where his mother and grandmother live is out in the valley."

"Danny Dryden? Daniel?" Diana exclaimed. "You mean . . . our Daniel?" She looked from Bishop to Hollis.

"I don't even know if it's possible, but it's what I've been fairly convinced of. Because I don't believe in coincidences, not like that would have to be," Hollis confessed, frowning. "Is it? Can one of your spirit guides be not a spirit? And a lot older than he appears in the gray time?" Her own theories aside, Hollis believed no one knew the gray time as well as Diana.

But Diana only looked baffled and uneasy. "I . . . don't know either. I don't think it's ever happened before."

Hollis looked at Bishop. "I'm betting you have theories. Do any fit this situation?"

Bishop looked at Finn. "Dryden is a Hales cousin—a first cousin, according to Megan's family. I assume they'd know for certain if, at the very least, he's shown any mediumistic tendencies."

"Yeah, related to the Hales that close they'd know. His mother was born a Hales. And now that I think about it, his grandmother was a Hales cousin."

"Does the Hales family history, that bloodline, show more signs of inbreeding than in the other families?"

Finn grimaced slightly. "Well, it isn't something anybody advertises, but my father always said the Hales should have gone outside the valley for mates a long time ago. Danny was the first son of his line in about three generations, and apparently his mother had several miscarriages before he was born."

"Is he known to have Talents of any kind?"

"Well . . . not that I ever heard. There are very few in the Hales family, even in the direct line, with Talent, and it's always, always the same Talent."

"Telekinesis?"

"Right. Difficult to control even when it's not a strong Talent. And it's usually not, at least not according to the family lore. Maybe because it's so rare nobody ever found a way for it to be really useful, so nobody was encouraged to use it. Controlling something like that is difficult, but necessary. Maybe because it's one of the few Talents that genuinely make people fearful."

"And it's not a Talent that can be used without the awareness of anyone watching," Bishop said.

"Yeah, exactly. Pretty damned visible if you move things with your mind."

"Could Dryden have another Talent?"

"Most of us have only the one." Finn glanced at Nellie. "Except a few Cavendishes."

"But it's possible?"

"Anything's possible—you know that. But if he has any Talent at all, much less several of them, he's hidden it very well."

"Maybe it's something that was triggered only recently," Hollis murmured, frowning.

Bishop looked at her. "The energy?"

"It's at least possible, isn't it? We know energy can affect abilities, even trigger them. So why not in him?" She looked at Finn. "Something's been nagging at me. The energy started increasing around here when Duncan Cavendish was building his power base, right?"

"It was beginning to affect some of us during the last year or so," Finn agreed.

"But it only became a real problem for people with Talents since Duncan was killed?"

He frowned at her. "Yeah. In the last few weeks. What're you thinking?"

"I don't know what I'm thinking. It just . . . bugs me."

Diana spoke up then to say, "But how was Daniel—Danny—able to do it? I mean, to get into the gray time? To be able to . . . manipulate that? And I know the guides are never as childlike as they appear, but—"

"So far," Bishop told her, "the best guess would seem to be that his primary ability, unlike that of his family, or any of the five families, is as a medium. We may never know whether he was born with the instincts to open a door into the gray time, as you were, or if it was triggered more recently and he somehow stumbled onto it."

Diana blinked at him. " 'Stumbled'?"

He shrugged slightly. "Sounds like he spent a lot of time on his own, up in the mountains. He may have been exploring his abilities as well as hiking trails."

Hollis said, "However he learned about the place—time—whatever—he must have visited, and more than once, especially in these last weeks. And he learned fast. Or, at least, learned enough to be able to manipulate some things in the gray time. Like his own appearance."

Steadily, Diana said, "Wait. You're telling me that a serial killer knows how to get into the gray time? By himself? I mean, I know there's been evil there before, but Samuel couldn't come and go at will. He needed us to open a door so he could get out."

Hollis, who understood better than anyone else just how creepy that idea was, nodded reluctantly. "Yeah, I think he can go there at will, and get out when he wants to. Not that I think he's a traditional—if I can use that term—serial killer. Which, as I remember, you were the first to question."

Diana looked as if she wanted to say something about that, but in the end just shook her head.

"I think Daniel wanted us to look for a typical serial," Hollis said, "and not look for personal connections to any of the victims. I mean, books, TV, and movies have pretty much educated way too many people about serial killers and how they hunt and prey on strangers. And about how we investigate crimes, especially murder. I think Daniel was trying to hide his connection to Megan."

Finn was frowning. "But Aylia Blackwood saw a serial killer hunting the five families."

Quentin shook his head. "Did she? I can tell you from experience that visions—that farseeing—is just a glimpse into a future that may or may not be set. Two members of the Five *have* died, and Simon was taken; she could have glimpsed just enough of that future to believe what it seemed to indicate. We interpret what we see, even if unconsciously, and filter it through our knowledge and experiences."

After a moment, Finn nodded. "Okay, that makes sense. But . . . is it why Daniel would have killed Cole Ainsworth and buried Simon alive? Just a distraction?"

Hollis said, "I think that was the plan, but the fact that he got so . . . enthusiastic . . . with Cole and played his little game in burying Simon is also because he's more than a little twisted and has been since he was a kid, according to what we were told by his pastor."

She filled them in on what she and DeMarco had learned, finishing with "Not that there's any evidence, especially after all this time, but the spirit of the old man I saw in the restaurant was definitely Lucius Matthews, and I believe he was trying to warn me about Daniel. I think he was probably Daniel's first victim, killed because Daniel didn't want him talking to his mother. Or maybe just because he was angry."

Finn looked from one to the other. "You were both able to use your Talents in questioning Reverend Matthews?"

"We'd both dropped our shields," Hollis confirmed. "There had to be something he knew, or else why did the crows lead us there? So we probed."

"I thought you were having problems with this energy interference, like the rest of us."

"Well, that's another thing we may have figured out." Hollis exchanged a glance with her partner. "Even though you were all aware of the energy once Duncan began building his power base, it's only interfered with everyone's abilities *in the last few weeks*. Not before that. So what happened back in January? Duncan Cavendish was destroyed."

"Yeah."

"And Cavendish was after energy, sheer power to add to his own. Which he stole from psychics who were descended from the five families. I remembered something Geneva told me. That it was Duncan, with that weird energy-weaving Cavendish talent No offense," she added hastily to Nellie.

Nellie smiled faintly. "No offense. I think it's weird too."

Hollis smiled at her, then went on. "It was Duncan who figured out how to construct something they called a barrier to hold in psychic energy. I mean, it was something he came up with long before Bishop taught Nellie how to weave a similar thing to help contain her energy. Right?"

Finn answered, "Yes. What became obvious later is that he saw young psychics as a potential threat. Saw anyone with Talents he couldn't somehow control or repress as a threat. What he told the families, however, was that by allowing him to construct the Barrier in their children with Talents, it would allow the children to grow and mature until they were old enough to be able to deal safely with their Talents. He claimed they had to be at least thirty before they'd have the necessary control."

"Bastard," Hollis said without heat.

Finn nodded. "He was that. But he was convincing, at least during the last twenty years. A lot of parents remembered their own struggles to master their Talents and believed they were protecting their children by sparing them those struggles until they were older."

Bishop said, "But not the Deverells."

"No, not us. No Deverell took Duncan up on his offer."

"And," Nellie said, "a few of us had parents who didn't agree with Duncan. It's one reason my parents took me and left Salem when I was an infant. My father didn't want any of my Talents suppressed."

Hollis nodded. "Yeah, because what the Barrier really did was an extreme version of what Nellie's shields were designed to do, to hold psychic abilities inside, but completely dormant, so they were no threat to Cavendish. Not all the kids, as you say, not all parents agreed with him, but enough to make a real difference."

Finn nodded. "There were plenty over the years. They believed they were keeping their kids safe."

"Yeah. But here's the point. If Cavendish constructed those barriers, what happened when he was destroyed?"

They stared at each other.

"All of them," Hollis said softly. "All those psychics . . . waking up so abruptly when Duncan died. With no idea how to use their abilities, or to build real shields, or to channel energy. Unshielded psychic minds all coming alive in the same small valley at the same time, many of them very young. Expending energy they can't control. That's why it's affecting us. All of us."

TWENTY-ONE

Hollis drew a breath. "And that's why I believe that instead of raising our shields, making them stronger, we should lower them. When Reese and I dropped our shields completely in order to read the reverend, the energy wasn't painful at all. Still there, and we were still conscious of it, but it wasn't painful. And it didn't interfere with our abilities. I think our shields somehow interact with the energy, and *that's* what causes all the problems."

Slowly, Finn said, "So, by concentrating so hard on building our shields stronger, we've just been making things more difficult for ourselves."

"I think so."

"You think Daniel figured that out?"

Miranda said, "It may not have been a conscious thing for Daniel. If being a medium was something virtually unheard-of here, it's obvious he would have had to figure out for himself how to use those abilities. Probably how he was able to discover the gray time and explore it and what he could do there. Nobody told him it was something rare, so there were no constraints on him.

"The additional energy these last weeks could easily have made him stronger, perhaps even triggered another latent ability he's been exploring. Hollis, didn't Jill say some of Cole Ainsworth's internal organs were crushed?"

Hollis winced slightly. "Yeah. She said the damage had probably been done with a hammer or mallet. You're thinking he was sharpening his telekinetic skills?"

"I'm thinking it's at least possible."

"Great."

Finn shook his head slightly but said, "Okay, but what about you guys? He obviously went out of his way to—to use this gray time you're talking about. Why invite you to the party?"

"You told us Aylia Blackwood had her vision of a killer stalking Salem on Sunday night."

"That's when she told me about it, yeah."

Miranda lifted her brows at him.

"He knew?"

"We believe so. Word spread quickly—you told us that yourself. He had to guess you'd call Noah, and that he'd send a team in. He must have hoped that by giving Diana that very spooky visit to the gray time, she and Quentin would be the team sent. Neither of them is telepathic or empathic; he had a far better chance of hiding himself from them, at least from their abilities. He thought."

Hollis half raised her hand, as if to ask a question, then dropped it and muttered, "Oh, crap."

Bishop was smiling slightly as he looked at her.

She eyed him, then sighed and looked at Diana. "Dammit. I did get pulled in."

"What?" Diana frowned, then realized. "When I opened the door? But Daniel said we were both needed here."

"I'm guessing he was adjusting his plan once I popped in. Maybe why he showed us all those walking dead in living color. To shake us up. Me up. And I doubt he knew how powerful Reese is, if he even knew anything about him at all."

Before anything more could be said about that, Bishop looked at Finn and asked, "Are your people deployed?"

"Yeah. All around the Dryden place, as instructed. It's fairly isolated, farther out in the valley, and there's plenty of cover. It's a small farm, basically supplies the family with most of their food. No movement inside, but Daniel's Jeep is there."

Bishop started to speak, then turned his head sharply and looked at Hollis. She was very still, looking ahead of her with eyes narrowed as though gazing into a great distance.

"Hollis?"

Softly, she said, "Just woke up. She just woke up. She's confused and her head hurts. And she's afraid."

"Who, Hollis?"

She was still a moment longer, then caught her breath. "Aylia. Aylia Blackwood. He's got her."

THEY LEFT THEIR SUV and Finn's Jeep some distance from the small house and moved silently, armed and wearing vests, toward it.

Nellie had stopped protesting that there was any reason for her to be here, even though it had taken all the persuasion she had to convince Leo to remain in the Jeep.

"What if he gets out?" she whispered to Finn.

"He won't. You convinced him. And I locked him in."

"He's a Pit bull," she said witheringly. "If he wants out, he's coming out."

Finn smiled faintly. "He'll be fine, Nellie. And you stick close. I know you can take care of yourself, but still."

"I'm not calling down a storm," she warned, glancing up uneasily at the heavy gray clouds promising snow.

"I hope you won't have to."

Nellie knew he was just as tense and worried about Aylia as she was, probably more so, but appreciated the effort. But she couldn't help muttering, "For somebody who's *not* a cop I seem to end up in situations like this one way too much."

He sent her another smile but didn't reply.

Nellie rubbed her cold hands together, wishing she dared take her gloves out of her pocket and put them on. Not that they'd help get her warm, except by illusion. And she was very aware of her carefully woven shield, held in place because she really didn't need the gloves anymore. Anyway, she was more worried about Finn's now-lowered shield than her own, even though Hollis had told him she saw no sign today that anyone or anything was trying to break through his guards.

He didn't seem at all concerned about that. Dammit.

They already knew that the Dryden household was an armed one, with two registered rifles and, Finn guessed, at least a shotgun. Maybe more.

What they really didn't know was whether Daniel's grandmother and mother were at home. Nellie could hardly believe they would be, that Daniel would be keeping Aylia Blackwood prisoner in the same house if they were, but the possibility was there.

She was very conscious of both the heavy, moisture-laden cold air and the almost oppressive sense of what she now recognized as diffuse energy all around them. It sort of made sense to Nellie that Hollis was right in believing they could use that energy to enhance their abilities, just as Daniel had probably used it. Maybe was still using it.

She started to say something to Finn about that, then caught a hint of motion from the corner of her eye and saw Tia settle onto a low branch of a nearby tree. It was the first time she'd seen the crow—any of the crows—today.

"Tia's here," she whispered to Finn.

"I know. A couple dozen of her friends and family are all around us."

Nellie wasn't surprised he'd seen or sensed the birds, only that she hadn't.

"Your shield is the only one still up." He glanced at her. "I know you're still mad about Simon."

"He was *tortured*," she reminded him.

"Use your mad," he told her. "On you, mad looks good. Use it to help you focus."

She really wanted to ask him what he meant by saying mad looked good on her, but they caught up with the others just then and she made a mental note to ask him later. Maybe.

"What's the plan?" Finn asked Bishop.

They had already made a somewhat loose plan on the way out here, details to be worked out once they were on scene and could get a better sense of the situation. Neither Finn nor any of his deputies had ever been inside the Dryden house, so the only description he could provide had been a very, very general layout of the type of small, older farmhouse that was fairly common throughout the valley.

Between Bishop's team, Finn's deputies, and Nellie, they far outnumbered whoever was inside the house, but that would not necessarily be an advantage if they couldn't get in a position to prevent Daniel from holding Aylia hostage.

With a gun to her head, he could hold them off almost indefinitely.

"The plan," Bishop said in a voice hardly above a whisper, "is to get eyes in there. One way or another."

Finn eyed him. "I'm not going to like this, am I?"

Bishop appeared not to hear that.

"Of all of us, Hollis and Reese have the most skill and experience in handling energy," he said. "They need to get as close as possible to the house and find out if they can sense who's in there and where—and anything else they can. The rest of us need to be ready to move the instant we're sure where Dryden is and what exactly he's doing."

DeMarco eyed the house, separated from them now by the outbuilding they were sheltering behind and the rather junky yard. The gray day meant no bright sunshine, and there were various things between them and the house—such as an old tractor up on concrete blocks—that would provide cover to allow them to get right up next to the building.

The windows they could see appeared to be curtained, but it was a bit difficult to tell because of the almost eerie hardness of the gray light.

DeMarco and Hollis both nodded to Bishop, then drew their weapons, and in seconds had slipped away from the shelter of the outbuilding to begin crossing the yard.

AYLIA HAD GIVEN up trying to work her hands free of the cord that bit into her wrists. He had tied the knot tight. Her fingers were numb, virtually useless. Her ankles were bound as well. Not that she'd made any attempt to get away.

The knife he held looked huge to her, its blade wickedly serrated, and there was a look in his strangely pale eyes that made her cold to her bones.

"Always stick together, you women," he muttered, standing between the bed and the window. "I should have known you would. Mom and Gran are just the same. Telling me I can't control my Talents. Telling me what to do. Telling me . . . always telling me. Like you told Megan." With his free hand, he rubbed between his frowning brows fretfully.

"Danny, I don't know what you're talking about." Aylia kept her voice steady with an effort.

"You know exactly what I'm talking about."

"I don't, Danny. I'm sorry if you feel I've done something to . . . Wait, Megan? This is about Megan?"

Half under his breath, he muttered, "Why is it so bright in here?" Then added sharply, "Don't pretend you don't know. You told her to leave me."

"No, I didn't. Danny, are you—are you in pain?"

"Head hurts." He scowled at her. You're probably doing that too."

"How could I—"

"Probably a Talent you women keep to yourself. *I know.* You hide things. Like Megan hid things. But I can hide things too. I can. I hid things for a long time. When I realized *I* had Talents. That I could move things."

"Move things?" Aylia felt another jolt of ice. The most dangerous Talent of all, the most incredibly rare Talent, and this clearly unbalanced man possessed it?

He laughed shrilly. "Makes you nervous, doesn't it? I found out I could do that when I was a kid. When that old—when somebody was mean to me. It was stupid of him to have a gun right there, but he didn't know what I could do with it."

She swallowed hard. "Danny—"

"I didn't know either, not then. I could only do it when I was really, really mad. And it's . . . it's harder now. Even when I'm mad. Everything's . . . harder now. I can't even get back to that gray place, even though I've tried."

"Gray place? Danny—"

"I wanted to keep distracting them after they got here, but . . . Did you do that? Did you make it harder for me?"

"Danny, I promise you I didn't do anything to you."

He rubbed his forehead again and then shook his head as though trying to throw something off. "Must have been you," he muttered. "Your fault. All your fault. First you told Megan to leave me, and then you did something to mess up my Talents."

"Danny, I'd never do anything to hurt you."

He laughed again, more unsteady than shrill this time. "Think I'm going to believe you? After you tried to send Megan away from me? No. No, I don't believe you. And I'm going to fix it so you can never hurt me again."

―――――――――

NELLIE KEPT HER eyes glued to Hollis and DeMarco, impressed both by their silence and by the ease with which they crossed that dangerously exposed space, flitting from tree to bush to tractor, barely hesitating. They had separated almost at once, each making for a different side of the house, and though she didn't see them even look at each other, she knew they were communicating.

She hardly dared to breathe until they reached the house, and each took up a position between two windows, their backs pressed up against the house. She wasn't sure but thought she saw them both close their eyes.

It seemed only seconds later that she obeyed a gesture from Finn and stuck close to him as he and the rest of Bishop's team began to cross the space toward the house. Nellie had no idea what their two forward scouts had communicated, but judging by the speed and alertness with which everyone moved, time must have been short. She tried to move both quickly and quietly, keeping her eyes on Finn.

Again, it seemed like only seconds—or hours—before they were at the house, crouched low, the two of them plus Bishop on the same side as Hollis.

"I'm only getting two," she whispered to them. "Daniel and Aylia. Upstairs, I think."

"Think or know?" Bishop asked.

She went still for a moment, then nodded. "Know. Upstairs, dammit. In a bedroom. We'll only be able to come at them from one doorway, maybe two."

Bishop was already at the window, using a small, thin tool Nellie didn't recognize to slide inside the wooden sash and silently unlock the window. Then he was easing the window open and seemingly in the same action slipping inside the house.

The window was low, but Nellie was still glad of Finn's help and tried desperately not to make a sound.

And nearly cried out when she straightened inside and found herself staring at a bed only a few feet away. Lying across the neat bedspread was an older woman, perhaps seventy-five or even older, with snowy white hair. She was fully dressed, her hands folded peacefully over her lean middle.

Her eyes were open, reddened and unblinking as they gazed up at the ceiling. Her mouth was slightly open, her tongue protruding from between bluish lips. There were faint bruises on her throat.

Nellie had no idea how she managed to trap the scream inside her, but somehow she did. She watched as Bishop bent over the bed, his long fingers quick and deft as they checked for a pulse. Then he straightened, looked at them grimly, and shook his head once.

Nellie heard Hollis let out a slow breath, then saw her turn her face toward the doorway of the bedroom. Dimly, and then more loudly as she herself unconsciously concentrated, Nellie could hear the low drone of a male voice. Then a female voice, quicker but softer, holding a soothing note.

Aylia's keeping him talking.

I know, she answered Finn.

They slipped from the bedroom and out into a short hallway. Bishop paused to move noiselessly into a second bedroom, only a glance needed to show Nellie there was a younger woman, probably in her late fifties, on that bed, more sprawled than peaceful but with the same reddened, staring eyes, the same bruises on her throat.

Nellie had no idea why Daniel would have strangled his mother and grandmother, but horror didn't change her certainty that he had. When Bishop came out of that bedroom with another slight shake of his head, she merely fell in behind Finn and Hollis as they followed their team leader on down the hallway.

They entered the small front room, with its tiny foyer and painted wooden staircase leading upward, just as DeMarco, Miranda, Quentin, and Diana reached the same space.

To DeMarco, Bishop whispered, "Do what you can to dampen his abilities. If he's telekinetic, that's something we don't need working against us."

DeMarco nodded, his gaze turned toward the upstairs as he focused to employ a rare ability, one he seldom had cause to use. His immediate but slight frown was just as rare. "Interference."

Hollis was staring at him. "We've been able to use the energy." Her voice was hardly a breath of sound.

"I know. This is coming from him."

It was Bishop's turn to frown. "From him?"

"Yeah. I think . . . he doesn't know how to use the energy. He's trying to use his abilities but the energy's blocking him. Echoing back to him."

Finn whispered, "That's gotta hurt."

"It does. He's in a lot of pain."

Hollis said, "Then we'd better not waste any time getting to him. Only two rooms upstairs, both bedrooms, and there's not much space. I think he's in the eastern bedroom, on the far side, near the window. No place for us to hide."

"Aylia?"

"On the bed, tied up. He doesn't believe he has to hold her. He's . . . wary. She's talking to him, holding his attention." She tilted her head slightly, her gaze directed toward that distant bedroom, her eyes going even brighter than usual. "I can't really reach him, but . . . Aylia. I think I can reach her. Yeah."

"Careful," Bishop said softly.

"Right. She's trying to . . . reach him. She just needs to know . . . exactly what to say to him."

Bishop looked at her for a moment, then at Nellie. "We need Tia," he whispered. "And a few others. More than one crow needs to fly past that window, close, making plenty of noise. On my mark."

Without even thinking about it, Nellie nodded and reached out mentally for Tia, vaguely surprised when she was instantly aware of a strong channel of communication. Telling Tia what they needed was simple, and her acknowledgment and agreement just as swift and easy.

Nellie looked at Bishop, realizing only then that she had briefly closed her eyes. "They'll be ready," she whispered. "Just tell me when."

It was an old staircase but, remarkably, no creaking tread betrayed them as they went very slowly up. And they had caught two breaks: The very short upstairs hallway was dim, and the bedroom door was only half-open.

It was just enough to allow them to creep close. Without really thinking about it, Nellie refocused her attention in order to listen.

". . . wasn't your fault," Aylia was saying quietly, an oddly soothing note in her low voice. "How could you have known?"

"I don't believe you." His voice was deep but with a strained note, something in it with sharp edges. "She would have told me."

"Did you give her a chance, Danny?"

"It's your fault. You told her to leave me."

"No, Danny. She told me she was leaving Salem. She asked my advice. She was— She needed to start fresh somewhere else after what happened with Paul. But she didn't tell me about you."

"I— She said she was leaving. The night before, when I wanted to talk to her, she told me she was thinking about it. That she'd talked to you. I was afraid she'd already made up her mind. So I went to her house that morning. And she was all packed. Sneaking out. She was leaving. She was leaving and she was never coming back. She said she—she—"

"Had to get away from Salem? But it's what she needed, Danny. Because people were . . . were talking and pointing—"

"She lied at first. Said she just had an appointment in town. But she was all packed. She was all packed, and she knew I knew what she was doing. She was leaving me. I tried to get her to stay, but . . . She wouldn't listen to me. And—and I got mad. But I would've listened if she'd said anything else. If she'd told me. I would've!"

"I know that, Danny. I know you would have cared. That you wouldn't have hurt her if you'd known about the baby."

"She never said. Not anything about a baby." His voice suddenly rose higher. "But—I would've—I would've—"

They were just outside the door.

Now.

Bishop's voice was clear in Nellie's head. She instantly sent the signal to Tia, and in seconds heard a sudden, surprisingly loud roar of wings from the window.

Daniel made a startled, choked sound and was still turning toward the window, away from them, when the door of the bedroom slammed open. He couldn't get turned back around before Bishop and DeMarco were on him.

He was quickly disarmed by DeMarco, but he was strong. Luckily, not strong enough.

Hollis stood by the bed, her gun held ready just in case, but turned her head slightly to look down as Finn and Nellie untied the cord cutting sharply into Aylia Blackwood's wrists and ankles. She winced as circulation began returning to her hands and feet but kept her gaze on Hollis.

"Thanks," she said in a voice that shook only a bit. "Thanks for telling me what to say to him."

Hollis smiled suddenly, and it lit her face with warmth. "No problem," she said. "Study enough of these guys and you learn what pushes their buttons. And what keeps them from totally losing it. I'm just glad to know that sometimes broadcasting comes in handy."

EPILOGUE

The forecast storm finally hit Salem that evening, and though it was relatively quiet, snow fell heavily, large wet flakes that very quickly covered everything.

"You'll all be snowed in for a couple of days," Finn told Bishop. They were gathered in the large sitting room downstairs at Hales. There was a brisk fire in the fireplace, and they had the space to themselves.

"There are worse places to be snowed in," Bishop told him. "And while we're here we can help build the case against Daniel Dryden."

Finn eyed him. "Appreciate that. But you know whatever defense attorney he gets is going to raise hell about that drug you've got him on."

"Well, even though he clearly lacks the experience to be able to control his abilities with all the energy in the valley interfering, that doesn't mean he couldn't figure it out, given time. The drug will keep him from using his telekinesis to tamper with anything important," Bishop said. "Like the lock on his cell door."

Hollis was staring at him. "Yeah, about that. Since when do we have a drug that suppresses psychic ability?"

"Not all psychic ability. Just telekinesis."

"The question stands."

"Something we developed in the lab."

Hollis opened her mouth, then closed it. "I need to pay more attention to that lab the next time I'm there," she said finally.

"Different lab," Bishop said.

Hollis looked at Miranda. "He does that deliberately, doesn't he?"

"Does what?"

"You're getting as bad as he is."

Miranda smiled at her.

Whatever Hollis might have said was interrupted by a giant yawn she hastily covered with one hand. "Last night's catching up with me," she muttered. "And today. Well, at least Daniel was so eager to explain himself that his confession is pretty damned clear. Not much room for a defense, if you ask me. He's evil and probably crazy, but not clinically insane, I'd say."

Finn said, "No, hardly insane. And he didn't have to tell us much, really. You guys were right about him."

Diana said, "At least he can't go on killing now. And it's obvious he would have if he hadn't been stopped. Imagining all those grievances, being convinced that both Cole Ainsworth and Simon Cavendish had been after Megan."

Finn said, "At least he thought Simon had only smiled at her, and so deserved a chance to live."

Nellie shook her head, absently petting Leo as the dog sat beside her chair. He'd finally stopped sulking over having been locked in the Jeep and missing all the action. "And Cole was killed so horribly because he'd dared to give Megan a ride for a couple of days while her car was in the shop. Talk about obsessed."

"At least he had some reason for choosing the victims he did," Hollis said. "The men because he was jealous and Aylia because he was convinced she'd talked Megan into leaving. I imagine he would have convinced himself there were others threatening his relationship with Megan, invented threats if he had to. You heard how much he obviously relished what he did to Cole; he enjoyed himself too much to stop."

"It could have been a bloodbath," Finn agreed. "I hope I don't have to state the obvious about how grateful I am."

"You would have put it all together," Quentin told him.

"Maybe. Eventually. But not before a lot more people had died." Finn brooded for a moment. "No matter what, we'll nail his ass for killing his mother and grandmother. I still can't believe he did that just because he knew they wouldn't *approve* of him holding Aylia in the house. Christ, why didn't he just tie them up somewhere?"

Miranda said, "I think he'd wanted to kill them both for quite a while. It was obvious from what he said to us and to Aylia that one reason he spent so much time hiking was to get away from their domination. They tried to control him. To keep him close. Maybe because they knew what he was, or suspected. Either way, sooner or later, that need to control him was going to backfire."

Diana said, "Poor Megan. She was upset about Paul and turned to the one man who had done nothing but admire her since her teens.

At least that was what she believed. All she really wanted was a little comfort, a little solace. She didn't bargain on an obsession that would get her killed."

Hollis said, "Nobody ever does."

DeMarco eyed her, but all he said, to Bishop, was, "What was that he said about the gadget he rigged to control the air into Simon's would-be coffin?"

"That he found it on the Internet."

Hollis covered another yawn and said, also to Bishop, "You need to do something about that."

"About the Internet?"

"Yeah."

"Such as?"

"I dunno." She lifted a hand and sort of wiggled her fingers. "Do your Yoda stuff."

"I believe it's been said that the Internet is forever," he told her politely.

"All the more reason," Hollis returned. "You don't want to destroy my faith in you, now, do you?"

"I would certainly hate to do that."

"And it causes us a lot of problems, you know that. The Internet. An information superhighway for the bad guys."

"And for the rest of us."

"Yeah. Maybe a special pass or something."

"For the rest of us?"

"Why not? So we can use the Internet and the bad guys can't. You can do that. You're good with secret stuff."

"Hollis, I can't control the Internet."

"Have you ever tried?"

He stared at her, brows raised.

"Sleep on it. I'm sure you'll come up with something."

Bishop looked around at all the smiles and said dryly, "Don't encourage her."

Leo rested his chin on Nellie's knee and listened drowsily to chuckles from the humans. He knew them well enough to understand a release of tension. Still, they were very curious creatures.

Very curious indeed.

CHARACTER BIOS

HOLLIS TEMPLETON—FBI SPECIAL CRIMES UNIT

A slight woman of medium height, she has regular features that become memorable when animated, and extremely unusual and striking blue eyes that make her face unforgettable. Brown hair worn in a short, no-fuss style.

Job: Special Agent, profiler.

Adept: Her primary ability is as a medium, and she's the most powerful medium in the unit, but Hollis is unique in several ways, not the least because she has, from case to case, awakened or even created numerous other psychic abilities, more than any psychic in the SCU or Haven, more than any psychic Bishop has ever known. And those abilities tend to be full-blown almost immediately, though never perfectly under her control.

One theory that could explain Hollis's numerous abilities could be the extreme trauma of her psychic awakening (see *Touching Evil*), which was the most horrific and brutal on record. But other agents in the SCU and operatives in Haven have suffered extremely traumatic psychic awakenings without continually gaining new abilities as Hollis has.

She is unique within an extraordinary group of unique people.

In addition to being a medium, she is able to see auras, heal herself and others, and recognize true evil no matter how it attempts to hide itself; she possesses the ability to sense, define, channel, and use sheer energy, even dark energy, without being harmed by it; and most recently she has awakened or created an extraordinarily strong ability as an empath. She may also be clairvoyant, though she and Bishop disagree about it. And she consistently tests at the higher, more powerful end of the scale the SCU has developed to measure psychic abilities—with every new ability gained.

Hollis, more than any other member of the unit, is proving there may well be no limits to what the human mind can achieve.

Appearances: *Touching Evil, Sense of Evil, Blood Dreams, Blood Sins, Blood Ties, Haven, Hostage, Haunted, Wait for Dark, Hold Back the Dark, Curse of Salem*

DIANA HAYES—FBI SPECIAL CRIMES UNIT

Medium height and slender but athletic, she has the coppery hair and fair skin of a true redhead. Not beautiful, her vivid green eyes and slow smile make her more than attractive.

Job: Special Agent, profiler.

Adept: Medium, the only one in the unit able to open a door to something she calls "the gray time," which she believes is a sort of corridor between the living world and the spirit realm. It's a cold, gray, desolate place or time without either light or shadow, a place where Diana usually meets "spirit guides" who often appear as children even though they aren't, and who are somewhat cryptic in explaining what Diana is called there to learn or do. Diana is also able to see and communicate with spirits in the living world, though she seldom sees the recently dead.

Appearances: *Chill of Fear, Blood Ties, Curse of Salem*

DANIEL—APPEARING AS A CHILD, DIANA'S SPIRIT GUIDE. BUT WHAT IS HE REALLY?

REESE DEMARCO—FBI SPECIAL CRIMES UNIT

Tall, powerful, blond hair, and light blue eyes. Originally one of the former military "civilian" operatives for Bishop, Reese has specialized in the past in deep-cover assignments, some long-term, until he came formally into the SCU as an agent and was partnered with Hollis.

Job: Special Agent, profiler. Also a pilot and a military-trained sniper.

Adept: An "open" born telepath, he is able to read a wide range of people. He possesses a unique double shield, which sometimes contains the unusually high amount of sheer energy he naturally produces, a shield he can enclose Hollis within when necessary for her safety. He also possesses something Bishop has dubbed a "primal ability": He always knows when a gun is pointed at or near him, or if other imminent danger threatens. At least twice, that primal ability has saved the life of his partner.

Appearances: *Blood Sins*, *Blood Ties*, *Haven*, *Hostage*, *Haunted*, *Wait for Dark*, *Hold Back the Dark*, *Curse of Salem*

QUENTIN HAYES—FBI SPECIAL CRIMES UNIT

Tall, shaggy blond hair, and blue eyes. One of the earliest psychics recruited by Bishop, and already an FBI agent at the time, Quentin had a well-deserved reputation as something of a loner with a reckless, impatient nature, traits that have changed at least somewhat during his years with the SCU. Still tends toward humor, often of the flippant or gallows variety.

Job: Special Agent, profiler.

Adept: Quentin is a seer, precognitive, although for most of his life he never "saw" the future, just sometimes knew something would happen before it did. Meeting Diana Brisco and struggling to help the then-fragile psychic as well as solve a decades-old mystery in his own life, he begins to have actual visions, though they are still rare and extremely unsettling. He's one of the best at using the "spider senses" developed by first Bishop and then many in the SCU, able to enhance the usual five senses to an extraordinary degree.

Appearances: *Touching Evil, Hunting Fear, Chill of Fear, Blood Sins, Blood Ties, Curse of Salem*

NOAH BISHOP—FBI SPECIAL CRIMES UNIT CHIEF

Tall, wide-shouldered, athletic; night-black hair with a striking widow's peak as well as a streak of pure white at his left temple; pale gray eyes like tarnished silver. A twisted scar down his left cheek is barely noticeable unless he's tense or otherwise disturbed.

Job: Special Agent, Unit Chief, profiler, pilot, sharpshooter, and highly trained and skilled in several martial arts. Plus has mastered a number of esoteric skills often useful in his work such as lockpicking and a facility with computers close to that of professional hackers.

Adept: An exceptionally powerful telepath, an ability that has evolved, he also shares with his wife, Miranda, a strong precognitive ability, the deep emotional link between them making them, together, far exceed the limits of the scale developed by the FBI to measure psychic abilities. Also possesses an "ancillary" ability of enhanced senses (hearing, sight, scent), which he has trained other agents to use as well, something they informally refer to as "spider senses." Whether present in the flesh or not, Bishop virtually always knows what's going on with his agents in the field, somehow maintaining what seem to be psychic links with almost all of his agents, connected without in any way being intrusive, something that has also evolved over time. With some of them in certain situations he can actually communicate telepathically, something that has proven highly useful more than once.

Appearances: *Stealing Shadows, Hiding in the Shadows, Out of the Shadows, Touching Evil, Whisper of Evil, Sense of Evil, Hunting Fear, Chill of Fear, Sleeping with Fear, Blood Dreams, Blood Sins, Blood Ties, Haven, Hostage, Haunted, Fear the Dark, Wait for Dark, Hold Back the Dark, Hidden Salem, Curse of Salem*

MIRANDA BISHOP—FBI SPECIAL CRIMES UNIT

Tall, athletic, yet with centerfold curves; black hair and electric blue eyes. Possesses the sort of rare beauty that turns heads wherever she goes despite the fact that she does nothing to play up her looks.

Job: Special Agent, profiler, black belt in karate, sharpshooter.

Adept: Miranda is a telepath and a seer, remarkably powerful, and possesses unusual control, particularly with a highly developed shield capable of protecting herself psychically, a shield she's able to extend beyond herself to protect others. Shares abilities with her husband, due to their intense emotional connection, and together they far exceed the scale developed by the SCU to measure psychic abilities.

Appearances: *Out of the Shadows, Touching Evil, Whisper of Evil, Sense of Evil, Hunting Fear, Chill of Fear, Blood Dreams, Blood Sins, Blood Ties, Hostage, Haunted, Fear the Dark, Wait for Dark, Hold Back the Dark, Hidden Salem, Curse of Salem*

FINN DEVERELL—CHIEF DEPUTY, SALEM SHERIFF'S DEPARTMENT

Age thirty-two, six feet tall, blond hair, blue eyes. The Deverells are one of the original five families that founded Salem, town leaders, and each owns and operates one of the major businesses that keep Salem not only viable but flourishing. In the case of the Deverells, the family business is twofold, with Finn running Salem's one newspaper and a Deverell aunt in charge of the huge paper mill that produces not only the sort of paper people use every day, but also beautiful, specialized paper that is still made by hand using tools older than the town. Employing workers skilled in operating the machinery to produce ordinary paper as well as dozens highly skilled in producing the specialized paper, the Deverells pay very well, offer generous benefits and bonuses, and are considered one of the best families to work for. Like each of the other families, the Deverells tend to have, in every generation, at least one family member with a psychic ability, usually empathic. Finn is an empath.

Appearances: *Hidden Salem, Curse of Salem*

NELLIE CAVENDISH

Age thirty, petite, slender, brown eyes, and brown hair. Her father, Thomas Ryan Cavendish, left a mysterious message for her that brought her to Salem just before her thirtieth birthday (see *Hidden Salem*). She had no intention of remaining, but a deadly battle against an evil adversary leaves her at least temporarily in charge, the head of her family—one of the Five. Nellie is a rather extraordinary psychic, something she has hidden her entire life. Until Salem, where both her abilities and her understanding of them grow, and where she may or may not find the beginning of a new life.

Appearances: *Hidden Salem, Curse of Salem*

LEO

Nellie's black Pit bull. Not exactly an ordinary dog.

PSYCHIC TERMS AND ABILITIES

(As Classified/Defined by Bishop's Special Crimes Unit and by Haven)

Adept: The general term used to label any functional psychic; the specific ability is much more specialized.

Clairvoyance: The ability to know things, to pick up bits of information, seemingly out of thin air.

Dream-projecting: The ability to enter another's dreams.

Dream-walking: The ability to invite/draw others into one's own dreams. (This is a separate ability from "walking" in the gray time, a kind of corridor between the living world and spirit realm where Diana Brisco Hayes, medium, has walked most of her life.)

Empath: One who experiences the emotions of others, often up to and including physical pain and injuries.

Healing empath: One who has the ability to heal the pain/injury of another.

Absolute empath: The rarest of all abilities, this one causes the psychic to literally absorb the pain of another, to the point that the empath physically takes on the same injuries, healing the injured person and then healing herself or himself.

Healing: The ability to heal injuries to self and/or others, often but not always ancillary to mediumistic abilities. Sometimes ancillary to empathic abilities.

Latent: The term used to describe unawakened or inactive abilities, as well as to describe a psychic not yet aware of being psychic.

Mediumistic: Having the ability to communicate with the dead. Some see the dead, some hear them, and some both see and hear.

Psychic medium: A medium who sees and/or hears the dead and is able to interact with them.

Physical medium: A medium who interacts with spirits using all senses, including feeling the emotions and sensations of a spirit. Rare.

Precognition: A seer or precog's ability to correctly predict future events. Whether they are able to affect or change those events is a much-debated and uncertain question; attempts have produced mixed re-sults.

Psychometry: The ability to pick up impressions or information from touching objects. Sometimes linked with clairvoyance.

Regenerative: The ability to heal one's own injuries/illnesses, even those considered by medical experts to be lethal or fatal. (A classification that is unique to one SCU operative and considered separate from a healer's abil-ities; most mediums, however, have a remarkable ability to heal them-selves.)

Sensitive: Usually a latent psychic whose abilities have not been triggered but who is far more aware of the moods and emotions of those around them than a person without active or latent abilities.

Spider sense: The ability to enhance one or more of the "normal" senses (sight, hearing, smell, etc.) through concentration and the focusing of one's own mental and physical energy.

Telekinesis: The ability to move objects with the mind. Rare.

Telepathic mind control: The ability to influence/control others through mental focus and effort; an extremely rare ability.

Telepathy (touch and nontouch, or open): The ability to pick up thoughts from others. Some telepaths only receive, while others have the ability to send thoughts. A few are capable of both, usually due to an emotional connection with the other person.

UNNAMED ABILITIES INCLUDE

The ability to see into time, to view events in the past, present, and future without being or having been there physically while the events transpire. A kind of clairvoyance; also sometimes linked to precognition.

The ability to see the aura or another person's energy field and to interpret those colors and energies. Through experience, trial, and error, the SCU has come to a tentative understanding of what the different colors usually mean:

White = healing/protective

Blue/lavenders = calm

Red/rich yellows = energy/power

Green = unusual, tends to mix with other colors, peaceful

Metallic = repelling energy from another source or holding it in

Black = extremely negative, even evil, especially if it has red streaks of energy and power

More than one color in an aura is common, reflecting the outward sign of human complexities of emotion.

The ability to channel energy usefully as a defensive or offensive tool or weapon.

The ability to hide or disguise an object or person.

The ability to communicate with animals, which is part telepathy and part empathy—and part something else.

AUTHOR'S NOTE

The first books in the Bishop/SCU series were published back in 2000, and readers have asked me whether these stories are taking place in "real" time and if, at this point, more than twenty(!) years have passed in the series. The answer is no. I chose to use "story time" for several reasons, one being in order to avoid having my characters age too quickly. Roughly speaking, each trilogy takes place within the same year, with some overlaps.

So, from an *arbitrary* start date, the timeline looks something like this:

Stealing Shadows—February

Hiding in the Shadows—October/November

YEAR ONE:

Out of the Shadows—January (SCU formally introduced)

Touching Evil—November

AUTHOR'S NOTE

YEAR TWO:

Whisper of Evil—March

Sense of Evil—June

Hunting Fear—September

YEAR THREE:

Chill of Fear—April

Sleeping with Fear—July

Blood Dreams—October

YEAR FOUR:

Blood Sins—January

Blood Ties—April

Haven—July

Hostage—October

YEAR FIVE:

Haunted—February

Fear the Dark—May

Wait for Dark—August

Hold Back the Dark—October

YEAR SIX:

Hidden Salem—January

Curse of Salem—March

So, with the publication of *Curse of Salem*, the Special Crimes Unit has been a functional (and growing) unit of agents for about six years (although Bishop was searching for and recruiting psychics and building the base of his unit for at least a couple of years before the events of *Out of the Shadows*). Time to have grown from being known within the FBI as the "Spooky Crimes Unit" to becoming a well-respected unit with an excellent record of solved cases. A unit that has, moreover, earned respect in various law enforcement agencies, with word quietly passed from this sheriff to that chief of police that they excel at solving crimes that are anything but normal by using methods and abilities that are unique to each agent, and that they neither seek nor want media attention.

An asset to any level of law enforcement, they do their jobs with little fanfare and never ride roughshod over locals, both traits very much appreciated, especially by small-town cops and citizens wary of outsiders. They regard both skepticism and interest with equal calm, treating their abilities as merely tools with which to do their jobs, and their very matter-of-factness helps normally hard-nosed cops accept, if not understand, at least something of the paranormal.